SHANDY GAFFE

"Explain yourself, sir!"

"Great Scott! I do believe I've been mountain-climbing in my sleep. I beg your pardon, madam. The intrusion was involuntary."

One did not, after all, expect to come upon what had looked from below to be an exceptionally large squirrel's nest, only to find it neatly decked over with birch saplings, carpeted with balsam fir twigs laid in a carefully overlapping pattern, and occupied by a lady in a deerskin bikini reading Young's *Night Thoughts*.

"I am Professor Peter Shandy of Balaclava Agricultural College. And this is my young friend Cronkite Swope," Peter added as his companion hove into view. "We're fugitives."

Vane Pursuit

☞ P9-BBT-499

ALSO BY
CHARLOTTE MACLEOD

CHARLOTTE MACLEOD

Vane Pursuit

A PETER SHANDY MYSTERY

THE MYSTERIOUS PRESS

New York • London
Tokyo • Sweden • Milan

MYSTERIOUS PRESS EDITION

Copyright © 1989 by Charlotte MacLeod

Cover illustration by Mark Hess

Mysterious Press books are published in association with
Warner Books, Inc.
666 Fifth Avenue
New York, N.Y. 10103

A Warner Communications Company

Printed in the United States of America

Originally published in hardcover by The Mysterious Press.
First Mysterious Press Paperback Printing: March, 1990

10 9 8 7 6 5 4 3 2 1

For My Cousins of the Clan MacKay
and Their Families

ONE

"Hey, you! You kid! Get the hell down off that cannon."

Dr. Helen Marsh Shandy ignored the yell even though it came straight from the bullhorn throat of Lumpkinton Chief of Police Wilbur J. Olson. She merely wriggled her new pink sneakers into a more secure stance atop the Civil War relic across from the soap factory, made sure her telephoto lens was on tight, doubled checked her focus, squinted into her viewfinder, and clicked her shutter.

Olson yelled again. Helen clicked some more. Not until the chief slammed open the door of his cruiser and started trying to squeeze his fat legs out from under the steering wheel did she slip the expensive camera into its carrying case and swing herself to the ground.

"I'm sorry, Chief Olson, but I absolutely had to catch the soap-works weather vane against that magnificent sunset before the sky changed. This one's considered to be Praxiteles Lumpkin's masterpiece, you know."

And so it well deserved to be deemed. The hand-wrought copper silhouette, verdigrised with time and soap fumes, depicted a lanky man sitting in a round washtub. One skinny leg stuck out over the rim. His right hand clasped a long-handled brush with which he was scrubbing his back.

The left hand was raised in a gesture of triumph, clutching a small oblong object intended to represent a bar of Lumpkin soap.

Some townsfolk considered the weather vane nothing more than a fairly clean joke. Others thought it was marvelous. Chief Olson clearly didn't give two hoots for the itinerant weather-vane artist's chef d'oeuvre, or for Helen's explanation, either.

"Ungh." He began working his legs back into the cruiser. "Aren't you Professor Shandy's wife? I thought you worked in the library over at the college."

"Yes, that's right. I'm doing this for our files. Also for a pamphlet we're helping the Balaclava County Historical Society assemble as the result of a request from the Smithsonian. The society doesn't have the resources to collect the data, but we do and I'm it, so to speak. Praxiteles offers a fascinating field for research because he's left such an impressive body of work and has never been properly documented before. Unless you count a few snapshots Canute Lumpkin's grandmother took with a folding Kodak," Helen added fairly. "They didn't come out awfully well."

Chief Olson showed no interest in counting Canute Lumpkin's grandmother's snapshots. "Huh. So that's what they're paying you for? Some women would be home about now getting their husband's supper on the table. And they wouldn't have to write a cookbook to get it ready, either."

He curved his pouty lips into a mean little smile to show Helen he'd been joking, then resumed his customary scowl. "You looked like a kid up there."

The remark sounded like an accusation, but Helen decided she might as well annoy the old tub of lard further by taking it as a compliment.

"Why, thank you, Chief Olson. I'm sure you know better now that you've seen my face."

The curator of the Buggins Collection at Balaclava Agricultural College, to give Helen her proper title, was a remarkably pretty woman. Her petite figure, blond curls, pink sweatshirt, and blue jeans could have fooled a sharper eye than Olson's. To irk him further, she added, "Praxiteles was a great-nephew of Fortitude Lumpkin, who married Druella Buggins, as you doubtless know."

Chief Olson most likely hadn't known and clearly couldn't have cared less, though he wasn't quite dumb enough to say so to Mrs. Shandy. "Cussed kids are always climbing around on that cannon," he growled. "They fall and hurt themselves and their mothers come putting the blame on me."

"I suppose a lot of the parents work in the factory."

Helen nodded toward the three-story expanse of red sandstone and dirty windows squatting across the road from the grassy triangle on which the cannon sat. Both had been here since the late 1860s, the cannon's muzzle pointing straight toward the factory's tallow room within whose vats thousands upon thousands of beeves had over the years rendered up their fat to be converted by the alchemy of potash and perfume into Lumpkin's Lilywhite for lovely young ladies, Lumpkin's Latherite for dirty old men, Lumpkin's Launderite for the washing you love to hang, and no doubt a good many more subtle saponifications of which Helen knew nothing.

She did know, of course, that this vast enterprise had grown from the pans of lye soap Druella Buggins Lumpkin had concocted long ago from kitchen fat and wood ashes and which Druella's husband, Fortitude, had peddled among the surrounding hamlets out of saddlebags slung across the rump of his trusty mare Beornia. She knew how the tiny clearing Fortitude had hacked out of the wilderness to make a home for his bride had burgeoned into a village and then to a town—all of it built, metaphorically speaking, on Druella's lye soap. Much of Lumpkinton was still farms, some of it was bedroom for the nearby city of Clavaton, but the soap works here in Lumpkin Upper Mills was its major industry. Helen wondered how soon the picture might change. Some of the younger firebrands, notably one Brinkley Swope, head man among the sesses, were complaining that the outmoded factory wouldn't be operating much longer if something wasn't done soon to improve its facilities and manufacturing methods.

Only two weeks ago, Brinkley's brother Cronkite, demon reporter of the *Balaclava County Fane and Pennon*, had published a feature story about the slippage of the Lumpkin works in the world soap market. Feeling was said to be running as high as feeling ever got to run in so stodgy a place as Lumpkinton. However, Helen Shandy noticed no sign of impending riot as she bade Chief Olson farewell and headed her own car back toward the old Horsefall place, where she'd left her husband in amiable conclave with their friend Henny.

Hengist Horsefall, to give him his proper name, not that anybody ever used it, was well into his eighties. Peter, who wouldn't see sixty for a while yet, appeared a mere stripling beside him. The two were sitting out on the front porch, contemplating the sunset and stoking themselves up for the evening meal with preprandial sips of Henny's Aunt Hilda's damson gin while Henny's nephews Eddie and Ralph finished up the chores with the help of various offspring. Inside the house, nieces-in-law Marie and Jolene, a few greats, and a great-great or two were getting supper.

The Shandys hadn't meant to stay. They'd driven over to Lumpkin Corners to take pictures of some of Praxiteles Lumpkin's other artifacts, including a particularly interesting one owned by Henny himself that depicted a rooster standing on a pig's back. The Horsefalls, one and all, had insisted the Shandys take potluck with them; so Peter had remained as willing hostage while Helen, who'd saved the best till last, hoping for a fine sunset, had gone off alone to Lumpkin Upper Mills to complete her day's agenda.

It was largely thanks to Peter that the Horsefalls still owned the family farm.* It had been Helen who'd helped them sell some of their antiques for enough money to build on a big wing and house the whole clan in a style they'd never expected to enjoy. The Horsefalls could have sold the

Wrack and Rune (1982).

weather vane, too, and wound up with sufficient wealth to build themselves a mansion, but they didn't need a mansion. They liked the old place the way it was and they were all fond of the pig and rooster; so here they were and there it was going to stay and Helen Shandy was glad. She kissed her husband, was hugged by several Horsefalls, including Henny, who wasn't about to pass up the chance to embrace a pretty woman when he might never get another, and accepted a tot of damson gin.

"Well, how did you make out at the soap works?" Jolene asked her. "Did you get your pictures?"

"I hope so," Helen replied. "The weather vane looked pretty good in the viewfinder, anyway. But I almost wound up in jail for taking them."

"What do you mean? Did Soapy Snell come out and start throwing his weight around as usual?"

"No. What happened was that I'd climbed up on that old cannon in the middle of the road in order to boost myself high enough to get a decent shot. Chief Olson happened along in his cruiser just as I was ready to shoot, and took umbrage. He thought I was a kid," Helen added rather smugly.

"Olson hates kids," grunted Young Ralph, who counted among the grown-ups now that he was a student at Balaclava.

"And he's really got a thing about that cannon," added Ralph's sister Hilary, a beautiful brunette of about fifteen and a half. "You'd think he was General Grant or somebody." She giggled. "Brinkley Swope's crazy about the cannon, too. Cronkite says Brink's planning to sneak out some dark night when nobody's looking and shoot it off."

"Blow hisself to hell an' gone if he tries," snorted Henny. "That damn cannon's prob'ly rusted out so bad inside it'd bust its bar'l if Brink so much as stood near it an' let off a real good—"

"Uncle Henny," snapped Jolene.

"I was goin' to say sneeze." The octogenarian's washed-out blue eyes were as innocent as a newborn lamb's. "Quit pickin' on me, can't you?"

"That cannon's not rusted," said Eddie. "The GAR used to

keep it swabbed out long as there was any of 'em left alive, then the VFW an' the American Legion took over. Anyways, I don't s'pose Brinkley meant to stuff the damn thing full of grapeshot. A little black powder wouldn't hurt any."

"You never can tell what those Swope boys will do. And by the way, Hilly," her Aunt Marie added with a lift of the eyebrows, "what were you doing talking to Cronkite? Isn't he a little bit old for you?"

"He's twenty-five. Nine years isn't so much difference."

"Nine and a half, surely?"

"Anyway, I think older men are more interesting."

"Oh, you do, do you?" said her mother. "Seems to me last week you were finding Tommy Lomax pretty interesting and he's not even fifteen yet. You listen to me, young lady. If I ever catch you on that motorbike of Cronkite's, there'll be some fur flying around here and I don't mean maybe."

"Mama, for goodness' sake!" Hilary protested. "Cronkite gave a talk Sunday night at youth group about being a reporter and we got to ask questions afterward. I asked him one question and he answered. Big deal! He wasn't talking to me specifically, I was just one of the gang."

"Well, that's what you'd better keep on being, as far as I'm concerned. Those Swopes have a peculiar streak in 'em a yard wide, if you ask me."

"Now, Marie, there's a damn sight worse than the Swopes around here," said Ralph. "Huntley and Brinkley are doing all right at the soap works, and they pull their weight around town. Hunt's on the finance committee, and Brink practically runs the Lumpkinton Militia. Cronk's kind of a loose wheel, I have to admit, but I guess you have to be in his kind of job. How are you making out with the weather vanes, Helen?"

"Quite well, I think. I've done yours, the two horses on the old Lomax place, Gabe Fescue's cow kicking over the bucket, the big donkey and carrot on the Lumpkinton Town Hall, the figure of Justice on the county courthouse over at Clavaton, the 'Onward, Christian Soldiers' one on the Methodist church down below you, the two roosters and the grasshopper over in Balaclava Junction, the blacksmith at

Forgery Point, and I was lucky enough to catch that lovely mare and foal on Mrs. Peavey's barn over in Hoddersville before the barn burned down."

"That was an awful shame," said Eddie. "Beautiful old barn like that, been in the family since the year One, just about. They blamed the fire on wet hay smoldering in the loft, but Joe Peavey's a damned careful farmer. He swears it was set. The arson squad didn't find anything, though."

"They never found the remains of the weather vane, either," said Helen. "I've got my suspicions about that, but I suppose we'll never know. But anyway, counting the soap works, I'll have nine so far and Peter has a line on another Praxiteles 'way up in Maine at a forestry school where one of his old classmates is president. It's a lumberjack felling a tree. Peter wrote asking if we could come up and take photographs. We're going to make a vacation trip of it. Peter's classes were over this past week, you know, and I've taken a leave of absence from the library to work on the weather vane project. They've asked him to speak at next year's commencement. He's going to give a speech and sing 'Trees' for an encore. Aren't you, dear?"

"No, I think I'll leave that out of the program. Madam, do you realize we've been imposing on these good people for upward of four hours? It's half-past nine and pitch-dark out."

"Oh, what's the hurry?" Jolene protested. "We don't get to see you that often. Here, Peter, let me het up your tea for you."

"No, really, we mustn't," Helen protested. "We never intended to stay at all and we haven't even fed our cat. Jane will be furious. This has been lovely, but we've got to scoot. Can I help clear the table first?"

"With all these hired hands sitting around doing nothing? I should say not. Come on, kids, stir your stumps. Marie, how about a piece of your layer cake for Helen to take home so she won't have to think about dessert tomorrow?"

"We'd love a piece," said Helen, "not too big a one, please. Peter eats too many desserts as it is. So do I, I'm ashamed to admit."

Actually Helen wasn't more than a comfortable pound or two over the optimum weight for her delicate frame. Peter's five foot seven or eight was pretty well upholstered, but he was of a stockier build and much of what he packed was muscle. Internationally renowned as a horticulturist and agronomist, Professor Shandy still believed the best teaching was done out in the turnip fields, and could still outspade and outfork the burliest students in his classes.

Peter, Helen, and assorted Horsefalls were standing around exchanging the usual last-minute remarks when old Henny picked up his ears.

"Hark! That's the fire whistle."

They all fell silent, counting the hoots.

"Six an' three," said Ralph. "Gorry, that means the soap works!"

Then came two more hoots, louder and longer. "General alarm," yelled Eddie. "Come on, boys. See you later, Peter. We got to get down to the fire house."

He, his brother, and four of the oldest sons made a beeline for the door, grabbing boots and rubber coats as they ran. Peter and Helen quit saying they must be going, and went. Already a faint whiff of smoke was drifting over the hillside.

"God, it smells like a giant barbecue," Peter remarked as he steered carefully down the rocky dirt driveway. "I suppose that's the soap fat burning. I can remember a pan of grease catching fire on the wood stove at the farm when I was a kid. My cousin Gordy panicked and heaved a dipper of water on it, which only spread the flames. My grandmother laid him out in lavender afterward because she'd had to use up her whole keg of pickling salt putting out the fire."

"This one's going to take more than pickling salt," Helen remarked soberly. "Look, Peter, see that red glow in the sky? We must be three miles from the factory. Can you imagine what it's like over there? How do you suppose it got started?"

"Lord knows, but I expect it wouldn't have taken much. A mill that age would have been all wood construction except for the brick. Get a mile or two of planks and beams that have been soaking in soap fat for a century or two and one spark from an electrical short circuit, or an oil-soaked cleaning rag that some damn fool left to smolder in a closet, would set the whole place off. It would be like lighting a giant tallow candle."

"But they've always been extra careful about fire hazards," Helen protested. "Mrs. Lomax told me so. Those Swope boys who work there are her nephews or something, and they tell her everything. Not that she wouldn't know anyway. You know how she is. But anyway, she says they give everybody a strict warning lecture their first day on the job. They have no-smoking signs all over the place and fire drills every few weeks. Cigarettes have to be left with the timekeeper and anybody caught with a lighter or even a single match in his pocket gets fired on the spot."

Peter shook his head, as if to clear it. "Did she happen to mention whether they're still working double shifts?"

"I know they are. I saw the day shift going off and the night people coming on while I was taking my pictures. Darling, I know we ought to stay clear of the area, but isn't there some way we could at least find out if everybody got out all right?" Helen begged. "I don't think I can bear not to know."

"There's a place called Lookout Point over toward Lumpkin Upper Mills. It's far enough from the factory so we won't be in the way of the engines. We ought to be able to see what's happening and there's bound to be somebody around who'll know whether there've been any casualties. Lucky we left our birdwatching glasses in the glove compartment."

By the time they got to Lookout Point, the smell of the fire was enough to sting their eyes and throats even though the wind was blowing toward the east and they were half a mile westward. Through their field glasses they got a clear view of the burning factory down in the valley. Flames were shooting far above the building, scattering burning debris over the road, the fire trucks, and the roofs of nearby buildings. Helen saw one ember land on the cannon where she'd been standing a few hours ago. To her surprise, it set off a strange, bright fizzing flash.

"Peter, look quick! The cannon's on fire."

"Can't be. No, by George, you're right! That looks to me like black powder burning. It must have been fresh, too. Powder gets damp quickly."

"There certainly wasn't any when I climbed up. I made sure the cannon was clean before I risked my pink sneakers. Silly of me, I suppose, but I always feel there's something extra special about new sneakers. Oh, how ghastly! The whole roof's caving in. Can't the firemen do something?"

"I don't think they're even trying to save the factory. They know it's hopeless. All they can do is try to contain the fire and protect the surrounding properties."

"Another of Praxiteles Lumpkin's weather vanes gone." Helen sighed. "Both in the same week, and both by fire. You know, Peter, that's awfully strange. The one I photographed this afternoon was right in the center of that section of roof we just watched fall in, but I didn't notice it falling. Goodness knows there's plenty of light to see by even if the smoke is so thick. Did you see it?"

"No, I didn't, now that you mention it."

"You don't suppose some brave soul dashed up and rescued the weather vane?"

"I expect they were too busy rescuing themselves," Peter replied somberly. "I just hope they all got out."

As Peter had predicted, they weren't alone on Lookout Point. Other spectators were crowding around them, looking far more worried than excited. Peter and Helen could overhear their anxious conversation.

"There's Bob Giberson down there wetting his roof with the garden hose. If only the water pressure holds out! Oh my God, look! The porch is on—nope, he got it out."

"You can damn well bet Soapy Snell's porch isn't on fire. Where is he? Can you see him anywhere? Say, mister, could we borrow your glasses a second?"

"By all means." Peter handed them over.

After a minute or so, the other man returned them. "Nope, I can't see him. Probably home countin' his money. Huh! Chief Olson's down there screwin' up the traffic."

"He would be."

"I wanted to go help, but they wouldn't let me past the fire line. Got engines there from Clavaton and Hoddersville and everywhere."

"They say half the cars in the parking lot were on fire before most of the people in the factory knew what was happening."

"Anybody get caught inside?"

"Clem says they all made it out but Caspar Flum. Cas was in the tallow room, naturally. That seems to be where it started. Huntley Swope tried to go in after him, Clem says, but it was a solid wall of flames. Huntley's clothes were on fire when they hauled him back; I guess he's burned pretty bad. The police ambulance whooped him off to the Hoddersville Hospital."

"That'll be something for his brother to put in the paper, I reckon."

"Yup, there's Cronk down there now taking pictures an' hectoring the fire chief. Where's Brinkley, I wonder?"

"Brink's on days this week. I saw him down at Johnny's Spa, just after he got off his shift. He was buying cigars for his father-in-law. They got the old man living with them now, him and Cynthia. So Cas Flum got caught in the fire? God, that's awful! Poor old bastard must have worked in that tallow room fifty years or more. Well, at least he won't be out of a job like the rest of the town."

"Think Soapy Snell will ever rebuild?"

"Who knows? I don't see how they could have enough insurance on that old firetrap of a building to make up half of what it'd cost 'em to put up a new building at today's prices. Soapy won't give a damn. He's got plenty. Be just as well pleased to retire, I shouldn't wonder."

"I don't know what people are going to do if they don't rebuild. Wind up slinging hamburgers at fast-food joints, I expect, or clerking in supermarkets. This is one hell of a situation, if you ask me. Boy, if we ever find out who fired that cannon—"

"You surely don't think the cannon had anything to do

with starting the fire? Hell, that old popgun couldn't shoot a hole in a paper bag."

"Who says it couldn't. Sure made one hell of a bang, didn't it? We heard it clear up here to our place. The wife and I ran out to see what the hell was going on and the tallow room was all in a blaze as if a bomb went off inside. I never saw the like before. And, believe me, I never want to see it again."

"But you can't even aim those old cannons like the modern ones."

"What's to aim? The damn thing was pointed right at the tallow room window and not more than twenty feet away. Cas could look straight into the muzzle. He used to kid about being under bombardment."

"But a cannonball wouldn't start a fire even if it landed plunk in one of the vats."

"You wouldn't use a cannonball. You'd ball up some rags around a rock or something, ram it in on top of the powder, and it'd be on fire by the time it left the cannon. Wouldn't travel far, but it wouldn't have to. Can you imagine what a wad of blazing rags would do to a vat of hot tallow?"

"I wouldn't want to be around when it fell in, that's for sure. But who'd be fool enough to take that risk?"

"Somebody was fool enough to fire the goddamn cannon. You can't get around that."

"Aw, it could have been coincidence. Maybe some kid shoved a big firecracker down the barrel."

"Well, I expect we'll find out fast enough, if there's any of us left alive by morning. Cripes, this smoke is getting to me. I'm going back in the house."

TWO

Peter and Helen had had as much as they could take, too. They drove home with the car radio on, catching emergency bulletins first from the Clavaton station, then from the network. Jane Austen was waiting for them inside the house, indignant at having been left so long, notwithstanding the fact that Mary Enderble had dropped over to open a fresh can of cat food and hold Jane's paw for a while after Helen had telephoned from the Horsefalls'.

They tried to apologize, but she turned up her nose at the smell of smoked soap fat and stalked off in a huff, so they went upstairs to shower and shampoo. Once rid of the stench, they changed into clean night gear, put their stinking garments down cellar to be washed or outdoors to be aired, as the case might be, and at last persuaded Jane to join them in front of the television set.

Seeing on the screen snatches of what they'd already watched live was rather an odd experience, but it didn't last long. Caspar Flum was the big news. His death was official. The *Fane and Pennon*'s archives had furnished a lovely picture of Mr. Flum beaming among his tallow vats on the occasion of the factory's centennial in 1972. There was a more recent shot of him accepting his fifty-year service pin from the august and, needless to say, spotlessly clean hand of President Soapy Snell.

Mr. Flum had been a childless widower, but the newshounds had managed to round up a sister and a couple of nephews, all of them bleary-eyed from tears or smoke or both, and none too eager to parade their grief in front of the camera. They were unanimous in agreement that tallow had been Caspar Flum's life. The sister was willing to allow that maybe perishing among his vats was the way Cas would have wanted to go, but the less inarticulate of the nephews blurted out that he'd still like to get his hands on the murdering son of a bitch who'd fired that cannon.

No, he hadn't seen it fired. Nobody had, as far as he knew. But it must have been the cannon that set off the blaze because what the hell else could it have been? It just went to confirm the big bang theory, the other and presumably more studious nephew added, having at last got his Adam's apple free from his collar.

The sister contributed the further information that Cas had always been a good brother to her. She'd already bought his birthday present a month ago and what if the store wouldn't let her return it after all this time? Her voice became totally choked with tears, and the cameraman at last showed the decency to move on.

"Poor woman," Helen commented. "I don't know why they always have to go pestering the families at times like this. Let's have a spot of brandy, dear. I'm ready to drop and so are you, but we probably won't sleep without something to settle us down."

The brandy must have worked; the pounding on their front door at half-past seven dredged them both from fathoms deep. Peter stuck his head out the window without bothering to open his eyes and yelled, "Hold your horses. I'm coming." He then held a brief wrestling match with his bathrobe, borrowed his slippers back from Jane, and went downstairs.

The too-early visitor was Cronkite Swope, begrimed, bedraggled, reeking like a smoldering tallow vat, and tottering from exhaustion. Peter grabbed him by the arm.

"For God's sake, come in before you fall down."

He steered the young reporter through to the kitchen,

shoved him into a chair, and began making coffee. "Want some juice?"

"Huh?"

"Here, drink this."

Swope examined the glass of orange juice as though it might have been an apport from the astral plane, finally appeared to remember what it was for, and drank. Perhaps the fruit sugar revived him to some extent. He shoved back his chair and stood up.

"Mind if I wash?"

"Go right ahead. In there."

"I know."

Swope had visited the Shandy house a number of times since Peter had, by several odd twists of circumstance, become the resident sleuth of Balaclava Junction and environs. He found the downstairs bathroom with little difficulty and emerged somewhat less begrimed though no less kippered. "Professor, you've got to help us."

"What's the matter, Cronkite?" Helen was downstairs now, looking far more human than either of the men in her fleecy pink bathrobe and cerise slippers with pompoms on the toes. "Sit down, Peter, I'll do the coffee. Who wants bacon and eggs?"

Without waiting for an answer, she got out the big frying pan and began rooting in the refrigerator. "You've been up all night, I'll bet, Cronkite. Did they get the fire out?"

"They got the flames down, but it keeps starting up again. It'll probably go on smoldering for a week, the fire chief says. Thanks, Mrs. Shandy, I guess I could use some food. Though I sort of remember eating a doughnut from the Red Cross canteen sometime or other."

"Here, take one of these muffins to gnaw on till the eggs are ready. Would you like a bowl of cereal?"

"This is fine, thanks. Gosh, I didn't realize how hungry I was. But it doesn't feel right, sitting here."

"Why not?" Peter wanted to know. "What's eating you, Swope?"

"It's my brother."

"Huntley? We heard he was burned trying to rescue Caspar Flum. He's not—?"

"No, Hunt's doing all right, the last I heard. It's mostly on his arms and chest. His shirt caught fire. He'll be awhile healing and they had to dope him up for the pain, but it could have been worse. It's Brink I'm worried about."

"Brinkley? What happened to him?" Helen asked. "He wasn't in the factory, was he? We heard somebody mention that he'd been working the day shift yesterday."

"That's right. No, Brink's okay physically. But while he was taking his sister-in-law over to see Hunt at the hospital, somebody heaved a cannonball through his picture window with a burning rag tied around it."

"My God!" said Peter. "Did it do much damage?"

"Set fire to an arrangement of silk flowers and dried native grasses, retail value forty-nine dollars and fifty cents, that his wife Cynthia won at the raffle when they opened that new flower shop in the mall. Lucky Cynthia's father was in the house with the kids and hadn't gone to bed yet, or the place might have gone up in smoke and them with it. And whoever threw the cannonball would have blamed the fire on a burning ember and got away with it." Swope jabbed his fork savagely into a fried egg.

"So somebody actually believes Brinkley fired that old Civil War cannon into the tallow room?" Helen asked incredulously.

"Somebody, heck. Everybody, from what I was hearing all night at the fire. Even the volunteer firemen were all sore as boils about losing their regular jobs. I don't have to tell you what the loss of the factory's going to mean to Lumpkinton, do I? It's the town's only industry. If they don't rebuild, it's going to do a real number on the real-estate tax base, which will hurt the families even worse than they're hurting now. I understand how people feel, but what gets me is how anybody in his right mind could think my brother would do a crazy thing like that. Just because Brink kidded about it a couple of times and I was dumb enough to—"

"Shoot your mouth off in front of Hilly Horsefall's youth

group last Sunday night," Peter finished for him. "But the kids knew you only meant it as a joke."

"Which wouldn't have prevented some smart little twerp from trying it out," the reporter said bitterly.

"But how could they have got their hands on gunpowder?" Helen wanted to know.

Cronkite snorted. "Are you kidding? Half their fathers probably belong to the Lumpkinton Militia and have black powder for their muzzle-loaders. If three or four of them each swiped half a cupful or so, that would be enough to do the job, I should think. Anyway, if they walked into a gun shop and said they were buying it for their fathers, they mightn't have too much trouble talking the clerk into letting them have a pound or so. Or they could get one of the big guys to buy it for them, same as they get their beer. There are screwballs enough around. That bunch up on Woeful Ridge would do anything, so long as it was what they think of as real he-man stuff."

He meant a group of self-styled survivalists who met on weekends to hone up their machismo. Cronkite had held a personal grudge against them ever since he'd tried to get an interview and had been ignominiously run off, but most of Balaclava County took them as a crude joke.

"Woeful Ridge is a long way from the soap factory," said Helen. "Have another egg. So what you want is for Peter to find who really shot off the cannon, right?"

"I want him to help me find out how the fire really got started. Brink says he didn't fire the cannon. He doesn't believe the ball would have gone through the window anyway on account of the trajectory, whatever that means."

"It means the ball most likely wouldn't travel in a straight line," Peter explained, "and you'd have the devil's own time figuring out just where it would go, unless you'd fired a number of preliminary shots to get the range, which obviously wasn't done in this case. I'm inclined to agree with your brother, but I expect we're going to have one hell of a job figuring out what actually did happen. Is anything at all left of the tallow room?"

"There's not much left of the whole factory except a few jagged hunks of brick and mortar and a lot of ashes, as far as I could see."

Helen's face twisted. "No sign of the weather vane, I don't suppose?"

One might have thought she'd just laid a roc's egg. Young Swope stared at her for fully ten seconds, a piece of toast halfway to his mouth, before he realized what she was talking about. "The weather vane? Oh, that's right. You're doing a feature article for the *Fane and Pennon* about them."

"Am I? I didn't know."

"Well, I assumed that had to be why you were going around taking all those pictures. I mentioned it to my editor and he's pretty interested. But, gee, I don't know, Mrs. Shandy. It'll be a while before those ashes are cool enough to sift through. If they did find the weather vane, I don't suppose there'd be much left but a blob. I'll mention it to the firemen, though, if you want."

Cronkite drank the rest of his coffee. "I hadn't thought about the weather vane. It's a shame, isn't it. I always liked that skinny old guy in the tub."

"So did I. Let me get you some more coffee. So, Peter, what are you going to do?"

"Well, er—"

"Yes, dear?"

"Well, drat it, Helen—"

"I understand perfectly, dear. The Enderbles are primed to take care of Jane, and you can get your meals at the faculty dining room."

"And where will you be, for God's sake?"

"In Sasquamahoc, Maine, naturally. You don't think I'm going to sit here twiddling my little pink thumbs and let another Praxiteles Lumpkin weather vane melt down before I've even got to take a snapshot of it?"

"But you can't drive all that way by yourself!"

"I certainly can, but what makes you think I'm going to? Daniel Stott's off at the pork breeders' convention and Iduna will jump at the chance to go with me. We can stay with our old buddy Catriona McBogle. She was a visiting author in South Dakota when I was librarian there. We both boarded with Iduna. That was while Iduna was still Miss Bjorklund, the buggy-whip magnate's daughter," Helen explained to Swope.

Catriona McBogle was the name that caught the reporter's attention. "Isn't she the woman who writes all those goofy books? What's she doing in Maine?"

"Writing more goofy books, I expect. She loves it there. Cat says you can be as insane as you please and nobody pays the least bit of attention. Iduna and I had better take the Stotts' car, don't you think, Peter? You'll want ours to go detecting in."

"I could rent one if you'd be more comfortable driving ours."

"Borrow the *Fane and Pennon* staff car," Cronkite offered through a poorly concealed yawn. "I can ride my bike."

"Cronkite, why don't you forget about your bike for a while?" said Helen. "Go upstairs, take a shower, and get some sleep. Peter, find him some towels and pajamas. I'll be up to change the bed as soon as I've finished my coffee."

"Sit still, I can manage. Come on Swope, you're dead on your feet."

"I don't want to put you to any trouble. I'll just get back on my bike and—"

"Fall off the other side. You're in no condition to go anywhere."

"Well, if you're—"

Another yawn interrupted whatever Swope was going to say. Peter took him by the arm and steered him stairward. Helen was thinking seriously about another swallow or two of coffee when the telephone rang. Old Henny Horsefall was on the line.

"Helen? Got a new wrinkle for your weather vane story."

Henny's yarn went on for quite a while. The gist of it was that everybody but himself and a few of the youngest children had gone off to the fire—some to join the volunteer firemen, some to help out at the Red Cross canteen, some to gawk from a safe vantage point. He'd finally got the kids to sleep, but he himself had stayed outside, on the qui vive for any stray ember that might find the way to their hillside.

None had, not surprisingly, but long about ha'past one he'd heard a noise out by the barn. He'd hotfooted it over there and be cussed and be damned if there wasn't two grown men up on the roof fiddling around with the weather vane. He'd had the hose nozzle in his hand so he'd guv a squirt and a holler, then run in for the old over-and-under and fired a blast out the kitchen winder.

By the time he'd got back to count the corpses, they'd made theirselves skeerce, didn't leave no ladder nor nothin'. He'd set up till daylight waiting but nothing else happened. The pig and rooster were still where they'd been ever since Praxiteles Lumpkin helped Henny's great-grandfather put them there.

But Henny had got to thinking. So this morning, soon as he and the kids got through milking, the younger men being still at the fire and the ones who'd straggled home too beat to find the cows, let alone the teats, he'd called up old Gabe Fescue. Gabe was the one who owned that other weather vane Helen had took the picture of, the cow kicking over the bucket. After hearing Henny's story, Gabe had gone out to take a gander at it, and be further cussed if the dern thing wasn't gone, slick as a whistle. Didn't Helen think that was the damnedest, and what did she think Peter would think?

"I expect he'll think pretty much what you and I are thinking," she told him. "The fire made a good excuse to go crawling around people's roofs and somebody who knew what those weather vanes are worth took advantage of the chance. That's terrible, Henny. It's hard to believe anybody would stoop so low."

"Seems to me they had to climb pretty high."

"Oh, Henny! You know what I mean. But that's a point to consider. You say you didn't see any ladder, so how did they get up on your barn? That ridgepole must be upwards of forty feet high, isn't it?"

"I guess likely. Mebbe they come in one o' them hook an'

ladder trucks that was screechin' and' hootin' around all night. Can't say I noticed any, an' I got to admit that might be kind of a hard thing to overlook. What I think is, they must o' snuck into the barn, clumb up into the loft an' out that little winder in the back where the swallows go in an' out of. There's an old ladder nailed to the wall that my father put up once when he was doin' some work on the roof. 'Twouldn't be too hard for an able-bodied feller to get up that way. I done it myself a few times when I was a dern sight sprier than I am now. They could o' used a rope an' pickaxe an' them pointy things on their boots if they was too scairt to tackle it bare-handed like I done. I seen 'em mountain climbin' that way on TV."

"And they'd have had the rope to lower the weather vane by if they'd got it loose, which thank goodness they didn't. But what a shame about Mr. Fescue's losing his cow. I'll speak to Peter, Henny. He's upstairs just now, putting Cronkite Swope to bed."

"What's the matter with Cronk?"

"He's dead beat, that's all."

If Henny hadn't yet heard the rumor about Brinkley Swope, Helen was not about to spread it. "I expect Peter will be out to see you after a while. Thanks for calling, and keep an eye on your weather vane."

She hung up. Peter came downstairs while she was still standing beside the telephone.

"What's up?"

"Something strange." Helen told him about Henny's call. "He asked for you. I said I thought you'd probably drop out to see him in a while."

"M'yes. It mightn't be a bad idea to check out the Methodist church, the county courthouse, and the rest of your list while I'm about it. You wouldn't happen to remember the Flackleys' telephone number at Forgery Point?"

"It's in the book. If you don't mind, though, I'd like to phone Cat McBogle first. I think Iduna and I had better get our expedition under way right now, before that firebug moves on to Maine."

THREE

Helen went upstairs to pack. Peter sat down with the phone book and began dialing. As far as he could learn from the puzzled souls whom he sent outdoors to check on their weather vanes, none of the other Lumpkin artifacts on Helen's list was missing. If she was right about the soap factory's man in the tub, though—and after Henny's call, it seemed more than likely she was—somebody had just pulled off a damned profitable night's work.

Others might have found it hard to believe anybody would pay thirty or forty thousand dollars for an old-time joke that time had turned into folk art. However, after the way his wife had parlayed Hilda Horsefall's grandma's courting sofa and a dozen or so other odds and ends into a handsome addition to the Horsefall homestead, two new trucks, some first-rate farm machinery, and the finest herd of Guernseys in the county, Peter was not about to dispute anything she told him about antiques.

Not that he'd have doubted Helen's word in any case; she was a librarian, and librarians were never wrong. He wished she weren't going off without him, but he understood why she felt she ought to. Furthermore, it was probably better for her to get away from here till he could get a handle on what in tunket was happening to Praxiteles Lumpkin's weather vanes. Mrs. Shandy's picture-taking had stirred up a good deal more interest in them than anybody had ever shown before, except maybe Praxiteles's lady friend, if he'd had one. These clandestine collectors, whoever they might be, might logically consider Helen their chief threat to what appeared to be shaping up as a highly successful operation.

Peter made one last phone call, to the editor of the *Balaclava County Fane and Pennon* to let him know his star reporter was catching forty desperately needed winks in the Shandy guest room. Then he decided he might as well stroll up to Valhalla, the hill above the campus where Professor Stott's substantial house stood cheek-by-jowl with the president's mansion.

"I'm going to see whether Iduna wants me to bring the car around," he called up the stairs.

"That's a good idea, dear," Helen replied. "She may need some help with her luggage; her back's been bothering her lately. I'll be ready by the time you get back here."

Dan Stott had finally put his old Buick out to pasture and bought a new station wagon. Sturdy, comfortable, and capacious, this would be just the ticket for the two women to travel in. Peter felt a little better helping Iduna Stott pack in a vast picnic hamper, a beverage cooler, two suitcases, a raincoat the size of an army tent, and a coat sweater big enough to accommodate several Helens or one Iduna, as the case might be.

"Well, that ought to hold you ladies awhile. Want me to drive as far as our house?"

"No, I'll do it. Helen can spell me after a while, once we're on the road."

Getting from Valhalla to the Crescent, where the Shandys lived, took longer driving than walking, since they had to circle all the way around the college. Iduna handled the wheel as nonchalantly and expertly as she did her pie dough.

"My, isn't it awful about that fire? What do you suppose those poor folks that worked in the mill are going to do now? Can't even drown their sorrows at the Bursting Bubble. I heard on the news it burned right to the ground. Nothing left but a few broken beer bottles and a nasty smell."

"Then they'll just have to stay sober, collect their unemployment, and pray something turns up before it runs out, I guess," Peter answered. "At least they haven't lost their houses."

"Not yet, anyway. Land knows what'll happen if it gets so they can't meet their mortgages. Whatever possessed that man to shoot off that darned cannon, I wonder?"

"How do they know it was a man?" Peter asked her. "Are they even sure the cannon was fired? Did anybody see it happen?"

"It didn't say on the news, but they're asking anybody who might have seen something to come forward. The trouble seems to be that there's never much doing on that side of the factory after dark, unless something's happening at the schoolhouse, which of course there isn't now that classes are through for the summer and they're closed for repairs. Going to put in a new boiler, Mrs. Lomax tells me, and paint all the classrooms. She's got a cousin on the maintenance staff."

"Name me something she hasn't got a cousin on," Peter grunted. "One thing sure, that school's going to need repainting now a damned sight worse than it did before."

"Won't it, though? Greasy soot all over everything. I'm glad I don't have to wash the windows. Well, at least it'll make a few extra jobs for some of the men, not that the women don't need 'em just as badly. They're going to miss being with their friends, you know. That's the tough thing about keeping house, it's lonesome not having anybody around to talk to. Which is one reason I started taking in boarders back in South Dakota. The other reason was that I needed the money after the buggy-whip business went bust."

Iduna uttered a ladylike snort of self-deprecating laughter. "I guess that's why I'm so wrought up about those factory workers. I know how it feels to be used to cream in your coffee every day and lamb chops on the table whenever you felt like 'em, then suddenly finding yourself with a big house on your hands and nothing much to run it on. Well, I suppose they can count one blessing. It was the Bursting Bubble that burned down instead of the schoolhouse. At least folks won't be tempted to blow their unemployment checks on booze they can't afford and are better off without. We saw too darn much of that back home after the buggy-whip factory had to shut down. They get depressed, you know."

"Can't blame them for that."

"You don't have to tell me, Peter. I was pretty down in the dumps myself after my own house got blown away by the tornado. All the family photographs, Poppa's mustache cup and everything just gone with the wind. It's a terrible feeling, like standing on the edge of a cliff and feeling the ground crumbling away under your feet. And now they say the remains are beginning to foam."

"Foam?"

Iduna nodded. "Yup. It's the soapsuds coming out. From all that water they've been squirting on, you know. Better than smoke and flames, I suppose, but they're frothing out all over the road and people's yards and getting into cellars and spoiling gardens. And of course the dogs and cats and kids are running out and getting soaked and tracking 'em into the houses. They're not nice, clean white suds, either—there's ashes and dirt and heaven knows what mixed in. From what I saw on the morning news, it's just one great big gooky mess over there. Everybody's fit to be tied and you can't blame 'em. I bet if they ever find out who started that fire, they'll tar and feather him and ride him out of town on a rail."

Peter was not happy. "What if he turns out to be a her?" he suggested without much hope.

Iduna shook her silver blond head. "He won't. Women have more sense. Look, there's Helen bringing her stuff out. I declare to goodness she looks younger now than she did in South Dakota. Don't you just love those little bitty pink sneakers? Helen always did have the cutest feet. Ready, ma'am? Your taxi's waiting."

"Just about, I think."

Helen's luggage consisted of one small suitcase, a few garments hung inside a plastic cleaner's bag, and a large canvas tote bag crammed full of books. Iduna chuckled when she saw the traveling library.

"Kind of coals to Newcastle, isn't it, lugging books to Cat McBogle?"

"Look who's talking," Helen retorted. "Set these in beside that pantry Iduna's got in there, will you, Peter? You know darn well Cat started cooking the minute she found out we were coming, Iduna. Anyway, Cat and I have the same recurring nightmare, that we'll find ourselves stuck away somewhere without a solitary thing to read."

"Don't they have a library in Sasquamahoc?"

"That seems to be a matter of opinion. Cat says it's eight feet square and open one afternoon a week from three to six o'clock. She does have access to the college library, but the only books in there are either about tree fungus or else the poems of Joyce Kilmer. Cat stocks up whenever she hits a bookshop and buys a lot through the mail, but it's hard on a person with a two-book-a-day habit. Let me just run back and say good-bye to Jane."

"Give her my love." Iduna settled herself more comfortably behind the wheel and checked her custom-made seat belt. "See you on Friday, Peter. Daniel's due back Saturday noontime, and I need time enough to have a decent meal ready for him when he gets home."

"I'm sure he'll be ready for one," said Peter. He'd never known a time when Dan wasn't. "Have a good trip, Iduna. I'd better go see if Helen has any last-minute nagging to get out of her system."

His true objective was to stock up on a few extra conjugal embraces to tide him over through the week, but Helen was encumbered by the phone.

"I shan't be here, but my husband will," she was saying. "He'll make sure Cronkite gets the message just as soon as he wakes up. No, no trouble at all. Please don't hesitate to call us anytime. You'd better try to get some rest and keep your spirits up. Give our best to Mrs. Lomax and tell her she mustn't even think of coming to us this week. You need her more than we do."

Helen put the phone back. "That was Huntley Swope's wife," she told Peter. "She called the paper trying to get hold of Cronkite and they told her he was here. She wants him to know Huntley came out of the anesthetic a little while ago and said he'd watched a soldier throw a bomb into the tallow room. She wants Cronkite to put that in the paper. I gather her object is to take the heat off Brinkley."

"Fat chance," Peter grunted.

"I know, dear, but at least it may make the poor woman feel a little better to know she tried. She's been sitting up all night long with her husband and sounds as if she's worn to a frazzle. Mrs. Lomax is taking care of the children. Aunt Betsy, she called her. So you'd better not count on getting any cleaning done while I'm gone. I feel awfully mean, running out on you like this."

"It's a far, far better thing you do." Peter didn't want to tell her so to her face, but he was relieved to know Helen would be safely out of the way for a few days. "How did Huntley know it was a soldier?"

"Darling, how do I know? Maybe the man was carrying a flag and beating a drum. I expect Huntley was still pretty groggy when he spoke to her. He may be able to do better when he wakes up again."

Helen picked up the pink sweater she'd left hanging on the newel post and slung it around her shoulders. "They had to give him another shot, poor man. Mrs. Swope says they're going to keep him sedated for a day or so, till he's over the worst of the shock. Well, I mustn't keep Iduna sitting there. Take care of yourself, darling. I've left Cat's number on the telephone pad. Give me a ring when you find a chance."

"You call me as soon as you get there, just so I'll know you made it."

"All right, dear. If you're not around, I'll leave a message with the Enderbles. Mary's going to keep an eye on Jane. I told her you'd probably be in and out a lot. You behave yourself, young woman."

Helen gave the cat a last tickle under the chin and went back out to Iduna's car. Peter stood up on the doorstep with Jane in his arms, watching them off. When his wife blew him a kiss, he waved Jane's tail in farewell, but he didn't smile.

"Poor Peter," she told Iduna as they turned out of the Crescent, "Cronkite Swope staggered in this morning looking like the wrath of God and stuck him with another detecting job. Not that Peter was in any rush to turn it down, I have to admit."

"Oh well, it'll be a change from teaching," Iduna replied comfortably. "Like Daniel going to the pig growers' convention. Darn it, look at that. Another little kid on a bicycle, wobbling all over the road. I wish their mothers would keep 'em in their own backyards till they learn how to ride the darn things. I always pass 'em at about two miles an hour with my heart in my mouth. What's Cronkite want Peter to detect? Who set fire to the soap factory?"

"As a matter of fact, yes," said Helen. "People are blaming Cronkite's brother Brinkley."

"Brinkley? I thought he worked there himself. Martha Betsy Lomax told me Brink was real high up in the sesses. Lucky I do the crossword puzzle when Daniel doesn't beat me to it, so I knew what she was talking about. At least I think I did. I expect sesses are sort of like jelly molds, only for soap. Brinkley hadn't been laid off or anything? Martha Betsy gave me to understand he was a good, steady fellow. Nice wife, pretty house, two kids, doing just fine and everybody happy. What makes anyone think he'd do an awful thing like that?"

"Brinkley once made a silly joke about wanting to fire the old cannon that sat pointing toward the factory," Helen explained. "And Cronkite rather dim-wittedly repeated the story to a youth group last Sunday night over at Lumpkin Corners. The cannon apparently did get shot off just before the blaze in the tallow room went up, which started the whole thing, as you've no doubt heard since you've been watching the news. Peter doesn't believe the shot could have started the fire, but obviously a lot of other people do."

Iduna still wasn't convinced. "How could they tell the cannon was fired? Did anybody see it happen? They didn't say so on the news."

"Then you can bet there were no witnesses. I don't know,

Iduna, I suppose the firemen looked down the barrel and saw gunpowder smudges, or whatever it is one's supposed to see. I myself happened to notice what Peter said must be gunpowder burning on the breech, or whatever they call it. I'm not much up on cannons. Anyway, the place at the back where they shove the stuff to make it go off. Remember how we used to get those packets of firecrackers with the fuses all twisted together that you had to untangle before you could light them? And if you happened to pull out a fuse, you'd break the firecracker in two and light the powder so you'd get a fizz instead of a bang? Well, that's how it burned."

"I used to break mine on purpose," said Iduna. "I liked the spits better than the bangs. I suppose it's more sensible not to sell 'em any more, but I can't help thinking it's kind of a shame kids can't get to celebrate the Fourth of July the way we used to. What happens nowadays is, they get hold of 'em anyhow, one way or another, and shoot 'em off any old time they feel like it. Doesn't mean anything and scares the dogs just as bad as it ever did. Land's sakes, our old Rover used to crawl under my folks' big double bed the afternoon of the third and not come out till noon of the fifth. We'd have to poke his food in after him with the end of a broomstick. Which didn't stop me from having my fun like the rest of the crowd, I have to admit. Kids are awful, aren't they? By the way, did you know I'm going to be a step-grandma again?" Iduna added just as proudly as though kids weren't awful at all.

Conversation drifted off into matters obstetrical, and Helen was as well pleased that it should. She was relieved to get away from the stench of burning fat that seemed to have got into her nose and lodged there; from the thought of Huntley Swope all bandaged up in a hospital bed and his worn-out wife huddled beside him; from the ugliness of that window in Brinkley's pretty house, broken by somebody who believed the sess man had been fool enough to kill the old tallow man and throw half the town out of work for the sake of a silly joke.

Those who hadn't been too badly injured or too totally

exhausted from fighting the fire would be heading over to the county seat by now, Helen supposed, to line up for unemployment benefits. The ones whose cars had been destroyed would have to beg rides from those who still had some means of transportation. Or maybe the town would let them use the school buses. That would be a sensible way to cope, but would anybody think of it? Were the buses still operable? They'd been parked out back of the school, Helen remembered, all too close to the fire.

At least parents who'd worked at the factory would get to spend plenty of time with their children during the long school vacation this summer. That should make the youngsters happy, but how would they feel if Christmas rolled around and the unemployment benefits gave out and there was still no extra money for presents? It wouldn't matter so much, she supposed, if they were all in the same boat. Not getting anything when others got a lot was what hurt.

Well, Christmas was a long time from now and all sorts of things could happen in the meantime. The sky was blue, the road was wide, this was a great year for daisies and dandelions along the embankments. Helen relaxed in her seat and let the miles roll by. She'd take over the driving in an hour or so, and Iduna could spell her after they'd got up into Maine. Or was it down? No matter, they'd get there.

They'd probably have made better time if Iduna hadn't brought such a big picnic basket. The Massachusetts rest stops were nothing to write home about, but they did allow for getting out the thermos and an oatmeal cookie or two. Once the women were through the southeast corner of New Hampshire and over the bridge into Kittery, it was another story. They visited the handsome information center, went back outside to the pine grove, and carried their provender to one of the inviting picnic tables.

They dawdled their way through jellied consommé in little plastic cups, then Iduna set out chicken sandwiches with watercress and thin-sliced roast beef on rye with dilled cucumbers.

"There's lemonade if you want it, Helen. I brought two

thermoses. I figured we might be pretty well coffeed out by the time we got this far."

"I'd better stick to coffee. I didn't get much sleep last night, thinking about that fire."

They ate their sandwiches, with sweet green grapes and a perfect brie to follow. The basket still wasn't empty.

"I've got some jam tarts I was taking up to Cat, and a few oatmeal cookies left, unless you want to save 'em for later."

"Later, thanks," said Helen. "I'm stuffed to the eyeballs. That was a wonderful lunch, Iduna."

"Well, I thought we wouldn't need anything hearty since it's just us women. How much farther do we have to go, Helen? I'm about ready for my nap."

"Cat said it would be a little over two hours from here. I'm not a bit tired myself, so why don't I drive the rest of the way? We'll go straight on through and be there for tea. Cat always did like her cup of tea in the afternoon, remember?"

"As who doesn't? Oops, looks as though we're being invaded. We may as well stir our stumps."

Five youngish men were piling out of a big green van with a Massachusetts number plate that had pulled up beside the Stott wagon. Judging from the rods lashed to the top of the car, they were on a fishing trip. They must be either present or former servicemen, Helen thought, because they all seemed to be wearing assorted garments of olive drab or camouflage cloth and they all had their pantlegs tucked into the tops of heavy laced boots. Then it occurred to her that they'd probably been to L. L. Bean's on a previous trip.

Most of them were fairly unkempt about the heads and chins, but one, the only one whose fatigue jacket matched his pants, was both clean shaven and close-cropped. He swung his legs over the bench of the next table, looked squarely at the two women—he had round topaz-colored eyes like an owl's, Helen noticed—and gave them a boyish smile as he waited for one of the others to bring him a Coke and a bag of corn chips out of the vending machine. Perhaps he was only smiling at the size of their picnic hamper. Anyway, they smiled back as they left the grove.

"Nice-looking boy," Iduna remarked.

"He's no boy," Helen contradicted. "What do you want to bet he's the oldest one of the bunch? It's just that haircut and the catfish grin that fool you."

Helen spoke offhandedly, her mind on getting back into the mainstream of traffic. Was that tractor trailer truck going to veer over into the outside lane just as she pulled out? She decided she'd better wait till it got safely past.

"He looked familiar, but I can't think why. Probably reminds me of some student I've had a run-in with at the library. When some kid gives me that wide-eyed innocent look, I start wondering which of the more expensive noncirculating reference books he's trying to sneak out with. We librarians do tend to develop a strain of cynicism, I'm afraid. Let your seat back and shut your eyes, why don't you? I'll wake you when we get to Cat's."

FOUR

"Cat, your hair's as red as ever," cried Helen.

"Damned well ought to be. That stuff I use is up to five dollars and thirty-seven cents a bottle. Come on in and rest your toenails."

Catriona McBogle was about halfway between Helen and Iduna in both age and height. Her current weight could only be guessed at since she had on a pair of baggy gray cotton drawstring pants and an oversized white sweatshirt with black pawprints on it. They were, according to the caption that ran across what was presumably her bosom, the footprints of a gigantic hound.

"Leave your luggage in the car. Andrew can bring it in. He's out hoeing the potato patch just now. I told the old coot to weed the flower beds, such as they are, but he's deaf as a haddock when he chooses to be. It's the bleddy old feudal system. Andrew hoed potatoes for the people I bought the house from, so he's bound and determined to hoe potatoes for me if it kills us both."

"Why should it?" Iduna wondered.

"It might if she ate too many of them green," Helen pointed out. "Can't you get him to hoe onions instead, Cat? None of the onion family is poisonous. Père Marquette and his exploring party lived on wild onions all the way from Wisconsin to what's now Chicago in 1674. Did you know the name Chicago is taken from an Indian word meaning skunk place, supposedly on account of the wild leeks that grew there?"

Miss McBogle grunted. "What do you want to bet it was on account of Marquette and his crew? Wild onions are good for bee stings, hemorrhoids, carbuncles, and ringing in the ears, I know that. You drop the juice into the ear canal. Want to see where you're going to sleep?"

"I want to see the bathroom first," said Iduna. "You do have one? How old is this house, Cat?"

"Two hundred years, give or take a twelvemonth or two. A good deal of inland settling took place in Maine around that time. The house has been modernized, otherwise you can jolly well believe I'd never have stuck myself with it. Straight through the kitchen, Iduna, that door at the back. There's another john upstairs if you're desperate, Helen. I'll put on the teakettle and give you the grand tour."

They rejoined her a couple of minutes later, ready for their tour. The house wasn't small, but the rooms were few.

"It's the *reductio ad absurdum* of the classic Federal style," Catriona explained. "This big kitchen all the way across the back half of the downstairs, and two in front with a staircase between. Upstairs is the same except that the rooms are narrower because of the landing. And I've had the attic finished off because it was the only way to insulate without having the batts all custom tailored. Besides, I couldn't bear not to. Come and see."

"I'm still gawking at this fantastic kitchen," said Helen. "I assume that old wood-burning stove is piped into where the fireplace used to be. Imagine what it must have been like two hundred years ago with black iron pots hanging over the fire on cranes and a haunch of bear meat turning on the spit."

"And soot and cinders and flying sparks, and your face scorching and your bum freezing. And kindling to split and logs to lug in and smoke getting in your eyes and all the food tasting like finnan haddie," Catriona finished.

"Do you use the stove for heating?" Iduna asked.

"Not unless the power goes off or Andrew happens to be in one of his wood-chopping moods. Do observe my pictur-esque Early American thermostat and the delightfully quaint baseboard radiation. You may also note that behind this divider thing are an electric stove, an electric refrigerator, and an electric dishwasher. There's also a trash compactor that scares the heck out of me and one of those things that chop up the garbage and flush it into the septic tank, which I personally consider both impractical and decadent."

"Then why do you have them?"

"I'll tell you why. Because the people I bought the house from had an uncle in the appliance business and got them wholesale, that's why. Generally, I bung the swill out on the compost heap, hoping Andrew will do whatever you're supposed to do to make humus and then fork it out on the flower beds. But he never does," Catriona added petulantly. "Mostly, the skunks eat the garbage. The garden's not doing too well, but we do have handsome skunks. I see them pattering around the yard sometimes at night. They have the dearest little feet, like Helen's."

"Don't they bother the cats?" Iduna hadn't seen any cats as yet but couldn't imagine Catriona McBogle without a few.

"No, skunks and cats manage to coexist quite peacefully. It's dogs that get into trouble. Cats are much more intelligent than dogs, of course. Finished communing with the woodbin,

Helen? Come on into the parlor, generally referred to as the living room."

"How lovely," Helen exclaimed.

It was. For either aesthetic or budgetary reasons, Catriona McBogle had kept the furnishings simple: cherrywood tables and a walnut rocking chair, an overstuffed sofa and chair with faded blue slipcovers that had known the touch of feline claws. A smallish oriental rug, figured chintz curtains, and a stenciled border on Wedgwood blue walls above a cream-painted wainscot made a pleasant background for a few pieces from Cat's modest art collection. The room's great beauty, however, came from its perfect proportions and the views of meadow and wood framed by tall windows.

Catriona took her friends' praise as a matter of course. "It's not me, it's the house. Come and see my Early Bunker Bean dining room set. Fumed oak, I believe they called it when Mother was a girl. I fumed enough while I was stripping off all that dark brown gunk they'd covered it with, that's for sure."

"But the result was worth the effort," Helen said. The bold grain and soft taupish brown of the exposed oak was exactly right with the boxy lines of the table, buffet, and funny little squarish chairs with somewhat crudely carved backs. Fake William Morris via Grand Rapids, circa 1923, she guessed. The curtains were a different chintz, pink flowers and purple birds in a pale green jungle. The painted green walls had a different stenciled border that picked up the formal leafy shape of a large potted palm that stood on the buffet.

"I raised that palm from a pup," Catriona bragged.

There were more plants in raised stands that ran the whole length of one wall under more tall windows. Most of them looked as if they'd been through a tough winter.

"Carlyle and Emerson practice their stalking in them when it's too stormy to go out," she explained. "I usually eat my lunch in here. It's lovely in winter with the sun shining off the snow. Free solar heat. Come on upstairs."

"Hadn't we better do something about that teakettle first?" Iduna suggested gently.

"Oh, hell, I always forget." Catriona ran for the kitchen. "Damn thing sits here shrieking its head off. I don't know why the bloody scientists can't make them self-pouring. Have you noticed people have pretty much quit going around saying, 'If we can put a man on the moon'? Maybe you'd like your tea right now, before it turns to tannic acid. I made a batch of Joe Froggers."

She began taking down cups and filling a plate with fat molasses cookies the size of saucers.

Iduna opened the hamper she'd refused to leave in the car. "I brought some jam tarts."

"Gad, the expedition's well equipped. Anybody take milk and sugar? Neither of you ever used to, as I remember. How long can you stay?"

"We have to leave Friday morning so Iduna can cook a fatted calf for Daniel," Helen told her. "Do you think you can stand us till then?"

"Probably, if I strain myself a little. Oh, it's so good to see you! Here, Iduna, you pour our tea for us the way you used to do in South Dakota when we mushed in out of the blizzard with icicles hanging off our noses. What lovely times we had."

"It seems as if we'd never been apart," said Helen. "I must say I've never fully accepted the time-like-an-ever-rolling-stream concept."

"Why should you?" Catriona passed her the Joe Froggers. "Time has been abolished. It's nothing but a bunch of quarps and quiffs these days. Quarps and quaffs, in Andrew's case. I personally can't make head nor tail of quantum mechanics, but it certainly is thought-provoking, as Professor Haseltine used to say about the hash at the college cafeteria. How did you two ever wind up married to professors? I suppose they both know all about quantums."

"What Daniel knows about is hogs, mostly." Iduna bit into one of Catriona's giant cookies. "My, these are good. Do you ever hear from Professor Haseltine?"

"Speaking of professors," said Helen, "I'd better call Peter and let him know we've arrived before he has the state police out looking for us. May I use your phone, Cat?"

"Of course. Use the one in my office, why don't you? It's straight at the top of the stairs."

Catriona McBogle's office was thirty-odd feet long and about nine feet wide. Which was typical of Cat, Helen decided. At first she thought working here must be like writing on a streetcar, then she decided it was more like being on the deck of a ship. There was a window on the front, and two more on one side, along with a huge chimney and a dinky little stove inside the fireplace. The other side was all bookshelves. Cat's own books had three shelves to themselves; Helen hadn't realized how prolific her former fellow boarder had been during the intervening years. She was interested to notice how many different editions of a single book there could be. The translations were a bit disconcerting. Whatever must *The Case of the Undarned Sock* or *The Baffling Affair of the Spearmint on the Bedpost* read like in German or Japanese?

She wasn't getting any answer on the phone. Peter must be off counting weather vanes and Cronkite Swope either dead to the world or up and away. She tried the Enderbles and got John.

"Oh, Helen. Good to hear your voice. Made it all right, did you? You've missed Mary by a whisker, she just this minute went over to have a little visit with Jane. Want me to holler out the door?"

"No, it doesn't matter a bit. I promised Peter I'd let him know we got here. Maybe you could buzz Mary at our house and ask her to leave a note on the kitchen table. He has my friend's number if he wants to call me back."

Helen exchanged a few more words with John on the subject of Sasquamahoc's local fauna, mainly to the effect that she herself hadn't seen any yet but she had it on good authority that the skunks all wore pink sneakers. Then, mindful of her hostess's phone bill, she hung up and went to get her tea.

"I was thinking," said Catriona, when Helen's cup had

been refilled and she'd been equipped with another Joe
Frogger she certainly didn't need but wasn't about to pass up.
"If we zipped over and took Helen's pictures today while the
light's still good, we'd have tomorrow free to go whale
watching."

Iduna set down her cup. "Whale watching? Whatever put
that into your head?"

"It's rather a done thing these days. Eustace Tilkey over in
Hocasquam has started running excursions on his lobster
boat, the *Ethelbert Nevin*. I haven't had a chance to go out
with him yet myself, so I thought it might be fun if we all
went together. Unless you'd rather do something else,"
Catriona added out of politeness.

But Helen and Iduna were all for the whales. "Those are
one kind of animal we don't have at Balaclava. Though we
do have President Svenson," Helen added out of fairness.
"How far from here is the forestry school?"

"About half a mile. We could walk it in ten minutes if you
feel like stretching your legs."

"I wouldn't mind a little stroll."

"Then why don't you and Cat go?" said Iduna. "I'll stay
here and wash up the dishes. Maybe I could get supper
started, Cat, if you'll tell me what to fix."

"We'll bung the dishes into the washer and supper's all
fixed except for heating it up and putting it on the table,"
Catriona told her firmly. "If you're tired from the ride, why
don't you stretch out on the sofa? Or sit on the terrace and
watch the swallows?"

"Now, that's a thought. They'd sort of get me in practice
for the whales. I think I will, then, if you don't mind."

Iduna picked up a magazine and headed out to the
old-fashioned wooden swing that sat under an apple tree near
the house. Helen and Catriona set off down the road.

"I could have offered to take the car," Catriona half
apologized. "I forgot walking isn't exactly Iduna's thing."

"Don't give it a thought. If she'd wanted to come, she'd
have said so. I suspect what Iduna really wants is a nap. She
dozed a bit on the way up, but you know what it's like trying

to sleep in a car. I don't suppose she got much rest last night. None of us did."

"Oh, on account of that fire in the soap factory? They had a snatch of it on the news last night. I wondered how near you were."

"Actually, Peter and I were right there. I'd been over in Lumpkinton taking pictures of the factory weather vane, oddly enough, just a few hours before the place caught fire. We'd stayed to have supper with friends, and when they all rushed off to be volunteer firemen, Peter and I went up on a hill where we could look right down into the fire. You can't imagine how awesome it was."

"Sure I can. How do you think I make my living? Damn, I wish I'd been there. I understand by now the town's a seething mass of soapsuds."

"You wouldn't think it was funny if it were your house the suds were getting into," Helen rejoined somewhat tartly. "Or your job that had just got washed away. I don't know what those people are going to do for work."

"Won't the factory be rebuilt?"

"I have no idea. Even so, it would take a long time."

"Oh, I don't know," Catriona demurred. "These days they prefabricate everything and stick up buildings overnight. Just truck in the hunks and whomp 'em together. With robots, I believe. You did bring your camera?"

Helen started to laugh. "I may have aged a few years since you last saw me, but I'm not quite senile yet. It's in this little blue bag over my shoulder."

"Oh, is that what the bag's for? I thought perhaps Iduna had packed us a lunch," Catriona replied somewhat regretfully. "As far as age is concerned, you look younger now than you did in South Dakota. So does Iduna. What's her husband like? Five foot three and skinny as a rail, I'll bet. Little men always go for big women."

"Not Daniel. He's taller than she and what you might with all temperance call portly. Actually, Daniel looks a great deal like a particularly handsome and distinguished pig. He was a widower with two sets of quadruplets, all married and fecund. Iduna's up to the eyeballs in grandchildren and loving it. None of them live very close, so she doesn't get stuck with a lot of babysitting, but they visit back and forth. She gets to cook huge holiday dinners, which she adores doing as I don't have to tell you. She also does some teaching in the home ec department and attends a good many of the college social events. Daniel used to be rather stodgy, but she's loosened him up. They performed an exhibition tango together at the alumni ball last month. It was lovely."

"I can imagine," said Catriona, who no doubt could. "So what's this windmill project in aid of?"

"Weather vanes." Helen explained about Praxiteles Lumpkin and the Smithsonian. "He used to travel around with a few sheets of copper, a bag of tools, and a jug of hard cider lashed to the back of his faithful mule Apuleius. The jug was for bait, to help him wheedle the local blacksmith into letting him use the forge. The cider worked quite well, except for one time when he found himself traveling just behind a temperance evangelist."

"These things are sent to test us, no doubt. I can't think what else they're good for."

"Neither can I. Of course, a good many of Praxiteles's weather vanes have been destroyed one way or another. Most of them sold for junk and melted down, I suppose, though it breaks my heart to think so."

"Blah. Your heart isn't broken that easily. How come you married Peter Shandy? You never married any of the others who kept panting down your neck."

"Our president's wife doesn't stand for any shenanigans. Besides, Peter's the kind of man one feels like marrying."

"Would I have felt like marrying him?"

"Quite possibly, but I'd never have let you. Anyway, you have Andrew."

"I do not have Andrew in the carnal sense, thank God for small blessings. Our relationship is purely that of lady of the manor and loyal serf. Or so I like to believe, though I have to admit Andrew has never quite grasped the principle of serfdom. You wait and see, I'll wind up having to eat all those damn potatoes, get fat as a pig, and become a hissing and a byword in the streets of Sasquamahoc."

"But think how nice and warm you'll be next winter," Helen reminded her. "You know Mrs. Beeton said there was no better insulation than an inch or so of extra fat on the ribs. Is that the forestry school we're coming to? Oh, I think I see the weather vane!"

She scrabbled her field glasses out of the blue bag and trained them on a spiderlike object she'd discerned atop a huge old barn. "It's glorious. Can we walk faster? I can't wait."

Catriona McBogle shrugged. "*De gustibus et coloribus non est disputandum.* I must say, I never thought to see the day when the blond bombshell of the ALA would be turned on by a weather vane."

FIVE

Do we have to get permission?" Helen asked as they neared the barn.

"Shoot first, ask later is what I'd do," Catriona replied. "Anyway, I thought you had permission."

"I suppose I do, now that you mention it. It just seems a bit brassy barging in like this. I'll have to stop in and pay a courtesy call on President Fingal, anyway, and explain why Peter couldn't come with me."

"Oh, Guthrie isn't one to stand on ceremony. Stall around awhile and maybe he'll have gone home. You don't want to waste the light, do you?"

"Good point. There is a lot of it, isn't there? The quality of the light up here is incredible."

"It's just that we have more room to put it in," Catriona replied modestly. "Maine's bigger than all the rest of New England put together, you know. As big as, anyway. Or so I've been told. I haven't taken the measurements myself. If I did, I'd most likely get them wrong. Do you want me to hold your bag or anything?"

"No, thanks, I'll be wanting it. I think what I'd better do is climb up on the fire escape of that building over there so I'll be more on a level with the weather vane. What is it, a dormitory?"

"Yes, but don't worry. I doubt if there's anybody inside. Summer sessions won't be starting for another week or so, I believe. At least I haven't heard any shouts of 'Timber' lately. Go ahead, they don't have any campus cops here. Just brawny lumberjacks with double-bitted axes. Hurry up, the thing's starting to wiggle."

The breeze had been almost too light to be felt on the skin. Now it was strong enough to move the vane so that the lumberjack felling the tree was directly broadside to the dormitory. Helen ran up the open iron steps to the topmost platform, leaned out over the railing, her telephoto lens in place and her shutter finger ready, waited for the vane to settle, and snapped.

She took exposure after exposure as the sun and shadows cast marvelous color effects on the oxidized copper. Wanting some black-and-whites, too, she fished an already loaded duplicated camera out of her blue bag.

As she was switching the lens, she became aware that the dormitory was not empty. From somewhere inside, she could hear male voices. Young men, from the sound of them. As why wouldn't they be? Intent on getting the right focus and fretting lest the wind take a sudden notion to change direction, Helen paid no attention to what was none of her business anyway until one place name caught her ear.

The only other time she'd heard Woeful Ridge mentioned had been last night at the Horsefalls', just before the fire alarm had gone off. She forgot for the moment what she was doing up here and strained to hear more, but the students either stopped talking or left the dormitory. On their way to the dining hall, most likely. She'd better get a move on, herself. Iduna was no doubt beginning to feel a trifle peckish.

Helen managed to get some excellent broadside shots before the wind freshened enough to be bothersome. Then she picked her way down, wondering why she hadn't been nervous coming up, and grievously smudging her new pink sneakers on the iron treads. Soot, she supposed, from wood fires in old stoves. One might think a forestry school would have heard about catalytic combustion.

One might also consider that Sasquamahoc, like other schools, was no doubt feeling the pinch of inflated overhead costs. She dusted off her sneakers as best she could and asked Catriona where they'd be likely to find President Fingal, assuming he was still around.

They tracked him to his office in the administration building. He said he was pleased to see them and looked as if he meant it.

"This is great, Mrs. Shandy. Sorry, it's Dr. Shandy, isn't it? Or Dr. Marsh? Or Marsh-Shandy, or Shandy-Marsh?"

"It's Helen, please. You call my husband Peter, don't you?"

"I've called him a few other things in my time, the old—" President Fingal caught himself. "And he calls me Guthrie, as I hope you will. We were in college together, as he may have mentioned."

"Any number of times. Peter was sorry he couldn't come with me as we'd hoped. I expect you've heard about the big fire down our way."

"Yes, I saw it on the news. Don't tell me Pete's a volunteer fireman these days?"

"No, he isn't, but it's rather an all-hands-to-the-pumps situation just now." Helen didn't see why she had to go into details. "He was asked to stay and help and didn't think he ought to refuse. So I came along to Catriona's with a mutual friend. Peter's hoping to get up later."

"I hope he makes it. It sure would be nice to see old Pete again. Now what were you planning to do about our weather vane, Helen?"

"Actually I've already done it," she confessed. "The light and the wind were exactly right as we came on campus. Cat said you wouldn't mind if I just went ahead and took some shots, so I did. Can you tell me anything of the weather vane's history? How did it come into the school's possession?"

"By accident, far as I know. It was on the barn when Old Hickory bought the place. That was what they used to call Eliphalet Jackson, who founded the school. We're not so old as Balaclava, but we do go back a ways. The barn's all that's left of a farm that used to be here. The house and the other outbuildings had burned down, which is how Old Hickory managed to get the place cheap. Cheap being practically for nothing in those days, or we'd probably never have got started."

He brought an old scrapbook of newspaper clippings and class photographs: small groups of short, dark, thickset men who made Helen think of bears wearing plaid shirts and heavy dark work pants tucked into high laced boots. They all had their axes with them.

"Old-time woodsmen didn't like to be parted from their axes," President Fingal explained. "They were pretty fussy about taking care of them, too. They'd smooth away at the handles till they got just the heft they wanted and kept the blades honed till they could shave with them, though I don't suppose many did. I've heard a man could pick up an axe in pitch dark and know whether it was his or somebody else's just from the way it felt in his hand."

He turned to another class photo. "Our boys have always looked pretty spruce, comparatively speaking. Years ago, the school blacksmith used to cut their hair and trim their beards with the horse clippers. We've got a set of real barber shears and clippers now," the president added proudly. "We like to move with the times, though they kind of get away from us now and then. The real old-time lumberjacks tended to get a trifle unkempt after a winter in the woods. My grandfather used to tell me what they looked like coming out in the spring. They'd be farmers, a lot of them, and they'd hire out to lumber camps after harvest was over. Sewn up in their winter long johns, like as not. By the time they got out, the horses would have grown long winter coats and the men would have hair down over their shoulders and beards to their waists."

He turned a few more pages. "There, I knew I had a picture of one somewhere. That's my Great-Uncle Mose. Looks like a wild animal, doesn't he? Gramp took that with an old box Brownie. He said you could hardly see Mose's face, just dirt and hair. Aunt Laviney had to shave and barber him and give him a bath before she was sure she'd got the right husband back. Not but what she might as soon have had somebody else's, from a few things I've heard."

President Fingal shook his head and shoved the scrapbook aside. "You couldn't blame the men. Those lumber camps weren't always the height of class, you know. Some of them did pretty well by the loggers, but Gramp said Mose wound up in one where all they had for bedding was piles of straw on the floor and one great big blanket. The men would lie down in their clothes, then the ones on the outsides would take hold of the blanket and spread it out over the whole pack of them at once. Maybe they took off their boots, but I wouldn't want to bet on it. Hope I'm not offending your aesthetic sensibilities, Cat."

He grinned at her and she grinned back. "You know me better than that, Guthrie. Well, I expect we ought to be moseying back to the house. We left our friend Iduna Stott communing with the swallows."

"Maybe you two would like to bring her over here to dinner tomorrow noontime?"

"Thanks, but we're going whale watching with Eustace Tilkey. How about the day after?"

"Sure thing. Just let us know you're coming, so's we'll have time to lay the plates over the spots in the tablecloth and pour a little extra water in the soup. Nice to meet you, Helen. Say hi to Pete for me."

"I'll do that, Guthrie. He'll probably be phoning me this evening. Oh, by the way, where is Woeful Ridge?"

"Cussed if I know. I never heard of it."

"Likable fellow," Helen remarked as they left the school. "He reminds me a little of Smokey the Bear. Do you see a lot of him, Cat?"

"Off and on. Guthrie's pretty busy most of the year, and so am I. Nobody ever believes writers do any work, but we do."

"Yes, I know," Helen replied demurely.

"Oh, that's right. Welcome to the club. How's the book going?"

"Rather well, considering nobody ever expected *The Buggins Family in Balaclava County* to be a runaway best-seller. They've just run off a second printing. The first one was two thousand copies. That's not bad for the Pied Pica Press, you know."

"Not bad at all," Cat agreed. "Maybe I can work in a quote from it in my next book and give sales another boost."

"Don't you dare! I've already let one idiot who calls herself an author use some of my genealogical material, which she of course carefully and properly attributed to me, only she got my dates mixed up. I've been getting polite letters of inquiry from complete strangers wanting to know how I could possibly have made such an imbecilic mistake."

"Don't let it upset you too much. Everybody comes a cropper sooner or later. As Harry Truman used to say, 'If you can't stand the heat, get out of the typewriter.' "

"I thought professional writers used word processors these days."

"Not me, kid. If God had meant us to spend our lives staring at green neon letters on a dinky little screen, She'd have given us styrene eyeballs is how I look at it. Are you hungry?"

"Cat, for goodness' sake! I've been eating all day!"

"That's beside the point."

"True enough," Helen conceded. "I expect I'll be able to

eat when you get around to serving, but don't hurry on my account. What's Guthrie's wife like? Or doesn't he have one?"

"Oh, yes. She's seven feet tall and has a beard."

"You're making that up."

"Certainly I am. She's less then seven feet tall and has only a small mustache. Her name is Elisa Alicia and she makes wreaths of dried apples and pillows filled with bulrush fuzz."

"What for?"

"I've often wondered. Elisa Alicia also brews potions and decoctions. Two months ago, I asked her for a charm against publishers. She promised to get right to work on it, but so far she hasn't come up with anything."

Cat picked a ferny sprig of young tansy. "Well, you can't hit a home run every time, I suppose. Elisa Alicia's coltsfoot poultice is said to be highly efficacious, but I forget what it's supposed to cure. Tansy applied externally to the sexual organs is said to promote fertility. The Indians used to bind it around their heads to cure the hangovers induced by the colonists. Do you suppose there might be some connection?"

"Anything's possible," Helen replied cautiously. "I'm not much up on tansy. Did you learn this stuff from Mrs. Fingal?"

"Ms. Quatrefages, if you please. Elisa Alicia is her own woman."

"She doesn't sound much like yours. Elisa Alicia Quatrefages . . . I've heard that name before. I wish I could remember where. Have she and Guthrie been here long? Do the students call him Woody?"

"Of course. He's not bad on the guitar, actually. We'll get him to sing "The Wabash Cannonball" when he knows you a little better. Guthrie was born in Sasquamahoc and never left, except when he was off to college. He came back and worked in the forestry service for a while, taught at the school for several years, and stepped into the presidency when his predecessor got felled, as they say in silvicultural circles. I forget whether old Prexy was hit by a falling limb or succumbed to Dutch elm disease. It was something arboreal, anyway. As to how Guthrie acquired Elisa, I couldn't say. The general assumption among the locals is that he went out on a field trip and found her under a rock."

Helen chuckled. "Cat, you're a dreadful woman. Can't you think of something good to say about Elisa?"

"Yes, I can. The good thing about Elisa is that she's not around here much. As soon as the moon turns gibbous, she packs up her accumulated wreaths and pillows and tootles off to Boston or New York. To peddle them, she claims. I personally suspect she does a brisk little sideline business in murrains and blights among the upwardly mobile. However, I shan't expand on my theory. I can see you've come all over sweetness and light since your nuptials. Whatever happened to the mordacious Marsh of yesteryear?"

"What's happened to Iduna is more to the point." They were within sight of Catriona's house by now. "I don't see her on the terrace."

"I hope the black flies haven't got her." Catriona quickened her pace. "Those blasted things chomp a hunk out of you, then you swell up in agony for a week and have scars on your soul forever after."

However, they found Iduna unchomped and unswollen. What had enticed her inside the house was obviously the telephone. She was talking into it when they entered.

"Oops, here they are now. I'll put her on the line. It's Peter, Helen."

"Good, I was hoping he'd call."

While Iduna went with Catriona into the kitchen, Helen took the receiver. "Hello, darling. What's happening?"

"Huntley Swope's conscious and sticking to his soldier story, but nobody seems to be buying it. The God-awful soapsuds around the factory are boiling up higher by the minute, and so is public feeling."

"What do you yourself think?"

"Drat it, Helen, how can Huntley be lying? He doesn't know Brinkley's getting the blame for starting the fire. Nobody's been allowed to see him except his wife and the hospital staff, and they've surely had sense enough not to say anything that might have upset him. According to his wife, Huntley tells a perfectly clear story. He says he'd been downstairs telling Caspar Flum to send up another batch of grease or some damned thing. The intricacies of soapmaking are beyond my grasp. Anyway, he was on his way back to his office and stopped at a window in the corridor just outside the tallow room."

"Wanted a breath of fresh air, I suppose," Helen prompted. "I noticed when I was taking my photos that all the windows were open and they hadn't any screens. I wondered how they kept the bugs out of the soap. Sorry, Peter. What then?"

"As he was standing there trying to get some of the fat out of his lungs, he noticed a youngish fellow with what he describes as soldierly bearing, wearing what appeared to be army fatigues with the pantlegs tucked into high boots, paratrooper style, walking briskly down the road. When he got parallel with the tallow room, the man didn't even look in, just whipped something out of his pocket and flipped it sideways through the window."

"Could Huntley see what he flipped?"

"No," Peter answered, "but he has an impression it was approximately the size of a lemon. He was all set to yell at the man when he heard a tremendous bang and saw flames spurting out the window next to the one he was looking from. He ran back to haul Flum out, but the doorway was a wall of flames. It doesn't seem to remember much after that, poor fellow, till he woke up in the hospital."

"Had he been able to get a good look at the soldier?"

"Not really. It was dark by then, of course. The factory windows cast some light on the road, but it doesn't seem to have helped a great deal. He thinks the man was beardless and had his hair cut short, but that's the best he can do. Nobody's son was home on leave and nobody recalls having seen a stray military man around, so naturally they all think Huntley's making up a yarn to protect his brother."

"But there's no reason for him to tell a lie if he doesn't

know his brother needs protecting," Helen protested. "Can't people see that?"

"They can't believe he doesn't know. It'll straighten itself out sooner or later, I suppose. Did you get your photographs all right?"

"Yes, dear, no problem. I shan't know how good they are till I get the films developed, and this doesn't look like the kind of place where I'd be able to do that in a hurry, but I used both cameras, so one of them must surely have worked. We saw your old friend Guthrie Fingal. He's awfully nice, Peter." Helen thought perhaps she wouldn't say anything about the as yet unseen Mrs. Fingal. "Oh, Peter, a funny thing happened. I was upstairs in one of the dormitories so that I could be at eye level with the weather vane, you know."

She decided further not to mention that she'd been at the top of a fire escape. Peter did have some quaint ideas about the frangibility of wives. Cat would be amused, no doubt.

"Anyway, a couple of students, I suppose they were, happened to be talking in the next room and one of them said something about Woeful Ridge. I asked Woody where it was, but neither he nor Cat had ever heard of the place. Wasn't that an odd coincidence? You remember Cronkite Swope mentioned Woeful Ridge last night when he came to the house?"

"Yes, I remember."

They talked a little while longer, but Helen thought Peter sounded somewhat abstracted toward the end. He must have been thinking about something else. She wondered what it was.

SIX

Peter was wondering, too. He wondered while he walked up to the faculty dining room and consumed a no-doubt excellent meal without noticing what he was eating. He wondered on his way back home and continued his musing as he watched the early news, the local part of which consisted mostly of dirty soapsuds. He was still wondering when Cronkite Swope slunk up to the door, steeped in gloom.

"Can I come in for a while, Professor?"

"Gad, Swope, you look like a one-man funeral." Peter ushered him into the living room. "Nothing direful on the home front, I hope?"

"Not specially." The young newspaperman sank into the easy chair that was usually Helen's and took Jane Austen on his lap for solace. "It's just that I'm not used to being treated like a skunk at a wedding. Over in Lumpkinton I can't even interview the man in the street without getting my head chewed off."

"Bad as that, eh?"

"Worse. I went to Clavaton and tried to dig a story out of Mr. Snell. All he'd say were things like 'I have no information at this time' and 'That will have to be decided by our board of directors.' The only piece of information I got out of him was that he didn't even know the factory was on fire till it was all over. He'd been in West Clavaton the whole time playing his bass viol with some chamber music group he belongs to. I wrote it up with the headline 'Snell Fiddles While Factory Burns,' but my editor killed it. He's afraid Snell will take away his advertising if the factory ever gets going again."

"The ways of editors are beyond our ken, Swope. Any more news on your brother?"

"Hunt's about the same, last I heard. Brink's had to board up his windows and evacuate his wife and kids to her folks' house in Hoddersville. Mum's cousins Clarence and Silvester Lomax are guarding Brink's place so a mob doesn't burn it down while he's gone. I don't know what to do, Professor."

"Then might I suggest taking a ride out to Woeful Ridge?"

Cronkite was surprised. "I guess so, if you want to. How come Woeful Ridge?"

"Because I've lived in Balaclava County upward of twenty years and never been near the place, but you're the third person who's mentioned it in the past twenty-four hours, so now must be the time. What's it like?"

"Scroungy and desolate. Rocks and weeds, mostly. The kind of place that makes you feel like sitting down and having a good cry. Don't ask me why, it just seems to hit everybody that way. You weren't planning to blow your brains out or anything?"

"By no means, Swope. My wife wouldn't stand for it."

"And you have Jane to think of." Cronkite tickled the white bib under the little tiger lady's chin, patently relieved to evoke a purr instead of a growl for a change. "Want to go now? We can take the staff car to save getting yours out."

"Have you eaten?"

"My mother made a pot of chicken soup to take to Huntley, but the hospital says he can't have any, so she's making me eat it instead. Every time I drop in at the house to use the phone, she shoves another bowlful at me. I had two at noontime and three more since then, so I'm not particularly hungry. If I were, I could probably lay myself an egg by now. If you're really serious about Woeful Ridge, Professor, I think we ought to be shoving along. The place isn't much in the daylight and I expect it'd be nothing at all in the dark. Besides, I think the were-wolves come out then."

The *Balaclava Fane and Pennon*'s staff car was a 1974 Plymouth Valiant, not much for looks by now but still capable of forward motion, so forward they went. The motion continued a good deal longer than Peter had bargained for.

"What a dull road. I hadn't realized Massachusetts could come up with such a long stretch of nothing in particular."

"It gets duller as we go along," Cronkite assured him, and sure enough, it did.

"Those survivalists you mentioned last night certainly haven't picked much of a place to survive in," Peter observed after a while. "What do they do out here?"

"Get closer to the earth. At least that's what one of them told me when I tried to get an interview out of him. He emphasized his point by ever so accidentally knocking me down and rubbing my face in the dirt while six or eight other creeps stood around laughing themselves sick. I expect what they mainly do is sit around and drink beer and tell each other lies about what big macho he-men they are. I don't expect we'll see anybody there tonight. They're pretty much weekend survivors as far as I know. If I haven't got my signals crossed, this is where we turn off."

The dirt road wasn't really fit for anything but all-terrain vehicles, but the staff Plymouth did its best. Damn shame to have put the brave old hack to the trouble, Peter decided when he got his first sight of Woeful Ridge. The place would have made a pretty fair setting for one of Thomas Hardy's gloomier novels, he thought. There didn't look to be much else it was good for.

As they left the car and began scrambling through the weeds and over the rocks, Peter amended his first impression. This granite hogback, its north side eroded by time and weather into a natural escarpment, would make an excellent place to crouch behind if one happened to be into guerrilla warfare and had anybody out front to shoot at. For want of anything better to do, he began searching the grounds behind the exposed rock. It was bare—not a twig, not a pebble, not so much as a bug.

"What are you looking for, Professor?" Cronkite asked.

"I don't know, Swope, but what I'm finding is nothing at all, which strikes me as being rather peculiar. You'd think someone had gone over this place with a vacuum cleaner."

"Maybe the survivalists don't want to mess up the environment."

"The hell they don't."

Peter was really curious now. He was running his hands over the rock, and finding a couple of chipped-out grooves into which dirt had been carefully rubbed so they wouldn't look too fresh. Kneeling, he took a beeline sight through one of them into the trees that surrounded the ridge. Then he walked down the escarpment, straight toward one tree he'd picked as his mark.

"Look up there, Swope. They've been doing some target practice lately."

"Well, sure, what would you expect? They're probably all hunters, or think they are. Get half a skinful and stand out here blazing away with their deer rifles just for the heck of it."

"Whoever did this wasn't just blazing away."

Peter had his field glasses up to his eyes, studying a large knot that looked as if it might have been hollowed out by woodpeckers. In fact, the center had been systematically chipped away by bullets, not one of which had strayed into the periphery.

"Here, take the glasses and see for yourself. That's expert sharpshooting. And they've picked up all the shells and swept out any sign that they've even been here. Of course if they'd been a little smarter, they'd have strewn an armload of leaves and trash around to make the place look more natural."

"Gosh, yes." Cronkite swept Peter's binoculars in an arc. "Looks as if that whole grove's been attacked by a squadron of trained woodpeckers."

"I'll bet you'd find a spent rifle bullet at the back of every hole. What's down the back side of the ridge, do you know, Swope?"

"Not a heck of a lot that I can remember. There used to be a cave, but it didn't amount to much."

"Can you find it?"

"I guess so, only we'll probably have to fight our way through a lot of squirrel briars."

Interestingly enough, they didn't. There was a path, so well camouflaged as to be invisible to anybody who didn't know the terrain, but easy enough to get through once one knew it was there. Cronkite had no trouble leading Peter to the cave.

"It isn't much of one," he apologized. "Only about four feet deep."

"Let's make sure, shall we?"

Peter had had some experience in caves with more to them than met the eye.* He poked around, scrutinized a part of the back wall that appeared to be one thick slab of solid rock, put his shoulder to the nearer edge, and shoved. The cave was more than four feet deep.

"Neat," he observed. "Must be on a pivot. Looks as if somebody's been doing some blasting here. You wouldn't happen to have a flashlight on you, Swope?"

"Sure, Professor. It says in the Great Journalists' Correspondence Course, lesson thirty-seven, that an investigative journalist should never be without one because you never know. Sorry it's just a pocket flash. I have a battery lantern in the car if you want me to run down and get it."

"No, this will do." Peter flipped the switch. "Great balls of fire!"

"You can say that again," breathed Cronkite. "What the heck is it, some kind of ammunition dump?"

"I'd call it an arsenal."

Peter stared in near-total disbelief at the rifles, machine guns, flamethrowers, and World War II bazookas that hung

*The Curse of the Giant Hogweed (1985).

from racks spiked into the stone walls. Heavy cartons of ammunition and explosives were stacked on wooden pallets to keep them up off the damp floor. He and the reporter were checking them over with the help of Cronkite's flashlight when they realized they were not alone.

"Freeze!"

Cronkite Swope jumped about a foot and a half. "Huh?"

"I said freeze, creepo. One move and I'll blow your fuckin' head off."

"And your own as well." Peter had managed to swivel himself around so that he was halfway facing the burly lout in the commando suit. "Don't you realize what a ricocheting bullet could do among all this live ammunition?"

"Who cares? I'd die a fuckin' hero."

"You'd die a mess of raw hamburger and your fellow thugs would spit on whatever bits and pieces they could find. Do you think they'd waste any hero-worship on a fool who'd been stupid enough to destroy what they must have gone to a great deal of trouble to steal?"

Peter added a contemptuous snort for good measure. "Cozy little place you've got here. Mind taking us to your leader? I believe that's the correct thing to say in situations like this."

"I think it's name, rank, and serial number, Professor," Cronkite murmured. "Do you suppose it would be all right if we just showed him our library cards?"

"Okay, wise guys," barked their captor. "Outside."

"May I point out, sir," Peter reminded him, "that you're blocking the exit?"

"Huh? Oh." The man with the gun took a step backward. "Come out with your hands up and no funny stuff."

"This is hardly the moment for japery, sir."

Peter raised his hands as bidden. The roof, he noticed, was low and the blasting had left a good deal of loosened rock overhead as well as underfoot. He stubbed his finger, felt a wiggle, and grabbed the shard before it fell. The guard didn't notice, he'd stepped on one of the fallen rocks, turned his ankle, and inadvertently looked down. Peter made sure the man's finger was off the trigger, and threw.

The rock wasn't big enough to fell their captor, but it was hard enough to hurt. The man dropped his gun and grabbed for his nose. Cronkite rushed him. Peter rushed the weapon. They tied him up with his own and Peter's belt, commandeered his bandolier, and gagged him with Cronkite's necktie, a natty affair of shocking pink with a pattern of little green alligators. Then they headed for the staff car on the double.

Five more commando types were clustered around the vehicle, happily engaged in slashing the tires with large hunting knives and smashing the windows with rifle butts. Seeing their attention thus engaged, Peter and Cronkite decided not to interrupt them.

"Any idea where we're headed, Swope?" Peter panted after they'd slogged at high speed through several miles of wood and bog.

"Away from there is all I care about," his companion panted back. "Holy cow, Professor, those guys are a bunch of maniacs!"

"Your diagnosis seems a reasonable one to me. Did you happen to recognize any of them?"

"I don't think I stopped long enough to look. Maybe I would if I dared to sit down and think about them. Only I kind of suspect we hadn't better just yet. Don't you think we ought to be coming out someplace pretty soon? I just hope we haven't been traveling in a circle."

"I'm quite sure we haven't. I've been keeping the sunset at our backs as best I could the whole time. At this time of day, that means we ought to be traveling more or less due east, I believe. Does that mean anything to you?"

"Means we ought to wind up in Boston Harbor if we keep going long enough, I guess." Cronkite looked down at his formerly dapper light blue slacks and cream and red checked sports jacket. "I'm not exactly dressed for hiking. And I sure wish I'd remembered to bring a sandwich. You know,

Professor, I think we must be in that big tract of land that belongs to the Binks estate."

"Binks?" exclaimed Peter. "Wasn't he the old coot who took up cryonetics and had himself quick frozen?"

"That's right. He had this thing about wanting to see the new century in. He's not due for thawing out until December 31, 1999, and they can't do a thing about settling the estate till they find out whether it worked. The relatives filed an appeal in court, but they didn't get anywhere. The judge is rooting for Mr. Binks."

"Another triumph for modern technology. How big a place is this?"

"Almost twenty miles square, as I recall. How far do you think we've gone?"

"Four or five, maybe. It hasn't been easy going, as I don't have to tell you. Come on, Swope, we'd better push along while there's still some light left."

"Then what happens?"

"Then we manage as best we can. Here, have some chickweed."

Cronkite shied away from the bundle of small-leaved green stuff Peter handed him. "What am I supposed to do with that?"

"Eat it if you're hungry. Chickweed is a valuable antiscorbutic."

"If you say so. But I wish you hadn't mentioned hamburger back there." Cronkite took an experimental nibble. "I suppose we ought to be glad this isn't the hunting season."

"Don't delude yourself on that point, Swope. After what we've seen, those thugs won't dare not to come after us. More chickweed?"

"Not just now, thanks. It makes me feel too much like Bugs Bunny. But it did sort of take the edge off," Cronkite added politely. "Which way now, Professor?"

"Up, I think. If they happen to think of bloodhounds, this may help to put them off the scent. I hope."

They had come upon a wide mat of squirrel briars, pesky vines with stems like wire and thorns like barbs. In the midst of the briar patch grew two oak trees, the tallest they'd seen so far, so big that their branches intertwined. These were something of an oddity. New England woodlands are more likely than not to have been cut over or burned off at one time and another during the past couple of hundred years.

Peter couldn't understand how two sockdolagers like these had escaped destruction, but he didn't wait to ponder. Jumping for a low-hanging branch, he swung himself up above the briars and shinned along toward the trunk, Cronkite right behind him. It proved an easy tree to climb, the limbs spaced not too far apart. Peter was grateful for that, he was beginning to feel a mite tuckered out.

Moving from the first to the second oak was no great feat of acrobatics; they simply shinned out on a convenient limb and stepped across to one that was rubbing against it. Instead of crawling across and dropping off on the other side of the briar patch, though, Peter began climbing straight up.

"Where are you going, Professor?" Cronkite whispered.

"I thought we might as well reconnoiter while we still have a little light left. If there's a shortcut out of here, I'd like to know where it lies."

"You and me both."

Cronkite swarmed after him, trying not to pant. Peter had chosen this tree for his lookout post because it was the taller of the pair. He'd recognized it as a white oak from the rather evenly rounded lobes on the leaves and the relatively pale color of the bark. He knew that white oaks could grow eighty feet or more, and this one mustn't be far short of that. Eighty feet was a long way up for a middle-aged man who'd been fleeing a looney tune with a machine gun for the past two hours. He gritted his teeth and kept on climbing.

SEVEN

"Explain yourself, sir!"

"Great Scott! I do believe I've been climbing in my sleep. I beg your pardon, madam. The intrusion was involuntary."

One did not, after all, expect to come upon what had looked from below to be an exceptionally large squirrel's nest, only to find it neatly decked over with birch saplings, carpeted with balsam fir twigs laid in a careful overlapping pattern, and occupied by an elderly lady in a deerskin bikini reading Young's *Night Thoughts*.

"I am Professor Peter Shandy of Balaclava Agricultural College. And this is my young friend Cronkite Swope," Peter added as his companion hove into view. "We're fugitives."

"Indeed? From what, pray tell?"

"The answer to that may strain your credulity, madam, yet I assure you that what I have to say is both true and alarming. Our being here may be putting you as well as ourselves in a highly dangerous position."

"Then you had better tell me at once." The woman closed her book, first carefully inserting a tender young oak leaf by way of marker, and laid it aside on the fir twigs. "I am all attention."

Peter was no defeatist, but he'd already faced the fact that he and Swope might not get out of this escapade alive. Somebody had to know what was going on at Woeful Ridge. This woman might be crazy as a coot, she might even be a lookout for the survivalists, but she was the only person he could find to tell, so he told. When he'd finished his short but lurid tale, she nodded.

"Then that's what they're up to. I've been wondering, and I reproach myself for not having investigated. You must surely realize, however, that a woman in my position is forced to be protective of her privacy. I have no inclination to draw a pack of anthropologists out here to study me. I suggest that you and Mr. Swope sit here and recruit your vigor to whatever extent is possible while I don more suitable raiment. Our route will be somewhat arduous. Please help yourselves to the day lily buds. They're quite delicious this time of year."

Before either of them could reply, she was over their heads and out of sight among the foliage. Peter shrugged and took out his field glasses. Their arboreal hostess, however, had chosen her bosky roost for seclusion rather than observation. He couldn't see much except a family of flying squirrels in the tree he and Cronkite had just vacated. The parents were trying to get the kids off to bed and the cheeky little critters were insisting on one more practice glide.

Under different circumstances he'd have been charmed. As it was, he lowered the glasses in disgust and ate a day lily bud. He himself wouldn't have said quite delicious, but it tasted better than he'd expected. He and Cronkite had pretty much finished the lot when the woman slid back down the trunk wearing deerskin pants and tunic somewhat haphazardly laced together with thongs. On her feet were moccasins that looked even more handmade than the clothes. Peter wondered if he'd met the ultimate do-it-yourselfer.

"Now I feel a trifle more presentable. Winifred Binks, gentlemen, at your service. There is a search party composed of six men with what appear to be deer rifles and two rather stupid-looking dogs working their way downhill from Woeful Ridge. They're about to get stuck in Soggy Bog. I thought you'd probably want to know."

"Er—thank you," said Peter. "How did you—er—"

"I looked, of course. I have a very powerful telescope on

my observation platform up above. Feel free to look for
yourself if you wish, but I suggest the time might be better
employed in moving to a more secluded locale. Shall we?"

"But where can we go?" Cronkite Swope was too grown-
up to burst into loud wails, but he might possibly have been
wishing he weren't. "Wouldn't it be safer for us to stay up
here in the tree and—"

"Hurl coconuts down on their heads?" Miss Binks suggested brightly. "That might be a solution if we had any.
Come along, Mr. Swope. Follow me where the woodbine
twineth."

Peter and Cronkite thought the woman was indulging in an
ill-timed flight of poesy, but it turned out she wasn't. The
woodbine, which appeared to be merely picturesque festoons
between the oak and an adjoining sugar maple, had, they
soon discovered, been adroitly trained to mask a crude but
navigable suspension bridge woven from some fiber whose
nature they didn't pause to identify. They'd discovered there
was nothing like the baying of a distant bloodhound to put
that extra ounce of spring in the step.

Tired as they were, the two men kept pace with the
incredibly agile Miss Binks throughout a Tarzanian journey
of perhaps a quarter of a mile, during which they didn't touch
dry ground once. They did plunge into a pond or two and
spent a chilly five minutes picking their way along the pebbly
bed of a rushing stream, but mostly they kept to the trees.
Then all at once they shot feet-first down the hollowed-out
trunk of a dead maple tree and found themselves underground.

"This way." Miss Binks had dropped to all fours and
scuttled along what proved to be a well-dug tunnel some four
feet in diameter, shored up with slabs of bark, dry as a bone
and clean as a whistle. The tunnel was not very long and it
opened out into Bilbo Baggins's parlor.

"Snug," said Peter.

The room was all that and then some; more round than
square, more free form than circular. Along one side of the
room a bench of earth that was no doubt Miss Binks's bed

had been built up a foot or so, mattressed with a thick layer of spruce tips, and covered with deerskins. A couple of aged but clean woolen blankets were tidily folded at one end of the bed. Surprisingly, a battery-operated table lamp with a duck stamped on its shade sat at the other end on a kind of headboard that had been made by piling the earth another foot higher and facing it with a couple of rather badly charred boards.

More boards had been used to shore up the ceiling and build bookshelves in a hollowed-out niche. Miss Binks's library, Peter noticed, was an interesting mixture of the more serious-minded British poets in tooled leather and the collected works of Euell Gibbons and his ilk in paperback. Another niche was obviously the kitchen. Here were a board working counter, hanging bunches of dried herbs and wild onions, and more shelves. An old galvanized pail filled with water sat under the counter.

The larder looked to be well stocked, though Peter could only surmise what might be in the containers Miss Binks had cobbled together from birch bark and the baskets she'd woven of dried rushes. Some of the baskets were more recognizable as such than others. Practice still hadn't made perfect, but Miss Binks was learning. Another niche held a fire pit lined with clay, a few pots and pans, a stack of firewood, and a heap of kindling. All things in good order. Dogberry would have approved.

"The earth closet is down the back tunnel," said their hostess. "You'll find a pan of water and a bunch of soapwort if you want to wash. My establishment doesn't run to guest towels, but one manages well enough with a handful of dry grass, I find. I'll just light the fire to dry out your clothes and fix us some food. No doubt you're both ready for a hot meal by now. And perhaps a little nip to settle your nerves after your ordeal."

She went to her pantry and fished out a recycled preserve jar filled with something liquid. "I've never been able to make up my mind what it is that I make. Applejack, perhaps, or perry. Or arrack or slivovitz. It all depends on what I can find to put in. There are still some fruit trees on the estate. Sometimes I get apples, sometimes plums or pears. Mostly it's a peck of this and a peck of that and a bit of whatever else happens to present itself when I'm ready to fire up the still. Anyway, I've been drinking my private distillations for quite some time now, in moderation, of course, and the stuff's never killed me yet."

Astonishingly, she took down three unmatched but exquisite crystal goblets. "Professor Shandy? Mr. Swope?"

"I think I'll go and wash up first, if you don't mind." Cronkite was still essentially a strawberry-milkshake man.

Peter wasn't. "Delighted, Miss Binks, if you'll join me."

She poured out two fairly generous belts and handed him one. "I believe I will. I must confess that I don't generally travel at quite the pace I set tonight, and I find myself feeling a trifle unstrung. Now please do relax and make yourself at home, Professor. I'm not really geared for company, as you can see, but we'll manage. I hope you like deer meat."

"At this point I'd like anything from aardvark to zebra," he assured her. "I dimly remember having eaten some sort of meal before Swope and I left Balaclava Junction, but it seems to have worn off. How do you hunt your deer?"

Miss Binks smiled. "Oh, I don't hunt them. I merely acquire them. Deer get hit by cars, poor things, or wounded by hunters who are too inept, too lazy, or too drunk to track them down. I don't find many, of course, but then I don't need many. I sun-dry or smoke the meat and it lasts me for months, mostly in soups and stews. My preference would be to subsist on a purely vegetarian diet, but anybody living this kind of life does need some fat and protein. Luckily I prepared a pot-au-feu this morning so I shouldn't have to cook tonight. We'll heat it up as soon as the fire dies down a bit. No use setting a pot on until we have a decent bed of coals. I hope you like pokeweed? It's quite safe to eat, you know, as long as you pick the sprouts young, which I am always careful to do."

"Extremely wise of you," said Peter. He wondered if there was any pokeweed in Miss Binks's applejack, or slivovitz as the case might be. "Would it be rude of me to inquire what prompted you to adopt this—er—alternative life-style?"

"Not at all. I did it because I prefer a life of solitude and contemplation, because I was too flat broke to live any other way unless I went on welfare or found some kind of job, both of which I scorned to do, and because it's a way of claiming my inheritance. I expect you've heard about the bizarre thing that happened to my grandfather, the newspapers were full of it ten years ago. I may as well tell you I am confident my grandfather is dead. In my opinion, the poor old egg was absolutely cracked and that so-called scientist who talked him into the experiment was no more nor less than a murderer. The man's dead himself now, of course, so I expect you're thinking I shouldn't speak so harshly. He was found inside a refrigerator over in Lumpkinton, as you may recall, shot full of bullet holes."

"I remember our own Chief Ottermole mentioned the case," said Peter. "I didn't realize that was the man who froze your grandfather. Chief Olson called it a suicide, didn't he?"

Miss Binks sniffed a particularly haughty sniff. "I have always assumed it was Chief Olson's wife who did the deciding. She'd been a Binks herself, though hardly a close enough relation to justify all the airs she used to put on until Grandfather made such a laughingstock of the family name. I can see why she made her husband hush the case up before the newspapers made the connection, though I did think at the time she was rather overstepping her position. I myself am the only Binks left in the direct line."

"Then you—er—had expectations?"

"Great expectations, Professor. Grandfather himself had led me to believe so, before he got involved with Star Wars–style cryonics. As it stands now, the will can't be probated until he's declared legally dead. I found out the expensive way. Court costs today don't come any cheaper than they used to. I should have remembered my Dickens and Trollope."

She shook herself all over, like a dog coming out of the

water. "Well, what's done can't be helped. I got myself into a mess and have been trying ever since to make my way out. My first thought was to squat in Grandfather's house, but somebody burned it down before I could move in. Just as well perhaps. I'd have been caught and evicted, or put in jail, and my dear second cousin once removed would have had another scandal to hush up. Anyway, that's why you find me underground. Or overhead, as the case may be. I've often spent warm summer nights in my aerie, though I expect I shan't be doing that any more once your pursuers discover it. Assuming they do, of course." She didn't sound any too hopeful that they wouldn't, and Peter could offer no encouragement.

"It's dollars to doughnuts they will, I'm afraid. We did get mired in a bog for a while not too long before we found your tree. That might put the dogs off the scent, but I expect we left fairly obvious wallowing tracks. I'm sorry, Miss Binks."

"Why should you be? You couldn't have known I was in the tree, I'm far too rare a bird." She chuckled. "Here, have a little more of whatever it is we're drinking, though I'm afraid this is not my prime vintage. Last year's apple blossoms got pretty much knocked off in that big hailstorm we had, so there wasn't much of a crop. I was forced to eke out with elderberries."

"Nothing wrong with elderberries." Peter took another sip and rolled it around his mouth, wine-taster style. "On the whole and speaking as a layman, I should say elderberries were just the ticket. What's happened to Swope?"

"I expect he's gone exploring," said Miss Binks. "I've taken a tip from the woodchucks and provided my lair with a couple of extra escape hatches. These also serve as a means of ventilation. I do hope Mr. Swope hasn't taken a notion to poke his head out at the wrong moment."

"It's okay, I didn't." Cronkite emerged from the tunnel, his sky blue slacks now totally beyond reclamation but his face and hands clean enough for practical purposes. "Quite a place you've got here, Miss Binks. What's that machinery in the little room down the tunnel for?"

"It's my unlicensed still, and I'll thank you not to squeal on me to the revenue men. I'd better heat up the soup now. The fire's just about right."

"How do you manage about the smoke?" Peter asked her.

"No problem. There's a colony of skunks nearby. I just funnel the smoke through their den and nobody's ever noticed. If anyone did, I don't suppose they'd care to investigate. Nobody comes around here much anyway, you know, except an occasional hunter and those disgusting types who've infiltrated Woeful Ridge. They've stayed pretty much over there until now. I hope they won't take it into their heads to relocate. Ah well, we mustn't borrow trouble."

"Till trouble troubles you." Cronkite's remark was not tactful. Unfortunately, neither was it refutable. This remarkable woman must already be realizing that her unusual but satisfactory way of life was likely to go down the drain pretty soon unless somebody got rid of those yahoos. Peter wished desperately that he knew what they'd assembled all those grenades and bazookas for.

"Miss Binks," he said, "can you tell us anything at all about the so-called survivalists? When did you first become aware they'd taken over Woeful Ridge as a base of operations?"

"I believe it was just about two years ago. I don't go by any calendar except the seasons, you understand, so you mustn't ask me to be precise. My chief recollection is that I was nettled at having any kind of long-term encampment on what I like to think of as my private domain. Woeful Ridge isn't actually part of the Binks estate, but it's close enough to give me concern as to what happens there."

"Have you ever gone over to find out what they're up to?"

"Yes, once or twice when I was reasonably certain they'd all gone away. All I've found out so far is that they're meticulous about cleaning up after themselves, which relieves my fear that they might have turned the place into a dump, but doesn't really make me any happier. I never go near that end of the estate if I think they're around. Too many guns popping off. Since my whole object is to remain undiscovered, I could hardly blame them for shooting at the place where they didn't know I was, could I? One must be fair. It wouldn't matter if I were killed outright, but I'd hate to be lying out there wounded and helpless with nobody to find me."

"Naturally you would," Peter agreed. "Then you have no idea as to their identities?"

"None whatsoever. I've never been much of a mingler, even in what I've come to think of as my other life. I was brought up by an elderly aunt who in an earlier day would no doubt have been called a bluestocking. Aunt had no use for tea-party chitchat and neither do I. On the whole, she and I were quite congenial. Ours was not an unhappy life. I went to school off and on but found it desperately boring, didn't get on with the other children, and irritated the teachers by pointing out their mistakes. I must have been a detestable child," she added rather smugly. "What about some sassafras tea, Mr. Swope? The kettle should be hot by now. You needn't look so alarmed. Sassafras is an ingredient of root beer. The early settlers used to drink it by the bucketful."

"Oh well, sure, Miss Binks. What the heck?"

Throwing caution to the wind, Cronkite took a sip from the cup she handed him. It was bone china, Peter noticed, cracked and stained but still a lovely thing. Miss Binks caught his eye and chuckled.

"Part of my inheritance, Professor. One of the small treasures I've managed to salvage from the ruins of Grandfather's house. I used to poke around the ashes quite a lot when I was first living here, but I've pretty well stopped that. There wasn't much to find. Oddly enough, it's delicate odds and ends like this that appear to have survived. What's particularly interesting, I think, is that there are so few of them. I've never found one that was quite whole, and I've never found two that match."

"Are you implying that the house was looted before it burned?"

"I think so, yes. The furnishings were supposed to have been left as they were pending Grandfather's return or the settling of the estate, neither of which of course has yet happened. I've found a good many fragments of burned furniture, but nothing that would have been worth stealing. Cheap kitcheny pieces, from the servants' quarters, I expect."

"Have you any idea who could have done the stripping?"

"Somebody knowledgeable enough to weed out the good stuff," Miss Binks replied, "and clever enough to move it away without being caught."

"Wasn't there a caretaker who got killed in the fire?" asked Cronkite.

"Yes, that's right. The man was believed to have started the fire by falling asleep with a lighted cigarette in his hand, but there wasn't enough left of either him or the house to prove it. Joseph McBogle, his name was. I don't know anything about him except that he had a red-headed niece who came from some little town in Maine."

"Did you meet her?" Peter asked.

"Yes, briefly. Rather an odd duck, I thought. She'd driven since before dawn to get to the funeral, she told me, and was going straight back afterward. She'd meant to stay over with a friend, but one of her cats was ailing and she was afraid her hired man would dose it with rum and kerosene if she stayed away. She took her uncle back with her in a shopping bag. His bones, that is. They'd been packed into a little Styrofoam box, like a miniature casket. She found the thing revolting but was understandably reluctant to repack the bones, so she simply popped the box into the bag to get it out of her sight. A reasonable thing to do, I suppose, but I did think it looked a bit *outré*. The bag had 'Drink Jersey Milk' printed on the side."

"M'yes, I see what you mean. But you didn't know Mr. McBogle?"

"Never laid eyes on him. He wasn't one of the old servants, you know. The lawyers for the trust hired him as a caretaker after Grandfather went to be frozen in California. I'd have thought Alaska, but there it is. Grandfather had pensioned off the others; I'd known them, naturally. I only went to Mr. McBogle's funeral because I felt Aunt would have expected me to represent the family. This was shortly after she died, while I was still living in Clavaton. I rather wished afterward that I'd taken the trouble to drop in on Mr. McBogle occasionally. I might have dropped a word about smoking in bed, but then I couldn't have known he did, could I? And anyway I don't suppose it would have done any good."

"Probably not," said Peter. "Miss Binks, have you ever heard of Praxiteles Lumpkin?"

EIGHT

Miss Binks's sparse eyebrows lost themselves among the wrinkles in her forehead. "Praxiteles Lumpkin? What an odd question. I'm assuming you refer to the antique weather vane man, in which case you're out of step with the times by almost half a century. Grandfather's weather vane, which is to say the one that used to be on the coach house and the only one on the estate, as far as I know, was a realistic, three-dimensional running horse in bronze. Victorian, you know, with lots of filigree around the letters and lightning rods to match along the ridgepole. Lumpkin's were simple two-dimensional cutouts, mildly amusing in a primitive, bucolic way, or so they always struck me. They'd be called collectibles nowadays, I suppose."

"M'yes, you may well say so," Peter answered. "The collector's usual modus operandi seems to be to snaffle the weather vane and then burn down the building, presumably to cover up the theft. Perhaps I'm being fanciful in seeing a parallel between several recent thefts of this nature and the possible looting and torching of your grandfather's house, just because they've all occurred here in Balaclava County."

"The more reason for lumping them together, I should say." Miss Binks got up off the couch where they'd all three been sitting, and lifted the lid off the soup pot. "Ready now, I believe."

She took three mismatched china bowls from her earthen pantry, dished up the soup with a long-handled tin dipper, and handed the bowls around. With his, Peter got a tablespoon with half the silver plate rubbed off, Cronkite a dinky scoop that must have been the sole survivor from a set of measuring spoons. Miss Binks used a strangely shaped object she must have fashioned herself from a piece of deer horn.

"This is terrific soup," Cronkite exclaimed after an experimental slurp or two. "I'm not going to ask what's in it."

"Just as well you don't." His hostess didn't sound a whit offended. "I can't for the life of me remember. Nor can I recall the last time I gave a dinner party. We used to occasionally, when Aunt was alive, but you're the first guests I've entertained here in the lair. I think lair has a much more picturesque ring to it than den, don't you? Now tell me about these other fires, Professor. When did they happen?"

"The latest and most serious happened only last night," Peter told her. "Are you familiar with the Lumpkin Soap Works?"

"Not to say familiar, but we used to ride over that way once in a while when Aunt was alive. I always liked their weather vane. I thought the skinny old man taking a bath on the roof was funny, but Aunt found it less than elevating. She was always trying to elevate me; she was very conscious of my position as Miss Binks. More so than I was, I have to say."

Miss Binks shrugged. "I've often wondered whether my subsequent futile efforts to gain control of Grandfather's estate were undertaken more as an act of filial piety than through any genuine inclination of my own. In which case, I played the fool with my money and deserved to lose it, but that's water over the dam and I can't honestly say I care much. I'm probably happier as I am. Healthier, certainly. More soup, Mr. Swope?"

"Thanks, I'd love some, if you can spare it."

"My dear young man, I have a pantry twenty miles long. Don't worry about my running out of food."

She refilled his bowl. "But getting back to the soap works, are you telling me that enormous brick building actually caught fire and burned down? How could such a thing happen?"

"They think my brother Brinkley set it," Cronkite mumbled through a mouthful of boiled greens.

"Your brother? Why ever would he do a thing like that?"

"He wouldn't. But the factory workers all think he did because he's been on Mr. Snell's ear so much about modernizing the plant."

"Mr. Snell? Dear me, that takes me back to a place I don't particularly want to go. I remember Mr. Snell, unfortunately. Aunt and I used to see him occasionally at the Clavaton Civic Symphony concerts. We lived in West Clavaton, as I perhaps failed to mention. He played the bass viol, or thought he did, and pontificated a good deal about music, using the right words in all the wrong places. Oleaginous creature. But Mr. Snell was the orchestra's richest patron so they let him get away with it. Patronizing came cheaper than modernizing, no doubt. So Mr. Snell is still around? Did your brother work at the soap factory?"

"Yes, ever since high school."

"Then wouldn't it have been remarkably shortsighted of him to burn down his place of employment merely to emphasize a point of view? Can't anybody come up with a more reasonable hypothesis?"

"My brother Huntley, who's in charge of the rendering, claims he watched a soldier throw what was probably a grenade through an open window into one of the tallow vats."

"Well then," said Miss Binks, "what's the problem?"

"The problem is that nobody believes him except us Swopes. We know Hunt has no more imagination than a doorknob. He couldn't lie if he tried. Which doesn't stop the rest of the town from claiming he's just making up a yarn to shield Brink. They're so mad about losing their jobs, I guess they've got to blame somebody."

"Can't they track down the soldier and make him confess? Who is he?"

"Don't ask me. Hunt's not even sure he was a soldier. It was too dark out to see much. The guy could have been a marine."

"Or a sailor or a boy scout, perhaps?"

"Definitely not a sailor or a boy scout," Cronkite insisted. "He was wearing what looked like army fatigues tucked into high boots. His hair was cut real short, Hunt says, and he didn't just walk, he marched. Stiff and straight, you know, with his chin up. When he got abreast of the open window, Hunt says, the guy just flipped his hand sideways without even turning his head. This round thing about the size of a lemon flew through the air, then flames started shooting out of the window. Hunt tried to save Caspar Flum, the tallow man, but the doorway was one big wall of fire. Hunt caught fire himself."

"How dreadful! What happened to your brother?"

"They hosed him down and took him to Hoddersville Hospital. The doctors think he'll pull through all right, but he's going to need skin grafts on his arms and they're not sure yet about his left eye."

Miss Binks shook her grizzled head. "One leads such a sheltered life out here on the estate. Rather, one thought one did. I wonder if your search party has made it this far. Shall I reconnoiter?"

"You'd better not," said Peter. "If those bloodhounds are anywhere around here, they might get a whiff of you. Er—no offense."

"And none taken, I assure you. Actually I'm quite clean, all things considered. Your point is well taken, Professor Shandy, and I don't suppose it matters where they are. I took hunting hounds into my calculations when I planned my lair. Bloodhounds never occurred to me, I must say. However, the chances of anyone's finding this place are, I believe, virtually nil."

She ate the last of her soup in silence. Then she put down her spoon and said, "Mr. Swope, I've been pondering what you said a moment ago. Could that soldierly person your brother saw possibly have been fairish, about forty by now but probably appearing younger, very square in the shoulders and trim at the waistline, and walking as if he had a ramrod for a backbone?"

"Gosh, Miss Binks, he could have been. Hunt wasn't too clear on the details. They've been giving him a lot of stuff for the pain. Why? Do you know somebody like that?"

"In all my life, I've encountered only one person who has that knack of looking straight ahead and flicking something to the side with absolute accuracy. He's a distant cousin of mine named Roland Childe, who grew up not far from us in West Clavaton. Roland was one of those curly-haired little darlings who can grin and smirk and lie and sneak their way out of anything."

Miss Binks pursed her lips. "I remember one time while I was still in my teens, Aunt roped me into helping out at a Sunday School fete. Roland was there, unfortunately. He couldn't have been more than eight at the time, but he'd managed somehow to smuggle in a live frog. He bided his time till a bunch of children were gathered round the punch bowl, then tossed in the frog, which of course started kicking frantically. The punch was mostly grape juice, which spattered the girls' pretty little party dresses and the boys' clean shirts with horrid purple blotches."

"What a rotten thing to do," exclaimed Cronkite.

"It really was," Miss Binks agreed. "We'd had them playing musical chairs so they were all hot and thirsty and had to stand around waiting while we scalded out the bowl and made a fresh batch using the extra juice we'd thought would be plenty for a second bowlful. That meant we ran short, so nobody got quite enough to drink, which made the situation that much more unfortunate. The girls were sobbing about their dresses and the boys were snickering at them and acting silly, and of course dear Roland was all wide-eyed innocence. I could have whacked the little monster. I'm still sorry I didn't."

"What happened to the young rogue when he grew up?" Peter asked her. "Assuming, of course, that he was allowed to do so."

"He was, more's the pity. He was sent to a military academy. Roland had always been hipped on becoming a soldier of fortune. His father hoped a taste of army-style discipline would knock some sense into him."

"Did it?"

"I can't imagine anything could. Roland was as stubborn as he was stupid. He had a great gift of gab, though. He could run on in the most plausible manner and get everyone believing absolutely in what he was saying even though it made no sense whatsoever. At one of our legal go-rounds, he even tried to talk the judge into declaring him the custodian of Grandfather's estate. However, the documents he produced turned out to be spurious so he managed to persuade the court that he'd been the victim of a cruel hoax."

"Nice chap," grunted Peter. "But you have no idea where he is now?"

"None," said Miss Binks. "Roland's parents are still living in West Clavaton, to the best of my knowledge. I've had no contact with them since that debacle with the court. They took the view that I was the one who'd forged the documents in order to discredit Roland's claim, which was absurd in the first place. His parents are only distant cousins whom Grandfather never had any use for. Had I been the sort to stoop to such subterfuge, I'd have had sense enough to pick somebody who was at least on the right branch of the family tree, but naturally the Childes weren't about to admit that they're too low in the pecking order to count. Dear me, I have scrambled my metaphors, haven't I? We have dessert if you'd care for some. Teacake made from day lily pollen, with wild strawberry jam."

"That sounds delicious," Peter replied gallantly. In fact, it was. After a final round of sassafras tea, they were replete.

"And now," said their hostess, "I suggest we all turn in. There's no telling what tomorrow will bring, but whatever it is, I'm sure we'll handle it better after a good night's sleep. Let me see now, this presents an interesting problem for the housekeeper. I think what we'd better do is drag these spruce boughs down on the floor and spread them wide enough for the two of you to share. Luckily I have somewhat sybaritic tastes in bedding, so there should be plenty."

She was working as she spoke. "We'll put one blanket over the boughs and the other one over you. Keeping out the chill from the floor is the essential thing. Even though it's probably still quite warm outside, you see, the lair stays comfortably cool. Comfortable for me, anyway. We can leave the fire going if you like."

"But what about you, Miss Binks?" Cronkite protested. "We don't want to put you out of your bed."

"You won't, never fear. I shall retain all the deerskins for my own use. A few below, a couple above, and voila! I've slept much rougher than this before I learned how to make myself comfortable. Now, who wants first crack at the bathroom?"

Her guests both insisted Miss Binks go first, so she did. By the time Peter and Cronkite were ready to hit the spruce, she was fast asleep with a smile on her face.

Their own bed could have been a lot worse. And no doubt would have been if they'd climbed a different tree, Peter couldn't help thinking. He wondered whether there was a bloodhound stationed at each of Miss Binks's escape hatches, and decided there probably wasn't. She was too wily a vixen for those precautions she'd taken against hunting hounds not to be effective—unless, of course, they were Miss Binks's hounds and this cozy lair of hers was about to turn into a prison for Swope and himself. Time would tell. He pulled his half of the blanket up over him. It smelled of wood smoke. Better than burning soap grease. Much better. He shut his eyes and followed his strange hostess's example.

NINE

" 'Call me pet names, dearest, call me a bird,
   That flies to your side for one—.' Fried or scrambled?"

"The bird or your brain?" Helen asked. One couldn't help wondering with Catriona. "You're in splendid voice today, Miss McBogle. Wherever did you pick that one up?"

"From an old book called *Heart Songs*. It's right next to 'See at Your Feet a Suppliant One.' As I was endeavoring to ascertain, how do you want your eggs?"

"I'm not sure yet whether I want eggs at all," Helen demurred.

"Eat your eggs like a good girl and I'll show you a picture of Lillian Nordica with her straight-front corset on."

"You're all heart, Cat. How about just a cup of tea and a piece of toast for a poor tired librarian? What does one wear to a whale watch?"

"What do you care? It's not as though you were likely to meet any whales with whom you're personally acquainted. And if they don't know you, what difference does it make? I'm going to wear my fuzzy red running pants and my Save the Whales sweatshirt, and take my slicker in case they spout at us."

"Whales don't really spout at people, do they?"

"How do I know? I've never had a close encounter with one before. Or even a distant encounter, which I frankly think

77

I'd prefer. I suppose some whales spout and some don't. Or vice versa, as the case may be. White toast or brown?"

"Brown, please."

"That's a relief. I forgot to buy white bread, mainly because I never eat the stuff myself. White bread makes your eyebrows fall out."

"Does it really? I never knew that." Helen pulled a green-painted chair out from the kitchen table and sat down near the window where she'd be able to catch the morning sun. "I love your house, Cat."

"I love having you in it. It's been too long, Marsh old scout."

"Yes, it has. Isn't it awful how time flies? Or blips, or whatever it does. Come to think of it, an egg mightn't be such a bad idea, at that. Do we get lunch on the boat?"

"Madam, you are pleased to jest. I'm only hoping we get a halfway civilized john on the boat instead of an old bait bucket. I thought I'd pack us a few odds and ends of this and that, including a pint of spiced rum I bought last year to make fruitcake with and never got around to using. Spiced rum has a nice nautical aura about it, don't you think?"

"I think we'd have a nice, nautical aura about us if we drank any," Helen replied. "Don't you have something plain and wholesome, like scotch or bourbon?"

"Certainly I do. Which would be more medicinal in case of seasickness?"

"We're not going to be sick, Catriona. We're going to watch the pretty whales and have a lovely time. Seasickness is all in the mind."

"I thought it was in the inner ear."

"Whichever." Helen waved a dismissive hand and began eating the herb-stuffed omelet her hostess had produced, seemingly by accident. "Where's Iduna?"

"Up, I think. What will she want for breakfast?"

"Just show her the refrigerator and she'll take it from there. I move you go ahead and pack us a picnic. Or should we stop along the way and pick up some sandwiches and things?"

"We might do that," Catriona agreed, "assuming there were any place to buy them. The road between Sasquamahoc and Hocasquam is not precisely the crossroads of America, my dear. Although I want to tell you we are getting into *la nouvelle cuisine* around these parts. Edna's Diner over in Squamasas has started serving fried clam tacos. Do you like mustard on your ham?"

"By all means. And cheese if you have it, and lettuce unless you think it will get too wilty. Iduna puts her lettuce in a separate plastic bag and doesn't add it until she's ready to serve the sandwiches."

"Iduna's out of my class. What do you yourself do?"

"Come to think of it, I don't do anything. Peter and I haven't been on a picnic since we were married, to the best of my recollection. We do eat out a lot, but it's usually with friends or at the faculty dining room. We live right on campus, you know. The dining room's just a couple of minutes from the house and the food's excellent. I expect Peter's there now, getting his breakfast. It's a relief not having to worry about his meals while I'm away."

She glanced at the kitchen clock. "I'd better run upstairs and get prettied up for the whales."

By the time she was back downstairs, showered and dressed in her blue jeans, her pink jersey and sneakers, and her heavy cardigan just in case, Iduna had worked her way through a plate of ham and eggs and taken over the picnic basket. Catriona was busy arranging a lavish buffet for two Maine coon cats; one a glorious orange with russet markings, the other a more conventional black, gray, and white tiger.

"There, that ought to hold you ungrateful critters for a week or two. Be good cats and Mama will bring you back a herring. I always leave extra food, just in case, since the time I went down to Lewiston to give a talk at the college and got stuck in a blizzard."

"Do you let them out?" Helen asked.

"Oh, sure. Andrew will play doorman when he gets here. I have him trained not to show up before nine o'clock so that I can get a good start on my writing before he starts bending my ear about some damned thing or other. I don't want to rush you, ladies, but we'd better get rolling forthwith. The *Ethelbert Nevin* has to catch the tide or we'll spend the day on the mudflats. I don't know why Eustace thinks he can run excursions out of a tidal cove, but that's his problem, not mine. Mind going in my car? It's not so grand as yours, Iduna, but it does know the way."

It was as well they hadn't brought the Stotts' elegant vehicle, Helen thought as they wiggled and bumped their way up and down steep hills with hairpin curves and tiny wooden bridges at their bottoms. Cat took the roads at a steady fifty-five, slowing down to forty or so at the more spectacular hazards and delivering her friends to the dock in mint condition.

The *Ethelbert Nevin* wasn't much for looks, but probably was seaworthy enough. She—Helen knew, of course, that a vessel was always a female even when her first name happened to be *Ethelbert*—was a typical Maine-coast lobster boat. Rather larger than some, perhaps thirty feet in length, broad in the beam, with a good-sized open cockpit cluttered with gear Tilkey hadn't bothered to unload and a small enclosed cabin painted white but not recently. The middle-aged man who must be crew as well as captain, since he appeared to be the only one aboard, stood in the cockpit gazing morosely out over the gunwale. When he saw the three women getting out of Catriona's equally middle-aged American car, he straightened up but didn't look any happier.

"Thought you wasn't comin'."

"Eustace, you told me eight o'clock sharp," Catriona protested. "According to my watch it's only six minutes to."

"Ayup. I ain't arguin' with no redheaded woman. Come aboard if you're comin'. Here, gimme that basket. This all you got for dunnage?"

"What did you expect us to bring? We weren't exactly planning to spend the night."

"Hell, that don't make no never mind. I git 'em comin' with movie cameras an' telescopes an' duffel bags an' foldin' chairs, enough culch to last 'em till doomsday. Well, might's well set down an' take a load off your feet. Looks as if you've got 'er all to your ownsomes this mornin'."

That would have been fine with the three women, but their luck didn't hold. Eustace had his engine idling and was starting to cast off the mooring lines when a large green van hauled up to the dock and five young men bounded out, yelling and waving twenty-dollar bills. They ran down the dock and clambered aboard the *Ethelbert Nevin*, much encumbered by a superfluity of equipment.

Two of them had binoculars and enormous suitcases, one had a video camera and an immense gadget case. One, for some unfathomable reason, carried a light little fly rod and a creel big enough to hold a whale. The last one had a tackle box but no rod. By the time they got themselves settled, there was hardly room in the cockpit to move, even with the suitcases lashed to the forward deck. Helen and her friends were beginning to ask each other with their eyebrows whether this had been such a great idea, after all, when two of the men leaped to cast off the bow and stern mooring lines, Eustace revved his motor, and they headed out to sea.

"Well, that settles the question of whether we go or not," Iduna chuckled. "Might as well make ourselves comfortable, if we can."

The influx of passengers had crowded the three women over to the port side of the boat, which was as good a place to be as any. They stowed their hamper as best they could under the bench that ran around three sides of the cockpit, and sat down: Iduna next to the cabin wall so she'd have something to lean against, Catriona next to her, and Helen closest to the stern.

Two of the newcomers sat on the stern bench, the other three along the starboard side facing the women. Even though four of them were practically indistinguishable, it didn't take Helen and Iduna long to recognize the group as the same fellows who'd parked next to them at the rest stop on the turnpike. Nor were the men slow to spot them. It was the clean-shaven one with the grin and the crewcut who spoke.

"Well, ladies, we meet again. How are you enjoying Maine?"

Helen had been right about his being older than the rest, she decided. It was the beards that put extra years on his companions, and the grin and the breezy manner that helped this one to give the false impression of youth. He must be forty or thereabouts, not that it mattered a hoot. If they were going to be jammed in here all day like peas in a pod, Helen saw no sense in being standoffish. She smiled back.

"Marvelous, so far. How about you?"

"We're having a ball. Is this your first whale watch?"

Helen said it was, and he said it was theirs, too. They exchanged a few more commonplaces, but it was hard to keep shouting back and forth over the noise of the engine and the *slap-slap-slap* of the water against the boat's hull. Pretty soon they both quit trying.

That suited Helen just fine. Men who laid themselves out to be fascinating and kept staring to make sure one was being sufficiently dazzled by their inanities were a type she could do nicely without. She laid a bet with herself that their chummy fellow passenger wouldn't sit in silence for long, though, and he didn't. His next ploy was to unfold a large map and make the men on either side of him hold it out flat while he expounded something or other with a great deal of pointing and gesticulating.

"Showing them what course he thinks we're going to take, I suppose," Catriona explained into Helen's ear. "Whales generally come up the Stellwagen Bank off Massachusetts into the Gulf of Maine, then swim out past the islands."

"Which islands?" Helen asked her.

"Whichever islands they take a fancy to pass, I guess. We have scads to choose from. The Great Glacier chewed up the coastline and spat out bits and pieces offshore, then the waves took it from there. If that gink tries to muscle in on us with his bloody chart, I move we mutiny."

The man with the map had finished lecturing his seatmates. Now he was hectoring the two in the stern to change places with the others so he could go through the whole performance again. Helen agreed that people with maps needed to be firmly dealt with.

He wouldn't bother Iduna, anyway. She was gently dozing, her face shielded from the sun and wind by an old-fashioned blue calico sunbonnet, and Helen's extra sweater tucked between her head and the side of the cabin as a cushion against the unending vibration and rocking.

After a while Helen began to wish Iduna didn't look so comfortable. She hated to disturb her friend, but she would rather like to get her sweater back. The sun that had been so bright when they started out was retiring behind what looked to her ominously like the approach of a fog bank. She wasn't frightened but she was getting awfully bored, crammed in here with nothing to do and nothing to see but choppy water.

The five male passengers seemed to be affected much the same as she. They'd quit their mild horseplay, put away the map, and fallen into silence. Even Crewcut wasn't talking. Helen hoped they weren't all going to be seasick. In such cramped quarters, that would be the ultimate disaster.

They were coming to an island. At least Helen assumed one could call it an island: a long, low grayish bump rising out of the water. Eustace cut his speed and steered the *Ethelbert Nevin* closer. The island opened one small eye. Catriona nudged Iduna.

"Wake up, quick," she whispered. "We've found a whale."

Iduna sat up straight, flipped back her sunbonnet, and turned to face the monster of the deep. The whale looked back at her. Quite unmistakably, it winked. Then it put down its head and sounded with barely a ripple.

Iduna nodded a pleasant good-bye. "Nice whale. Here, Helen, you'd better put this on. Wake me up when we meet another."

She handed over the cardigan Helen had been longing for, donned her own raincoat, flipped the sunbonnet brim back down over her face, and went back to her nap.

Now they were really among the islands, not very exciting ones so far, nothing but tumbles of rock with sometimes a little sparse vegetation and, on one, a weathered fishing shack. Far ahead in the channel another whale was so obliging as to breach, shooting its vast bulk clear of the water and landing with a horrendous splash. Catriona put her slicker on.

"Just as well the gamesome little dickens wasn't so close as the first. Having fun, Marsh?"

"I'm not quite sure," Helen replied honestly. "It's awesome watching something bigger than the boat cavort in the water like a kid at the beach. Why do they leap like that?"

"Sheer animal spirits, I expect. Whales have to get their kicks where they find them, Marsh. There are no bingo games in the ocean."

"Thank you for telling me. Where do you suppose Eustace parks his bait bucket?"

"I was beginning to wonder that, myself," her friend confessed. "Shall we?"

"Let's."

They picked their way through the men's impedimenta the few steps to the cabin overhang. The wheel was on the outside rear wall of the cabin, on the starboard side. Eustace was standing there, hands on the spokes, eyes on the channel. Without waiting for Catriona's question, he answered.

"Head's inside. Step down. Port door."

"Thanks, Eustace."

The cabin didn't contain much except a strong odor of engine, fish, and Eustace. They had no trouble locating the portside door; it was the only door there was. To go through, they had to step up, then down into a little well. Catriona hung back.

"Go ahead, Marsh. I'll wait. Watch out, there's probably another step inside. You okay?"

"Yes," said Helen, "but I can't find a light. I don't think there is one. Never mind, I can manage."

The plumbing was nothing fancy; still, it was better than a bait bucket. There was even an *Old Farmer's Almanac* with half the pages torn out hanging ready to hand. Helen found a tissue in her sweater pocket and used that instead, found another and saved it for Catriona. Iduna had some wash-and-dry packets in the picnic basket; she'd fish a couple out when they got back to their seats.

Because there'd been no light in the cuddy, Helen had wound up having to leave the door open a crack so she could see what she was doing. Cat had stood in the stairwell, holding the knob against a possibly embarrassing sudden swing. As they changed places, Helen was about to perform the same service for her friend, but Catriona shook her head. "You needn't bother. I've found my pocket flashlight. Go ahead before the smell gets to you."

Nothing loath to get away from the odor of bilge and fish, Helen stepped up into the cabin. She was just in time to see the man with the crewcut stand up behind Eustace, whip out what looked like a short piece of pipe, and whang it down with all his might on the boatman's head. As Eustace's knees buckled, Crewcut flicked his weapon sideways over the port rail and grabbed the falling body under the armpits. The man sitting nearest sprang up and grabbed Eustace by the feet. Together they swung the now inert form over the gunwale and let go. The first murderer smiled sweetly at his mates and sat down. The second remained standing and took Eustace's place at the wheel. A thoroughly professional operation.

Helen was quite sure they hadn't seen her. As soon as she'd realized what was going on, she'd ducked back down into the pit. The narrow cabin windows were filmed with oil and salt. She and Cat had shut the cabin door behind them when they went in, the natural reaction of two averagely modest, middle-aged women in close quarters with a boat-load of strange young men. Crewcut had probably counted on their doing so. The automatic gesture might have saved their lives, at least for the moment, but it had certainly provided an opportunity for Eustace to be robbed of his.

Now what to do? Stall for time and pray, was the best plan Helen could come up with. Say nothing to Cat or Iduna, assuming the latter had actually managed to sleep through a murder that was being committed practically under her nose.

If Crewcut had meant to kill her and her friends right off, surely he'd have kept the weapon with which he'd struck Eustace. Maybe he was planning to take them hostage, though Helen couldn't imagine why.

Well, there was only one way to find out. Helen waited till Catriona emerged from the cuddy, then opened the cabin door and walked ahead of her into the cockpit.

TEN

Naturally Catriona McBogle was surprised to find one of the passengers at the wheel. "Where's Eustace?" she asked him.

"Up front looking for whales," he grunted.

"What front? You mean that dinky little foredeck? In this weather? He must be crazy. Eustace! Ahoy! Come back here, you old coot."

She craned her neck forward into the gray mist that wasn't yet opaque but was thick enough to coat everything with slippery wetness. "Where is he? I don't see him."

"Then perhaps you'd like to go look for him."

That was the man with the crewcut. Without losing his amiable smile, he got up from the bench and grabbed Catriona by the wrists. The man who'd been sitting next to him snatched her ankles. Seeming to enjoy the woman's struggles and yells of outrage, they swept her off her feet and began swinging her back and forth like a couple of teenage rowdies clowning at the beach.

There was no time left to play it cool. Helen flew at the men, kicking, screaming, beating at them with her fists. Not to be left out of the fun, the remaining two sprang up and gave Helen the same treatment. Counting in unison, "One . . . two . . . three," the two hoodlums gave their captives three last, mighty swings and sent them flying over the side, into the ice-cold water.

Helen and Catriona came up close together, sputtering and

gasping. Something else hurtled toward them, came down, and bobbed on the water. It was, incredibly, the picnic hamper. Then came a splash like the breaching of a whale, and Iduna was beside them.

"I heaved the hamper overboard and jumped in after it," she told her friends calmly. "Thought I might as well save those hooligans a hernia, not that they deserve any consideration after the way they treated you. Here, girls, take hold of me. I'm good as a lifeboat any day."

It was true. Iduna's weight kept her bobbing on the surface like an inflated balloon. "Undo my sash, one of you. We'll tie ourselves and the hamper together the way mountain climbers do. That way we won't get separated."

That way they'd make an easier target, Helen thought. Rifle bullets were hitting the water all too near them. Then she realized the men weren't shooting at them, but at a whale that was coming up fast astern.

"They're trying to get that whale angry so it will come after us," she gurgled as she struggled with the wet knot at Iduna's waist.

"Damned fools." Catriona had captured the picnic basket and brought it up to their human raft. "Do they think whales are stupid?"

This one certainly wasn't. Sweeping past the pathetic little flotilla without a sideward look, the great beast headed straight for the *Ethelbert Nevin*. They could hear the yells, more shots, and a burst of speed as the murderous quintet tried to outrun a whale. The water that had gone dead calm with the onset of the fog was in a roil from the wakes of the boat and its dire pursuer. Iduna and the hamper floated with the waves; Helen and Catriona perforce went along for the ride.

They wouldn't be able to stay alive for long. Maine waters were too cold, Helen was thinking quite dispassionately as she tied one end of the long sash to Iduna's wrist, passed it through the handle of the picnic basket and then around Catriona's arm. Already her fingers were stiffening. She had a hard time making the knots secure. She saved her own till last because she, as the smallest and slimmest, would be first to go. They could untie her and let her sink. She didn't want Peter to see her all bloated and waterlogged. He'd be upset enough without that.

"Okay, Marsh, I'll do you."

Catriona had taken the sash from her. Helen could feel it going around her wrist, being pulled tight. Too tight. The circulation would be cut off. What difference did it make?

"Come on, Marsh! Kick your legs, move your arms. Get the old corpuscles racing."

Cat must be noticing what was happening to her, trying to make it not happen. Good old Cat. Helen attempted a few kicks. Her wet sneakers felt like divers' weights. The arms worked a little better, for a while.

She didn't remember giving up. She didn't remember much of anything until she began to feel her feet. They hurt like pins and needles, only much worse than when she sat at home reading with Jane Austen sleeping on her feet till the feet went to sleep also and had to be waked up again.

Her face hurt, too. That was because somebody was slapping it, shouting at her.

"Marsh! Come on, Marsh, wake up!"

"Umh." Helen turned her head to avoid another blow. "Stop it, Cat. I'm all right."

"You could have fooled us there a few minutes ago. Here, drink this."

That was Iduna, holding something to her lips. Whisky? Bourbon? Spiced rum? Helen didn't know and she didn't care. It burned and she could feel it, really feel it all the way down. She tried to sit up and realized she could.

"All better. I'm sorry. I hope I didn't cause you too much trouble."

"Oh, shut up, you old idiot."

Cat was hugging her. Cat's arms were soaking wet. They were all wet, and cold, and no doubt slightly hysterical. Except Iduna. Iduna was passing out paper napkins from the picnic basket to dry their hands on, and sandwiches still appetizing in their individual ziplocked plastic bags.

"The quicker we eat, the better. The calories will warm us up. Helen, I know you don't like sugar in your coffee but I'm giving it to you anyway. You need it."

"If you say so, Iduna." Helen drank meekly from the plastic cup, then bit into her sandwich. Ham and cheese. Lots of body-building protein. "Where are we?" she asked with her mouth full, "and how did we get here?"

"Same answer to both questions," Catriona replied. "Damned if I know. That nice whale saved us, making all those waves. We were just lucky enough to get washed up on one of the islands. It would, of course, have made a better story if the whale had carried us here on its back."

"I was the nice whale. Nothing like a few extra inches of blubber in a pinch." Iduna complacently helped herself to another sandwich. "My, these taste good, Cat. Good thing that hamper has a plastic lining. I was scared stiff the water would get in, but everything stayed dry as a bone, which I sure wish I was, myself, right now. I think what we'd better do is rig my raincoat for a lean-to, if we can find anything to hang it on, and scout ourselves up some driftwood for a fire. The sooner we get warmed up and dried out, the better we'll feel in the morning."

"Whatever you say, Captain." Helen's voice was choked. She realized to her surprise that she'd been crying all the time she'd been eating. "Sorry I'm being such a sissy."

"Oh, shut up," said Catriona. "It's just delayed reaction from the shock of getting pitched overboard into ice water."

"And not having meat enough on your bones to grease a griddle with," Iduna added just a bit smugly.

"I think it's mostly from having watched those men murder Eustace and throw him overboard while you were in the john, Cat, and Iduna was asleep."

Helen was surprised she could say it so calmly, but after what had subsequently happened to herself and the others, she didn't suppose any of them could be much affected by the boatman's gruesome death. Iduna went on eating her sandwich. Catriona expressed only professional interest.

"How did they do it?"

"The smiley one with the crewcut hit him over the head from behind. I'm not sure what with—it looked like a short stick or a piece of pipe."

"Billy club with a lead weight, maybe. Then what?"

"Then he grabbed Eustace around the chest and that one who had you by the ankles took his feet and they chucked him overboard. Just the way they did you and me, only not so—playfully."

She took another fit of shuddering. Iduna poured her a little more coffee.

"Get this into you, Helen, then I think we'd better find that driftwood before everything gets too damp to burn. I wonder how big a place we're on? There might even be a house."

There wasn't. Their haven was only an islet, not more than an acre overall, if that. They found not a single tree, but there were a few scrubby bushes that might serve after a fashion for their shelter. At least there was no scarcity of driftwood, nor were matches a problem. Cat's slicker pocket yielded a waterproof matchsafe as well as a jackknife they could use to trim back the shrubs into a shape that would accommodate Iduna's raincoat.

"Guthrie Fingal gave me these," she told them. "He says nobody should ever go anywhere without a knife and some matches. I thought he was being funny, but he swore there'd come a time when I'd be darned glad I had them. That's the one thing I can't stand about Guthrie, he always winds up being right."

"If he's so smart, how come he didn't give you a folding canoe?" What with the food, the exercise, the fire warming her bones and drying her clothes, Helen was getting her spirits back. "Has it occurred to either of you to wonder how we'll ever get off this rock?"

"Not to worry, Marsh. Another kindly whale will befriend us. Maybe that one who was giving Iduna the eye while we were on the boat will come back. Darn, I wish I hadn't mentioned the boat. It makes me remember poor old Eustace."

Iduna hadn't abandoned her role as chief comforter. "Maybe he was only stunned, and the water brought him to."

"To where, for instance? Eustace had no picnic basket to lean on, and I doubt very much whether he'd ever swum a stroke in his life. You'd be surprised how many fishermen can't. They get enough of the water just being on top of it. I feel I ought to apologize for landing you two in this mess."

"How could you possibly have known it was going to turn out like this?" Helen retorted. "We were just as keen on coming as you were. And we did get to see some whales. I didn't mean to sound pessimistic just now. Surely somebody will come looking for us sooner or later."

"Oh, yes. Once the fog lifts, word will get around that the *Ethelbert Nevin* hasn't come back and the Coast Guard will begin searching the channels. What concerns me, I have to say, is whether those birds who stole the boat might come back to make sure we really drowned."

"They won't," Iduna reassured her. "They're in a big hurry to get to Paraguay."

"Paraguay? In that old tub of Eustace's?"

"That's what they stole it for."

"Do you mean they joined the whale watch on purpose to hijack the *Ethelbert Nevin*?"

"Of course. Why do you think they brought all that luggage with them?"

"But that's totally insane. Who do they think they are, the Owl and the Pussycat? And why Paraguay? Paraguay isn't even reachable by water. Is it?"

"Down around the coast of Brazil to Uruguay, then up the Paraná River through quite a lot of Argentina," said Helen. "They must be out of their minds. How did you get on to Paraguay, Iduna?"

"Easy enough. Do you remember Mr. Bjornstern, who had my downstairs bedroom?"

"That sweet old man with the big white mustache he used to tie up in his napkin so it wouldn't drag in his soup? How could we forget? What about Mr. Bjornstern?"

"He was deaf, you know."

"Yes, I remember. We all paralyzed our larynxes screaming at him, then we discovered we could communicate just as well by simply mouthing the words and letting him read our lips."

"That's right. After you two left, I taught some of my other boarders the same trick. I had so much fun watching those conversations with everybody talking and nobody making any noise that I got pretty good at reading lips myself. So when I happened to notice what that fellow with the map was talking about, I decided I'd better go on making believe I was asleep and keep watch on what they were saying. Did you know you've been kept under surveillance for the past two months, Helen?"

"Me? You're joking. Whatever for?"

"On account of the weather vanes. That's what they're going to Paraguay for. As far as I could make out, they've got some crazy billionaire down there who collects antique weather vanes, and they're on their way to deliver a few that they've stolen."

"Praxiteles Lumpkin's weather vanes? I can't believe this! Where do they have them cached, did they say?"

"Right on the boat. That's why they had those big cases with them."

"But how could they?"

"Easily enough, I should think," said Catriona. "They'd have dismantled them and just packed the design part and the crisscross thing with the letters on it. The hardware that held them on to the roofs wouldn't be all that important to a collector, I shouldn't think."

"I suppose you're right. My God! That might have been a piece from one of the weather vanes he killed Eustace with. But this means we may still have a fighting chance of getting the weather vanes back. Surely the Coast Guard shouldn't have any trouble picking up the *Ethelbert Nevin*."

"Unless the whale caught up with her first."

Catriona realized she'd been tactless again. "What's far more likely is that they've piled up on another of these little islands in the fog. They'll be picked up like sitting ducks, weather vanes and all. You'll be a heroine, Marsh."

"A poor apology for one," Helen retorted. "You two are the heroines."

"Blah. Tell you what, let's all be heroines. I wouldn't mind another slurp of that coffee, but I expect we'd better save it for tomorrow's breakfast. Likewise the rest of the sandwiches. It may be a while before we're picked up, and there's no sense going hungry in the meantime. What else do you have in the basket, Iduna?"

"There's that lemonade you and I never got around to drinking yesterday, Helen. I forgot to empty out the other thermos. No reason why it shouldn't be fit to drink. Too bad we haven't a pan to heat it in, we could have hot lemonade and cookies for a bedtime snack. Not that I'm complaining, mind you. I'm just darn glad to be where I am instead of—"

She got control of her voice and went on briskly. "I left those oatmeal cookies in on purpose. I thought they might go kind of good on the boat. Here, Cat, try one of these, and a little lemonade. You'll have to use the same cup, we've only got three. Too bad I didn't think about bringing a jug of drinking water, but we've got oranges and grapes. They ought to help some."

Catriona put another piece of driftwood on the fire. It blazed up with magical blue and emerald and crimson and scarlet glints among the orange-yellow flames. Orange, Helen thought, the color of Hestia, goddess of the hearth. Home was where you hung your raincoat.

She sat between her two friends, watching the fire, nibbling at Iduna's wholesome cookie, sipping her small tot of lukewarm lemonade. After a while, Catriona began to sing another one of her old songs, a tune she'd found first in a John Buchan thriller and later in one of her grandmother's gospel music books.

" 'On the other side of Jordan in the sweet fields of Eden, where the tree of life is blooming, there is rest for you.' "

Helen joined in, then Iduna. " 'There is rest for the weary, there is rest for the weary, there is rest for the weary, there is rest for you.' "

Such is the resilience of the human spirit. They were having a singalong, here on an unknown lump of rock in the middle of nowhere. The fog was thick enough by now to cut with a knife, but who cared? They were snug, huddled under their bush with Iduna's raincoat bouncing the heat from the fire back to warm them all over and make them forget their clothes still hadn't dried. And probably never would, until they could get back where there was fresh water to rinse the salt out.

They were sheltered, they were fed, they were together, they were alive. For now, that was enough. They sang on and on: sweet songs, funny songs, rousing songs, college songs, silly songs. No sad songs, they'd had misery enough for one day. Iduna was a really good mezzo-soprano; she'd been soloist in her church choir back in South Dakota. Cat's voice wasn't much, but her repertoire was tremendous. Helen could at least carry a tune. Their attempts at harmonizing might not have struck all that euphoniously on a trained ear, but there was nobody to listen except perhaps for a whale or two.

And a flickering gray wraith that stole up toward their rainbow-colored campfire and stood watching them through the leaping flames.

ELEVEN

" 'Do you see what I see? Do you see what I see?' " Helen crooned the words of the Christmas carol softly, urgently.

"I don't know that—" Catriona stopped short. "Holy cow!" she croaked, "we've conjured spirits from the vasty deep. Speak! Speak, thou fearful guest!"

"Damned if I know what to say." The voice came low and trembling. The specter took another step forward and reached its shaking hands out to the fire. "Feels real."

"Cripes, I—" The apparition licked its pallid lips and seemed to fumble for words. "I thought you was them Lorelei like they got in the Rhine River tryin' to lure me to my doom. That really you, Cat?"

"Eustace! You're alive!"

"Guess it's kind o' beginnin' to look that way, though I sure as hell don't feel it. You ain't got a slug o' somethin' to warm a feller up, by any chance? I'm so cold my tonsils are froze to my windpipe."

Iduna, who'd been sitting stock still, her eyes as big and round as butter chips, heard the call to action. She whipped into the hamper, poured out a little of the hot coffee they'd been saving for breakfast, and added a sizable tot of the spiced rum Catriona had decided they might as well take along after all.

"Here, come around where it's warmer and drink this."

The boatman's hands were so numb she had to help him hold the cup, but once he'd got a couple of swallows inside him he began to steady down.

"By God, I needed that."

"How about a sandwich? We've got ham and—"

"Whatever you got, I'll take it. You sure you ain't a Lorelei?"

Iduna turned pink as a giant peony. "My husband calls me one sometimes. He can be quite poetical when he takes the notion."

"Husband, eh? I might o' known."

Eustace had taken a wolfish snap at his sandwich before he'd got it fairly out of its baggie. He took another before he'd quite finished dealing with the first and spoke with a full mouth and perhaps a full heart. "How come he lets a fine figure of a woman like you run around gettin' into trouble?"

"He had to go off and read a paper at a hog breeders' convention, so I came along with Mrs. Shandy to visit our old friend Cat. My husband's Professor Daniel Stott. She's Helen and I'm Iduna. Another sandwich?"

"Don't mind if I do."

"Eustace, for God's sake!" howled Catriona. "Will you quit the small talk and tell us how you got here?"

He chewed ham for a while, then shook his head. "No sense me tellin'. You wouldn't believe it anyways."

"Try us."

"You got any more o' that rum?"

"Oh, all right, you maddening old critter." Catriona slopped another inch or so into his cup. "There, that ought to be good for what ails you. Now what won't we believe?"

"What's happened to my boat?"

"Eustace!"

"Quit yellin', can't you? I got a right to know, ain't I? Is she here?"

"We don't know where she is," Helen took it upon herself to explain since Catriona had turned stubborn and preferred to fume in silence. "What happened was something we don't quite believe, either, but here's how it was."

She told it, every bit, while he sat gawking at her over his sandwich. "So that's how we got here. Now how about you? Surely you haven't been in that freezing cold water all this time?"

Eustace remembered the sandwich and took a bite. "Well, I have an' I haven't, as you might say. Now that I know I got hit over the head, it begins to make some kind o' sense, if you can call it that. Best I can tell you is, I was standin' at the wheel like you seen me doin' when you went into the cabin. Next thing I know, I was underwater fixin' to drown. Then I felt somethin' solid under me an' the water sunk, or else I riz up. Don't ask me which."

He masticated for a moment in silence. "Anyways, there I was, clear o' the water an' ridin' flat on my back lookin' up at the sky. One minute I was thinkin' it don't look so good, an' then I was thinkin' the hell it don't. I thought I was back aboard the *Ethelbert Nevin*, see? I figgered I'd been drug up onto the foredeck an' laid out to dry like a split mackerel. Then I knew I wasn't because we was travelin' at a pretty good clip but wasn't makin' any noise. So finally, by gorry, I got it figgered out. Like I said, you're not goin' to believe this, but—"

"A whale had come up under you and was carrying you

along on its back," Catriona finished impatiently. "What's so remarkable about that? It happens all the time."

"Like hell it does! I been puttin' out o' Hocasquam Cove ever since I was old enough to cut bait an' I ain't never heard o' nobody hitchin' a ride on a whale's back before like I done. You tryin' to take the wind out o' my sails?"

"I wouldn't dream of it. Actually, after we three went overboard, we were hoping to board a whale ourselves, but we weren't lucky enough. So you've been on top of that whale all this time?"

"Far's I know. Seem's like I must o' kept passin' out. I'd get my bearin's best I could, then I'd be someplace different. Then the fog come in an' I couldn't tell where I was an' didn't see's it mattered because I knew I was a goner anyhow. Sooner or later that whale was goin' to sound an' that'd be the end o' me. Only it never did, I don't know why. You'd o' thought it would o' wanted its supper. I sure as hell wanted mine, I can tell you."

"How did you get off the whale?" said Iduna.

"Got throwed. We was cruisin' along slow an' easy, not makin' more'n mebbe half a knot. That whale wasn't one to overwork itself, I got to admit, not that I'm runnin' it down nor nothin', 'cause it sure done right by me. But anyways the sky got darker an' darker an' foggier an' foggier an' the suspense was gettin' me down. I got to thinkin' what am I prolongin' the agony for?"

"Another cookie?" suggested Iduna.

"Thanks. So anyways, there I was. Might's well just slide off an' let the ocean have me, I says to myself. It'll get me sooner or later anyways, like as not. But I dunno. Seemed as if it was just too much bother. An' then be cussed an' be blowed if I didn't see this glimmer o' light off the port bow. I guess maybe the whale seen 'er, too, 'cause it sort o' rolled over an' threw me in the water. I says to myself this is it, an' I started to sink."

He stuffed the rest of the cookie into his mouth. "But cripes, first thing I knew I was touchin' bottom, an' I could hear singin'. So I thought to myself, here I am at the pearly gates an' I might's well go sign up for my harp lessons. So I kept walkin' shoreward an' here I am. An' mighty glad to be here, I don't mind sayin'. I might eat another couple or three o' them cookies if you got 'em to spare, Iduner."

"There's only one left, but you're welcome to it. Do you think this fog will burn off in the morning?"

"Might," Eustace conceded. "Then again, it mightn't."

"It's just that we'll be down to mighty slim pickings by tomorrow afternoon if it doesn't," Iduna apologized.

"Oh hell, we ain't goin' to starve. We could scrape mussels off'n the rock an' roast 'em in the embers, long's we kin keep the fire goin'. Eat seaweed if we have to. Fresh water's the real sticker. Don't s'pose you thought to bring any?"

"No, it never entered my head. We have half a thermos of lemonade, about a swallow of coffee apiece for breakfast, three oranges, and a fairly good-sized bunch of grapes. Those ought to help some. And I stuck in a box of wash-and-dry tissues in case anybody wants to clean themselves up a little."

"You also got the rest o' that rum," Eustace reminded her.

"Of which you're not going to get any more for a while, if that's what you're hinting at. From the way you described yourself going in and out of consciousness while you were riding the whale, it sounds to me as if you might have a mild concussion from that whack on the head those villains gave you. Alcohol's the worst thing in the world for a brain injury."

"Huh. Think I'm a sissy? I got a skull like a rock."

"With brains to match if you think you can con Iduna into giving you another drink," Catriona snorted. "You'd better wait and see how you feel in the morning before you go trying to make yourself any worse. We're not exactly geared to take care of invalids here. I wish we had a blanket or pillow to make you comfortable, but we don't."

"Hunh." For a wonder, Eustace managed to produce the ghost of a snicker. " 'Member when you come aboard this mornin', Cat? I says was that all you had for dunnage an' you says you wasn't fixin' to stay the night. Don't pay to go jumpin' to conclusions, does it?"

"Thanks for reminding me. I think I'll go hunt for some more firewood."

"Cat, please don't go wandering off by yourself in this fog," Iduna begged. "We have enough to last till morning."

Actually they did. As soon as they'd got themselves thawed out and fed after their escape from being drowned, Helen and Catriona had gone scrounging. They'd amassed a sizable woodpile, partly because they needed the fire for survival, partly because the exercise got their blood pumping again, partly because having something to do made their plight seem less dire. Things had begun to look a shade brighter now; Catriona gave in with a fairly good grace.

"All right, Iduna, I won't if it's going to upset you. I guess I'm just having a case of the fidgets. Why the heck didn't I think to bring my typewriter? And a battery to plug it into? That's the trouble with Western civilization, we're too bloody technologized. Look at me, I'm a keyboard junkie. If I were Abraham Lincoln, I'd just take a charred stick from the fire and scrawl algebra problems on the rocks."

"Why ever would you want to scrawl algebra problems?" Helen asked her. "You can't even balance your checkbook. At least you never could back in South Dakota. Besides, this fog's so thick it would wash them off before you got them solved. Shouldn't we be trying to catch some of the moisture for drinking water? We could set out all the plastic cups."

"How 'bout if we stick out our tongues?" Eustace grunted. "How long do you think Wedgwood Munce is goin' to leave us perched out here like a gaggle o' shags? Soon as Wedge notices the *Ethelbert Nevin* didn't come in overnight, he'll be out lookin', you kin lay to that. He won't quit till he finds us, neither."

"What makes you so sure?" Catriona grumbled. "Wedgwood Munce never impressed me as being any great ball of fire. The way I heard it, his brothers only finagled him the job as harbor master because they were sick and tired of having to support him."

"I ain't sayin' they didn't. What I am sayin' is that I borried fifty dollars off'n Wedge a ways back an' he's bound an' determined I'm goin' to pay 'im back this week, come hell or high water. He knew I was aimin' to take you three out whale watchin' today. Or yesterday or whenever 'twas. I told 'im so right after you called up to make the reservation. That meant I'd have your money on me by the time I got back, so it'd prob'ly be safe to say Wedge's been settin' in the dock ever since high tide with 'is cussed paw stretched out, waitin' to grab me by the pocket before I even got tied up. Cussin' me out by now, I shouldn't wonder, 'cause he's scairt the *Ethelbert Nevin*'s gone down with all hands an' he's out his fifty."

"Are you trying to be funny, Eustace? If so, I feel constrained to inform you that the humor of your remark eludes me," Catriona remarked coldly.

Iduna was more sympathetic. "Surely Mr. Munce won't want to take your money when he finds out you've lost your boat."

Eustace refused to be consoled by any false hopes. "Don't take no scholar to figure out you never met Wedge Munce, Iduner. Wedge is the meanest cuss from Kittery to Calais, bar none. I told 'im so to 'is face last time he tried to hit me up for the fifty. Wedge, I says, if there was two o' you, I'd kill one of 'em so's they wouldn't breed."

Eustace spat, turning his head genteelly aside in deference to the sensibilities of his feminine companions. "I never met only one other person who c'n get me riled up worse'n Wedge Munce, an' she's that woman Woody Fingal went an' got tied up with. What the hell's she call 'erself, Cat? Ambrosia somethin' or other?"

"Elisa Alicia Quatrefages, but don't ask me why. What have you got against Elisa Alicia, Eustace? I wasn't even aware you knew her."

"'Tain't my fault if I do. She's always down around the waterfront lately, gettin' in the way an' askin' fool questions. Last time I seen 'er, she had a camera slung around 'er neck like a goddamn tourist. I swear she must o' took fifteen or twenty pitchers o' the *Ethelbert Nevin* alone. I was settin' on the dock fixin' a lobster trap, an' she wanted me to pose for 'er. I says gimme ten bucks an' I'll pose for you standin' on my head playin' the harmonicker."

"Did she go for it?"

"Nah, just teeheed an' says she wasn't that int'rested, she was just tryin' to soak up the atmosphere. I had a bucket o' fishheads under the bench that I'd been kind of ripenin' for a week or two to see if they'd attract the lobsters any better'n the bait I'd been usin'. Cussed critters are gettin' so scarce these days you practic'ly have to swim down an' hand 'em a gilt-edged invitation to lure 'em into the trap. So I took off the lid an' slid the bucket under 'er nose. Here, I says, if it's atmosphere you want, take a whiff o' this."

"Eustace, what a rotten thing to do!" Catriona crowed. "Why the heck didn't you wait till I was around? What did Elisa Alicia say?"

"She said the smell was prime evil, which was layin' it on pretty thick for a few stinkin' fishheads, if you ask me. I smelt plenty worse. Anyways, she didn't stick around for another sniff, but be cussed an' be blowed if she wasn't back the next day wantin' to know if I'd like to charter my boat. I says who to, an' she says a friend o' hers. I says with me runnin' 'er, an' she says no, the friend wanted to run 'er hisself. So I says forget it, an' she left agin an' that's the last I seen o' 'er. Maybe you noticed I been kind o' peakin' and pinin' the last few days?"

He expected a laugh on that sally, so they all three gave him one. "Next time I see Elisa Alicia, I'll tell her how much you miss her," Catriona promised.

"Ayuh, you do that. 'Bout as much as I miss them gurry boils I used to git on my wrists when I fished the Grand Banks on the schooner *Rudy Vallee* with my cousin Tramwell. You'd of enjoyed Tramwell, Iduner. Ever meet 'im, Cat?"

"No, I can't say that I ever did."

"Well, you ain't missed a hell of a lot. Tramwell used to play the saxophone. When he wasn't playin', he was singin' through 'is nose like Rudy only a damn sight worse. God, Tram was awful! An' the hell of it was, on a boat there wasn't no way you could git away from 'im. Even out in the dories, you know how sound carries over water. He'd set there whinin' 'My Time Is Your Time' till you'd want to row over an' clout 'im one with an oar."

"What finally happened to your cousin?" As usual, Helen was after the facts. "Did he go on the radio?"

"Nope. He went overboard from the *Rudy Vallee* one night when the deck was iced up three inches thick. I always kind o' wondered who was behind 'im when he slipped but I never said nothin' to nobody. 'Twouldn't o' done no good an' I wouldn't o' blamed 'em much anyways. We put 'is saxophone in a gunny sack weighted down with a bowl o' cherries an' buried it over the side. Had to use canned ones but we figured it was the thought that counted. We all stood around to watch it go down, singin' 'Rocked in the Cradle o' the Deep' through our noses so's we'd have somethin' solemn an' reverent to tell 'is mother when we went ashore."

"That was kind of you," said Iduna. "These things mean a lot to a bereaved mother."

"Ayuh. I dunno how much it meant to Aunt Penelope. She was worse'n Tramwell about gettin' into vodvill. That was what she called it when they still had it. All she could think about was a herd o' fleas she was trainin' to start 'er own flea circus. She got Uncle Brockley so mad one day yakkin' about them fleas while he was waitin' for her to fry the fishcakes that he grabbed the Flit gun an' wiped out 'er whole act with one big squoosh. So Aunt Penelope snatched off 'er apron, left the salt codfish soakin' on the drainboard an' the pork scraps fryin' in the skillet, an' thumbed a ride to Old Orchard Beach. She got a job pullin' saltwater taffy an' shacked up with a feller who slung hamburgers in the next booth, an' they all three lived happy ever after. 'Specially Uncle Brockley."

Catriona was amused. "Why don't you tell that story to Guthrie Fingal next time you see him? What did Elisa Alicia's friend want to charter the *Ethelbert Nevin* for?"

"She never said an' I didn't feel like askin'. Say, you know, I just thought o' somethin'. Dunno why it didn't come to me sooner. Anyways, after I talked to you on the phone, Cat, I thought mebbe I better go down an' get rid o' them fishheads an' sort o' redd up the cockpit so's you wouldn't be ashamed o' me in front o' your friends from away. So I puttered around awhile, then it got dark an' I couldn't see to do no more, an' it wouldn't o' done much good anyways. But it was kind o' pleasant down there, so I just went into the cabin an' set—you know how you do."

"Why inside the cabin?" Helen asked him.

"I dunno. Felt like it, I guess. Anyways, I set there an' pretty soon I heard a bunch o' men come down on the dock. I thought maybe they was comin' to find out about the whale-watchin' trips an' I ought to give 'em a hail, but I didn't. They might o' been tourists just soakin' up the atmosphere like Elisa Alicia an' I'd had enough o' them kind already. 'Twasn't anybody I knew, that was for sure. An' now I'm willin' to swear it was them."

He didn't have to tell the three women whom he meant by them.

"They must have been coming to see whether the *Ethelbert Nevin* was a good boat to steal," said Iduna.

"Sounded to me as if they already knew she was, an' they just wanted to make sure she was where they could get hold of 'er easy. O' course, that wasn't how I heard it then, you understand, or I'd o' made damn sure they didn't. But like I says, I thought they was just checkin' 'er out to see if they wanted to sign on for the cruise. I figured either they'd come or they wouldn't. If they did, they was welcome. If they didn't, 'twasn't no skin off my nose. I had you three signed up an' that would give me enough to get Wedge Munce off my back, which was all I cared about. So there I set an' here I am." Eustace sounded disgusted with himself as well he might.

"What did they say?" Helen prompted.

"Well, they kind o' nattered back an' forth about was this the right boat an' then they decided she had to be 'cause she was the only one big enough to hold 'em all with what they had to carry."

"Did they mention what that was?"

"Nope, but they did say they still had one piece to collect. I s'pose they was talkin' about them damn big suitcases they brung with 'em. I don't recollect if they happened to mention where they was fixin' to collect it from. They was talkin' soft an' my hearin' ain't what it used to be. But then one of 'em said, 'Are you sure we can trust 'er?' An' the cocky one, though I didn't know it was him then, you understand, said not to worry, it was all goin' along slick as a weasel. That ain't quite how he put it, but it's what I took 'im to mean. Then they all laughed, sort o' down in their throats like as if they was afraid somebody was goin' to hear 'em. I dunno why they should o' been, 'less they'd spied me in the cabin an' didn't let on, not that I'd give a damn. So anyway, one of 'em says somethin' about at least she looked as if she'd hold together till they got to Paraguay, an' somebody else says, 'We got to be there by Saturday, right?' Then they went away an' I figured it was time for me to do the same, so I went."

"Paraguay by Saturday?" Helen shook her head. "Eustace, didn't that strike you as a totally crazy thing for them to say?"

"Can't say as it did."

"But don't you know where Paraguay is?"

"Someplace along the coast or the islands, looks like."

"Eustace, Paraguay is in South America."

"Ayup, an' so's Peru. An' China's in Asier an' Moscow's in Russier, an' Poland's in Poland an' Paris is in France, but I can show you all those an' a damn sight more on a map o' Maine. Can't say's I could put my finger on Paraguay offhand, but I got no reason to s'pose we ain't got one kickin' around someplace. How's about lettin' me bank that fire, Cat, so's she'll last us the night? We might as well try to grab ourselves a wink o' sleep."

TWELVE

"We're in luck, Professor Shandy. It rained in the night."

"Ungh?" For a moment Peter couldn't recognize the voice, or remember why he was lying on a bed of boughs at the bottom of a rabbit hole. No wonder he'd been dreaming about little cakes labeled EAT ME. Then it all came back to him.

"Oh, Miss Binks. Good morning. What time is it?"

"A while before sunup is the best I can tell you. I've been outside reconnoitering. Observation seems to indicate we're in the clear. The rain must have thrown the bloodhounds into confusion. Do you know, I shouldn't be surprised if that mess you and Mr. Swope made trying to get through Muddy Bottom may have confused your pursuers into believing you were both sucked into the quagmire. You didn't miss it by much, you know."

"Er—no, I hadn't realized." Peter would have been as well pleased if she hadn't told him, though he supposed he ought to be relieved that he was still around to be told. "So you think those goons have called off the hunt?"

"Appearances would so indicate, but vigilance should still be our watchword, don't you think? We must remember it was overconfidence that lost the British the Battle of Trenton."

Peter supposed they must, though he himself didn't particularly want to. He ought to be up and doing with a heart for any fate instead of lollygagging here among the spruce tips.

The spirit was willing enough, but what about the tensors and flexors? He tested a few muscles, counted his limbs and found them all present as far as he could tell without offending Miss Binks's presumed maiden modesty, and slid out from under the blankets.

Getting dressed was no problem. He'd slept in his clothes on the premise that they must be ruined already, so what difference would a few more wrinkles make? A glance at his pant legs confirmed his assumption. A rub of his chin told him that his whiskers had been waxing while the rest of him waned. How in Sam Hill would he and Swope be able to hitch a ride back to Balaclava Junction looking like a pair of skid-row bums? Asking this elderly spinster whether she happened to have a razor on the premises seemed to him both futile and a trifle indelicate. He prowled along the tunnel to the so-called bathroom and did what he could, which wasn't much.

Cronkite Swope was still asleep. Miss Binks didn't appear to mind a body sprawled on her parlor floor, so Peter decided he didn't, either. He hauled a short log near the fire to serve him for a stool and accepted the cup Miss Binks handed him. It was a mug this time, of thick white ironstone with a blue line around its cracked and discolored rim. The stuff inside looked like black coffee and smelled the way one might presumably expect rabbit-hole coffee to smell. Anyway, it was hot and wet. He took a sip and was pleasantly surprised.

"Ground dandelion roots," Miss Binks explained. "I wash them carefully, roast them by the fire till they're well browned all through, then pulverize them with my mortar and pestle." She nodded toward a foot-square slab of shale in which a dishlike depression had been worn. In the hollow lay a smooth granite pebble about the size and shape of a jumbo egg. "I find the flavor more delicate than that of chicory root, though I sometimes blend the two for a more robust brew."

Like any well-bred hostess, she picked up her own cup and settled herself facing him on another lump of firewood. "Now, Professor Shandy, I've been giving a good deal of thought to your next move. You won't want to go back to Woeful Ridge and try to salvage your car, I shouldn't think."

"Perish the thought," he assured her. "I doubt whether there's anything left to salvage anyway. The demolition crew had already made impressive headway when Swope and I took our departure. Unless they're incredibly stupid or cocky, they'll have dragged the remains away and ditched them somewhere by now. Burned it, perhaps, or dumped it in a quarry hole. This happens to be the *Balaclava County Fane and Pennon*'s staff car, you see. The name was painted on both front doors and across the trunk."

"Hardly a thing to leave sitting around," Miss Binks agreed. "The survivalists would hardly want to call attention to the possibility that it was they who'd effected your demise. Which they haven't, needless to say, but I do so hope they're convinced they have. I noticed a few bits and pieces of Mr. Swope's jacket and trousers caught on some briars beside the sinkhole, which may reinforce their conjectures. If Mr. Swope is a reporter, by the way, I sincerely hope you can dissuade him from printing anything about me."

"No fear," Peter assured her. "Swope's not one to bite the hand that feeds him. Er—that wasn't meant as a hint. We were planning to pick some chickweed for breakfast along the way," he lied bravely.

"Oh, come now, Professor! You can't be that tired of my cuisine already. I can't offer you bacon and eggs, but you might enjoy my amaranth pancakes with birch and maple syrup."

"They sound delicious," he lied gallantly, "but please don't put yourself to any bother for us."

"You're no bother, I assure. It's fun having someone to cook for again. Perhaps I've been lonely after all, though I hadn't meant to be."

"Have you ever thought of keeping a pet?"

"Not seriously. I suppose I might adopt a stray dog or cat if one happened along, but so far they haven't. I've nursed a few injured or abandoned forest creatures but always returned them to their natural habitat as quickly as possible. Having renounced domestication myself, I have no desire to foist it on my fellow wildlings."

Even as she made her declaration of emancipation, Miss Binks was bustling around her kitchen, the picture of domesticity, Mrs. Bunnykins style. If she'd left the hair on her deerskin garb, Peter thought, she could easily have passed for a burrowing mammal herself. Since he couldn't think of a way to be useful, he stayed on his log watching her measure out strange ingredients and stir them up, then slap spoonfuls of thin dough on a flat rock she'd been heating in the fire.

"Haven't a griddle and don't need one. These will be done in a couple of minutes. Shall we wake Mr. Swope? I don't want to seem inhospitable, Professor, but I'd suggest you two get on the road fairly soon."

"M'yes," said Peter. "It's a long walk back to Balaclava Junction."

"Around twenty-five miles, I should say," Miss Binks replied briskly. "Out of the question, of course. What I've been thinking is that you'd better go straight on to Whittington and either telephone a friend to pick you up or else rent a taxi. Which would cost the earth, no doubt. Not to be nosy, but do you have any money with you?"

Peter stuck his hand in his pocket, was relieved to find his wallet still there, and pulled it out. "About a hundred dollars. I expect Swope has a little money on him, too."

"An embarrassment of riches, I should say. You won't have any problem, then. Once we get you safely to Whittington, that is—which may take some doing. Mr. Swope, breakfast is ready."

"Huh? Oh. Sure."

With the resilience of youth, Cronkite bounded out of the blankets, dashed to the washroom, and was back by the time Miss Binks had flipped her first pancake. The cakes tasted rather strange but Peter and Cronkite ate them willingly enough with rather more than their fair share of Miss Binks's birch and maple syrup.

"Now," said Miss Binks when the plates were empty and she'd declined any help with the dishes, "how are we going to get you out of here?"

"I guess we'll just have to get up and go," was the best Cronkite had to offer, and in truth Peter could have done no better.

Miss Binks, however, soon demonstrated that her question had been purely rhetorical. "First, we'll need to do something about your clothes."

Peter wasn't too badly off in the dark gray corduroys and plaid flannel shirt that were his habitual off-duty garb. Although dirty, wrinkled, and torn in a few places, they were what any non-self-respecting knight of the road might be wearing. Cronkite's formerly pale blue summer-weight slacks and red and cream checked jacket were another, sadder story. Their hostess shook her head.

"There's simply no way you can show yourself on a public thoroughfare looking like that, Mr. Swope."

"But I'll have to, Miss Binks. It's either this or my birthday suit."

"Oh, I think we can do a little better than that. Let's see what my wardrobe has to offer."

Miss Binks darted into a tunnel the men hadn't yet got to explore and returned with an armload of plastic cleaners' bags. "I did bring some clothes with me when I moved into the lair. I soon realized they were hopelessly impractical for the kind of life I found myself leading, but I kept them anyway. One never knows when something will come in handy. Let's see, Mr. Swope. You're wearing what I'd call sneakers, though I expect you have a fancier name nowadays. Here's a baggy old sweatshirt that looks as if it might fit you. Why don't you put this on? We'll cut off your pant legs as high as decency permits and you can pass for a jogger."

"Hey, right on! Maybe I ought to shave first, if you don't mind."

"You have a razor, Swope?" cried Peter.

"Sure, I always carry one in my pocket. It says in the Great Journalists' Correspondence Course that there's nothing more off-putting to an interviewee than a reporter with a day's growth of whiskers on his face. And you can't always be running home to shave when there's a hot story breaking. You want to borrow mine when I'm through, Professor?"

"Please. I resemble a hobo enough without the stubble."

"The problem is not that you resemble a hobo, Professor," Miss Binks corrected, "but that you resemble the man those hoodlums found exploring their arms cache yesterday afternoon. What we really need to do is change your appearance entirely. This ought to do the trick, don't you think?"

She held up a full skirt of bright green cotton patterned in red and pink strawberries, and a plain green long-sleeved shirt that went with it. "These were my aunt's. Aunt bought them new shortly before she died, and I couldn't bear to give them away with her other things. She'd have wanted me to get some good out of them, and now seems to be the time. Aunt was quite a bit larger than I, and the skirt's elasticized in the waist. You should be able to get into them all right."

"But drat it," Peter sputtered, "I can't go parading down the road in a woman's clothes with a man's legs and a man's face."

"Nobody's going to see your face. We'll tie a scarf over your head and pull it well down in front. You wouldn't happen to have a pair of sunglasses with you?"

He searched his pockets again. "Er—my driving glasses. Yes, I have them."

"And your binoculars, too. Good man. You can carry my bird-watching book. As for your shoes, they're sensible enough and that's what counts. People expect bird-watchers to look a bit eccentric. You might shave your legs while you're about it. We can stain them tan with walnut juice."

She picked up a pair of scissors, good steel ones she surely had never retrieved from her grandfather's cellar hole, and went to work on Cronkite's pant legs. Peter resigned himself to being Miss Binks's aunt, picked up the green and pink garments, and went to prepare for his debut as a transvestite. When he got back to the lair, he was confronted by a new Miss Binks, smartly togged out in gray flannel slacks, a turquoise blue polo shirt, and fairly clean white sneakers.

She greeted him with the amusement he'd anticipated.

"Why, Professor Shandy, you're a picture no artist could paint! Stand still and let me tie this scarf so it won't slide off. Actually, I don't think we need bother about your legs. Those socks you have on will do well enough, since the skirt is so long. Aunt always believed in getting full value for her money so she bought everything a size too large, luckily for us. Mr. Swope, quit cowering in that tunnel and get your shorts and sweatshirt on. We really do have to be starting. It will be sunup soon, and the early morning cloud cover will be disappearing. Not that it's going to help us a great deal, I don't suppose, but we need every scrap of advantage we can scrape together. Just till we get clear of the lair, you know. We'll be in a less vulnerable position once we're on the bikes."

"Bikes?" cried Peter. "Miss Binks, you don't mean you have bicycles here?"

"You weren't supposing I'd expect you two footsore waifs of the storm to walk all the way to Whittington, were you? Or that I'd have been foolhardy enough to maroon myself out here with no means of transportation whatsoever? I thought Mr. Swope might sprint ahead on the two-wheeler, Professor, while you and I follow at a ladylike speed on the tandem. I must say I'm looking forward to getting dear old Daisy Belle out again. I haven't had anyone to ride with since Aunt died. I did try to sell Daisy with the rest of the household effects, but nobody made me an offer, so I brought her along. As I said before, one never knows, does one? The thing of it is, your chaps, if they're out patrolling the road, will be looking for two men on foot. One young cyclist by himself and two elderly ladies on a tandem ought to throw them off the scent, shouldn't you think?"

"I'm beyond thinking, Miss Binks. I can only hope. But how will you get your bicycles home?"

"I'll ride the two-wheeler, leaving Daisy Belle in some appropriate place of concealment. Perhaps you or Mr. Swope can help me retrieve her at a more convenient time."

"Sure," said Cronkite, "but what if somebody steals the old girl before we have the chance to get back to her?"

"Then we'll be spared the bother," Miss Binks replied briskly. "Are you quite ready, Mr. Swope?"

"I guess so. This sweatshirt's a bit on the tight side."

"Make believe it shrank in the wash. Shove the sleeves up so they won't look too skimpy. Here, wear my cycling helmet. It will abet the dissimulation. Come along, gentlemen. The south tunnel, I think."

This one didn't have to be crawled through, Peter was relieved to learn. How he'd have managed that in the late Aunt Binks's strawberry skirt was a riddle he was better pleased not to solve. They simply walked along, stooping more or less, depending on their respective heights, until they came to an apparently insuperable barrier. Miss Binks flicked it aside with one hand.

"Camouflage," she whispered. "I keep the end walled off to remind me not to step too far and fall in. This is an old well. Very convenient to draw water from in the winter but awkward to get out of without the drawbridge. Be careful going across, the bridge doesn't quite cover the hole."

The drawbridge was merely a short section of plank. It stretched across what looked to Peter like a yawning abyss and rested, securely he hoped, on the bottom one of a few iron cleats that had been driven into the stone side of the well. Miss Binks capered nimbly across, swarmed up the cleats, and nudged away a partly rotted wooden cover over which brush had been piled. Cautious as a fox, she poked her head up, looked, sniffed, and listened.

Once sure the coast was clear, she beckoned the men to follow. Cronkite climbed like a kitten on a curtain. Peter hitched up his skirts and did his best. The two men helped to replace the well cover and rearrange the brush, then followed their leader by a circuitous route to a somewhat boskier dingle than they'd encountered hitherto. Here, Miss Binks lifted a large clump of growing ferns to reveal a board-lined cache in which lay an assortment of wheels and handlebars.

Without wasting a word, this latter-day counterpart of Rima the Bird Girl picked out a wrench and a screwdriver from the cache and began fitting the pieces together. In two minutes by Peter's count, both machines were ready to roll. Miss Binks perched Audubon's *Field Guide to the Birds* conspicuously in the wire basket that hung from the tandem's front handlebars and nodded to Peter.

"Professor, you and I will wheel Daisy Belle out to where the ground becomes flat enough to ride on. Mr. Swope, take charge of the two-wheeler."

By now, both men would have followed her anywhere. They passed the vast cellar hole, still half-filled with charred wood and debris, struck an overgrown but passable drive, mounted their bikes, and after a few preliminary wiggles, were off.

Peter had never ridden a tandem before but he caught on fast enough. Miss Binks assigned him the rear seat, so all he had to do was stay on and keep pedaling. At first Cronkite lagged behind them. Once they were out on paved road and he knew which way to go, he swooped ahead, though not so far ahead as he'd have been able to go on a newer, faster bicycle. That was according to plan, they didn't want to lose each other.

The day was hardly begun. Not many cars were on the road. The first one that passed them honked its horn, and Peter's heart stopped. Miss Binks waved gaily and it went on.

"Amusing how drivers always honk at tandems, don't you think?" she called back over her shoulder.

Evidently she and her aunt had run into this sort of thing often enough before. Peter quit holding his breath; he was even beginning to enjoy the ride. Maybe he and Helen ought to buy Daisy Belle from Miss Binks, at a vastly inflated price. This amiable troglodyte seemed to have no use for money right now, but there might come a time when she'd be glad to have some cash on hand.

In any event, he'd have to make some kind of return for her incredible hospitality. But what could one give a woman so totally self-sufficient? Imported wines? Exotic teas? She'd probably turn them down, like Calvin Coolidge in his boarding-house days spurning fresh strawberries because he was afraid they'd spoil his taste for prunes.

Helen would think of something. He wouldn't talk about Miss Binks to anybody else; her fear of anthropologists was probably well grounded. But it was inconceivable that he wouldn't tell Helen. Damn shame Helen wasn't home now; she could have come after him and Swope in their car, and there'd have been no chance of a leak.

Hiring a car or a taxi would be too risky. Peter didn't want to get himself and Swope talked about, either—not until they'd managed to put that pack of wolves at Woeful Ridge safe in the zoo. They'd have to call somebody they knew.

Cronkite Swope's relatives were preoccupied with their own woes, and apparently all his neighbors had gone sour on the Swopes. His connections at the *Fane and Pennon* were no good; they couldn't be trusted to keep Miss Binks out of the paper. Peter ran through his own list of possibles.

The hell of it was, so many of his close friends had gone away on holiday jaunts as soon as classes ended. Dan Stott was off to his pig conference. President Svenson had taken his wife and their two youngest daughters to Sweden. Jim Feldster would come like a shot, but his wife would have the whole story and then some spread all over Balaclava County in no time flat. The Jackmans had left with their four youngsters on a camping trip nicely timed to coincide with the blackfly season. The Porbles and Goulsons were celebrating their respective daughter's and son's engagement with a joint sightseeing tour to the Library of Congress and Arlington National Cemetery. Peter's best friend, Timothy Ames, was in California dandling his newest grandchild on his knee. Tim's daughter-in-law had gone with him. But Tim's son Royall was at home, and Roy was a good scout. He'd call Roy Ames. Now if they could only find a telephone.

THIRTEEN

Maybe they'd needed their disguises, maybe they hadn't. At any rate, nobody tried to riddle the three cyclists with bullets, run them off the road, or even stop to pass the time of day. Peter and Miss Binks rendezvoused with Cronkite at a patch of conservation land just outside Whittington and managed to find a big fallen pine with a capacious hollow under the roots where Daisy Belle would have a fair chance of lying undiscovered until they could get back to reclaim her. They even spotted a Blackburnian warbler and made good use of the bird book and Peter's binoculars.

But it was high time to part. Dawn was by now fairly broken. Peter rolled down his trouser legs and gave Miss Binks back her aunt's skirt. He kept the spacious green blouse, which looked enough like a man's sport shirt to get by with and was long enough to conceal the indecent ravages to his nether garment. He insisted on knowing what she'd like by way of recompense, and she at last admitted to a hankering for some light summer reading, such as *The Brothers Karamazov* or the works of Henry James. Then she rode off on the two wheeler, still blushing from the hug and kiss Cronkite had given her in parting.

She'd told them there used to be a supermarket up the road not far from where they stopped. Cronkite jogged on ahead, Peter followed at a gentlemanly stroll. The store was still there, with a couple of pay phones beside the front door.

Peter told Swope why he'd decided Royall Ames was their best hope, and the young reporter readily agreed.

"Sure, Professor, go ahead. I can't think of anybody back home who's speaking to me anyway except my mother and my boss, and I wouldn't trust either one of them not to rat on Miss Binks."

So Peter called. Roy was awake and delighted to oblige. He said he'd be there in half an hour. Knowing Roy, Peter thought he most likely would. So there was nothing to do now except hang around. The store wouldn't be open till eight o'clock but they could see an all-night diner, relic of a vanishing breed, up the road a little way. Miss Binks's amaranth pancakes had been filling enough, but they did leave a peculiar taste in the mouth; a cup of coffee mightn't go amiss.

They walked up and had one. Cronkite decided maybe he'd stay and eat a jelly doughnut or two, so Peter walked back in case Roy came along, although the younger Ames couldn't reasonably be expected to arrive for another twenty minutes at the least. A man might beguile the time by telephoning his wife. He'd brought Catriona McBogle's number with him just in case. He hauled out a handful of change and dialed.

Nobody answered. He got his money back and tried again. Still no answer. He reached Maine information and checked the number in case he'd copied it down wrong. He hadn't.

There was a perfectly simple, rational explanation, he told himself. The women had gone for an early-morning bird walk. Or maybe they were over at the forestry school having a sunrise breakfast with Guthrie Fingal. He got hold of information again and asked for the school's number. Somebody answered this time, perhaps a dryad. Mr. Fingal was around someplace. Did Professor Shandy want to hold? Peter held.

Four quarters and a dime later, Guthrie Fingal came on the line. "Pete! Sorry to keep you waiting. It's kind of busy around here just now. We had a fire in our big barn yesterday morning and—"

"Oh, Christ, not you, too! Did they get your weather vane?"

"Huh? Wait a minute!"

The wait was a good deal longer than a minute. Peter stuffed more coins into the box and kept on holding.

"Pete? You still there? We can't find the weather vane."

"That doesn't surprise me in the least. Is Helen with you, by any chance?"

"No." The no sounded awfully curt. "She and Cat came over day before yesterday and took some pictures, but then they—"

"They what?"

"Pete, I don't know what to tell you. She and Cat and that other woman who came with them—I didn't meet her—" Guthrie was having a hard time. "They went whale watching in the *Ethelbert Nevin* yesterday morning."

"So? What about it?"

"Well, it's just that I tried to get hold of Cat last night and her hired man was there. He said the *Ethelbert Nevin* hadn't come in on the tide, so he thought he'd better drop over and feed the cats. I tried again this morning but— Now don't get all hot and bothered, Pete. Most likely what happened was that they got caught in the fog and Eustace—the guy who runs the trips—decided to lay up somewhere overnight. Wedgwood Munce, the harbor master, is going out to look for them as soon as the fog lifts."

"The hell he is! What's the bastard waiting for? I'll be up."

Peter slammed down the receiver. Where in tunket was Swope? Where was Roy Ames? Where, for God's sake, was Helen?

The only thing that saved his sanity was Royall Ames's insouciance about speed limits. Peter had barely finished loading off some of this anxiety on Swope, who stood there trying to look sympathetic while licking raspberry jelly from the corners of his mouth, when Roy's red compact car whizzed into the parking lot. They climbed aboard, fastened their seat belts, and told their tale. As agreed, they said not a word about Miss Binks. There was plenty to tell without her.

"Holy cow!" was Roy's reaction. "You sound like one of Dad's old John Buchan thrillers. First the weather vane robberies and the soap works fire and now a bunch of trigger-happy terrorists practically in our back yards. How the heck did they think they could get away with an operation like that?"

"From the look of things, they've already been getting away with it for two years or better," said Peter. "They're so well entrenched by now, that it would take a couple of regiments to roust them out. Unless the matter can be dealt with in a more—er—diplomatic manner. Or unless they decide to clear out and resettle now that they've been rumbled, which would be the smart thing to do. This will have to be reported, but I'm damned if I know whom to tell. What town is Woeful Ridge in, Swope?"

"Gosh, I don't know, Professor. I think it's still part of Lumpkinton. But I can't see that slob Olson handling a big case like this. Maybe the county district attorney?"

"Your guess is as good as mine, Swope. Whoever it is, you'll have to cope. I'm not sitting around here snarled up in a lot of red tape."

"But do we have to tell on them right away?" Cronkite protested. "Think what a scoop it would be for the *Fane and Pennon* if I—"

"Went back there alone and got your head blown off? Forget it, Swope. And you too, Roy, in case you were also entertaining any notion about playing commando. You have a wife to consider."

"Yeah, Laurie would kill me if I went and got myself shot. Say, Peter, you don't suppose there's a connection between the survivalists and the weather vane robberies?"

"I can't imagine why there should be, Roy," Peter answered wearily, "but that's not saying there isn't. I don't even want to think about that now. I just want to get to Maine and find Helen."

"More than likely you'll find her at her friend's house wondering where the heck you are."

"That's what I'm hoping, not that I want to cause her any

anxiety. But it may not be a wasted trip in any case. Guthrie Fingal just told me they've had a fire at the forestry school and the Praxiteles Lumpkin weather vane Helen went to photograph has turned up missing."

"Then there's your answer, Peter. Helen's not out in that boat at all, she's off tracking down Fingal's weather vane."

"If you think that makes me feel any better, young man, you're sadly mistaken. Can't you make this sardine can go any faster?"

An indecently short time later, Peter was in his own house, taking a fast shower, putting on trousers fit to be seen in, apologizing to Jane Austen for his past and future desertions, explaining to the Enderbles why he'd have to continue imposing on their good nature.

Fortunately the elderly couple's beneficence was without bounds. They wished him well, urged him to let them know as soon as he found Helen safe and sound as he surely would, and promised to keep Jane's spirits jacked up as high as possible under the circumstances.

Then he was in his own car, gassed up and rolling northward. He turned the radio on to keep himself from agonizing too much about where the center of his personal universe might have shifted to. Even Bach didn't help much, but the sound served to remind him that he wasn't alone on the road and he'd better keep a reasonable degree of attention on his driving.

He'd turn his mind to other matters, Peter determined. But he was on beautiful Route 495, not the villainous 128, and there wasn't the constant stream of hairbreadth escapes from sudden doom to keep him alert. He'd think about Miss Binks and her cryophilic grandfather. Helen had a penchant for the bizarre, she'd get a kick out of them.

It was no use. He might as well give up trying to kid himself into sanity and just think about Helen. Helen dignified and businesslike at the library, Helen in the kitchen making marmalade, Helen by the fireplace with Jane on her lap, Helen self-confident and learned in her doctoral gown lecturing to an enthralled audience, Helen enchanting in rose-colored silk at the faculty ball, Helen in bed wearing nothing at all. Was there no end to this wearisome road?

At the circle in Portsmouth he stopped for a hamburger and a cup of coffee, not because he wanted them but because he knew he ought to. The amaranth pancakes and dandelion brew had tasted better. He got back in the car and drove on. And on.

Once over the Piscataqua bridge and into Maine, he made great time. He did run into fog on the turnpike, but it wasn't thick enough to slow him down. It was barely noon when a narrow strip of wood nailed to a tree by the side of the road told him he'd reached Sasquamahoc. Guthrie Fingal's directions were a cinch to follow; there were so few roads to get lost on.

The first thing he spotted when he'd turned at the forestry school was the burned-out barn. A tall man in a plaid flannel shirt like the one Peter had left at Miss Binks's stood beside it, looking up at what remained of the roof. There was no mistaking that rawboned shape, that jutting chin. The red hair was faded to brown mixed with gray now, but otherwise Peter couldn't see that his former roommate had changed much. The creases around the mouth might be deeper, but the surprised grin was the same.

"Pete, you old warthog! Didn't lose much time, did you?"

Peter got out of the car, not realizing he staggered. Fingal had started walking toward the car; he broke into a lope. "Pete, take it easy! Are you all right?"

"Certainly I'm all right." Peter couldn't understand why Guthrie was looking at him like that. "Just a little stiff from driving. Is there any word on Helen?"

"I called the Coast Guard again about ten minutes ago. They've had a helicopter out looking, but visibility's been zilch out over the water on account of the fog. They say it's beginning to lift, though, so we ought to be getting some action. Want to take a run down to the cove and see if Wedgwood Munce has left yet?"

Peter started to get back into the car, but Fingal stopped him. "Why don't we take my Jeep? The road's not all that great. Want anything before we start?"

Peter shook his head. "I stopped along the road, thanks. It's good to see you, Guth. I guess I am a little whacked out, at that. I didn't sleep too well last night."

"You weren't worrying about your wife?"

"I didn't know there was anything to worry about. Actually I was worrying about myself and the young chap who was with me."

Peter had been meaning to tell his friend as much of the story as he could. Somewhere on the way up, around Billerica he thought it was, he'd remembered why he and Swope had gone to Woeful Ridge in the first place.

"This may not make much sense, Guthrie, but you'd better listen. There's a fairly good chance you may be involved in what's going on. I'm not sure when it started. How Helen and I got into it was through her getting a request from our county historical society for information about Praxiteles Lumpkin's weather vanes."

As they hurtled over the frost heaves and through the potholes, Peter explained about the fire at the soap factory and what it had led to.

"So you see, the burning of your barn follows the standard pattern."

"But that doesn't necessarily mean the same gang's responsible, if it is a gang," Guthrie argued. "Maybe somebody else twigged on to what must be a damned lucrative racket. Cripes, we had a case not far from here a few years back where some guys pinched the weather vane off the fire station—it was supposed to be worth $35,000. They didn't dare try to sell the thing because too many people would have known where it came from, so they held it for ransom. The town paid a thousand dollars to get it back. One guy was caught but he jumped bail. He was still on the loose last I knew. Maybe he got to hear about Praxiteles Lumpkin."

"M'well, that's possible, but Lumpkin's name isn't exactly a household word. Until Helen tackled the project, nothing at all had ever been published about Praxiteles as far as she could discover, not even his obituary. If some member of the Lumpkin family hadn't happened to take a few

snapshots and jot down a list of people who still owned
Praxiteles's weather vanes back around the turn of the
century, Helen wouldn't have had a blasted thing to go on.
The information just happened to turn up in an old file at the
Clavaton Library that nobody had looked into since Rin Tin
Tin was a pup."

"So you believe it was your wife's research that set off the
fireworks?"

"I'm not claiming anything of the sort. I suppose, however, that I have to grant the possibility. Helen hasn't tried to
hide what she's doing. There wouldn't have been any point in
that, since all the members of the society and no doubt a good
many other people knew our college library was being asked
to help get some data together. Helen was the logical staff
member to tackle the project. She's curator of a special
collection which has already given her plenty of experience in
historical research at the local level."

"Has she been getting her name in the papers?"

"Not about the Lumpkin project. Helen's kept her activities as low-key as possible. She intends to publish as soon as
she's got her material organized and doesn't want to scatter
the roses before they bloom, as it were. What I'm wondering
is whether we ought to be looking at this situation the other
way around."

"What do you mean, Pete?"

"Well, it strikes me as being pretty damned fortuitous that
this long-lost information happened to come to light just as
Praxiteles Lumpkin's weather vanes began disappearing.
Lately it seems they've been waiting till Helen takes her
photographs before they pull the snatch. That's what happened at the soap works and now at your school. I'm inclined
to suspect that whoever's behind the robberies figures some
public recognition from an eminently reputable source will
create a more lucrative market for his loot. It looks to me as
if Helen's been targeted for a patsy, and I'm damned well
going to put a stop to it."

But first he had to find her. Peter's state of mind wasn't

improved any when they swung by the cove where the *Ethelbert Nevin* ought to be tied up and wasn't.

"Eustace couldn't get in here now anyway," Guthrie explained quite unnecessarily, since the tide was flat out. "We'll go up to the head of the cove. It's deep water there all the time."

The *Ethelbert Nevin* wasn't at the head either, though Wedgwood Munce was—standing next to a fast-looking power boat that was tied up at the dock, squinting out to where the horizon would be visible in a while. Already a few darkish lumps that might be islands were beginning to show themselves through the thinning grayness. Damn the man, Peter thought, what's he waiting for? Yet he was relieved to have caught Munce in time. Guthrie stopped the Jeep and they ran to the dock.

"What do you say, Wedge?" shouted Guthrie. "Going out? This is my friend, Peter Shandy. He just drove up from Boston."

Peter hadn't, but he recognized the fact that, north of the Piscataqua, *up* and *down* acquired strange new meanings and *Boston* might be used as a portmanteau word for anywhere in Massachusetts. Some Mainers and a lot of New Brunswickers thought Massachusetts was actually in Boston. So did a lot of United States school children, like as not, if they thought about it at all, which was a doubtful premise. But the hell with that. He was in no mood for geography lessons. All he said was, "My wife's on the boat."

"Ayup," said Munce. "So's my fifty dollars Eustace Tilkey owes me. You comin'?"

Peter was first on board, Guthrie right on his heels. The harbor master's boat was a snappy twenty-two-footer with a lapstrake hull in highly varnished wood finish. Peter didn't give a damn what she was. She was afloat, and she could move. Once they got away from the dock, Munce made up for lost time. Guthrie stayed in the stern talking to him about what course Eustace might have taken. Peter went as far forward as he could get and stood straining his eyes into the mist ahead until the harbor master barked at him to sit down. He sat, but continued to strain.

Suddenly Munce exclaimed, "Wind's beginnin' to freshen."

"Thank God!" said Peter.

They most likely couldn't hear him back there, and what difference did it make? He wasn't talking to them. He was watching the fog getting blown to rags. After a long, long time he spied something, dead ahead.

"A light!"

"I don't see nothin'," Munce yelled back.

"Right ahead of us. Look!"

"By gorry, Pete, it is," yelled Guthrie. "Looks to me like a signal fire."

Munce gunned his motor for all she was worth. Peter cursed himself for having forgotten his field glasses and kept his eyes glued on that flickering speck. The speck grew to a dot. The wind was blowing their way and they caught a whiff of wood smoke.

Guthrie was in the bow now, too. "Can't be the boat burning. We'd smell gasoline. Must be driftwood."

He was speaking very quietly. Guthrie always did turn calm in a tight spot, Peter remembered. Oh, God, let it be Helen!

They'd passed a few obviously barren islets and a whale none of them even bothered to look at twice. Now they were approaching another dot of rock that wouldn't have been worth looking at, either, except for the fire that was burning on its highest point and the four little figures they could see capering like maniacs. Two were heaping more wood on the fire. One, by far the biggest, was waving something huge and white, like a bedsheet with sleeves. And another, the tiniest one, in a bright pink something or other, had its hands up to its mouth like a megaphone. Over the water along with the smoke from the fire and even above the noise of the motor, a sound came loud and clear: "Peter! Peter! Peter!"

FOURTEEN

"I knew it was you."

Helen took a firmer grip on the livid green shirt Peter had forgotten to change out of. "I knew it couldn't be, but I knew it was. How did you get here?"

Peter rubbed his mouth against her smoke-smelling, salt-tasting hair. "I ran, of course. Never mind me, what happened to you?"

No doubt there'd already been explanations, but he hadn't been listening. First things first. He did recall having agreed to remain on the island with Guthrie and the three women. There was no way the harbor master's open boat could have accommodated all seven in safety on the longish run back to Hocasquam. After Wedgwood Munce had collected his fifty dollars from Eustace Tilkey, the pair of them had gone off to meet a Coast Guard boat that was in the vicinity somewhere and lead it back to pick up the others.

Catriona was sharing a rock by the fire with Guthrie. He had his arm around her, no doubt in a spirit of neighborly camaraderie. Iduna was handing around a few jam tarts that the castaways had been saving for emergency rations in case they'd got stuck on the island for another night.

"We never did get to roast any mussels," she said somewhat regretfully. "Here, Peter, try a tart. No sense lugging them back to Cat's."

And Heaven forbid they should waste good food. Peter

accepted the pastry and fed most of it to Helen. Breakfast had been on the lean side, she'd confessed, and they'd lunched on five grapes apiece. They'd whiled away the morning searching the island for more firewood and for mussels or anything else that might be edible, but hadn't had much luck.

"We did find plenty of bladderwort," she told him, "but nobody quite knew what to do with it. Seaweed's awfully rubbery stuff to chew raw."

"Too bad there's no amaranth out here. Did you get any sleep?"

"Not a great deal. We were all four scrunched together under Iduna's raincoat, trying to keep warm. We'd given up on dry, of course. Eustace was not the ideal person to huddle with, I have to say. His clothes were so stiff with engine grease and fish oil that he smelled like a tugboat towing a garbage scow. I suppose I shouldn't criticize. The grease probably saved him from dying of hypothermia by repelling moisture and conserving some body warmth while he was riding around on the whale."

"Perhaps you might elucidate," Peter suggested. "Why was Eustace riding a whale? Did it ram the boat and sink you?"

"No, the *Ethelbert Nevin*'s all right—or was, the last we saw of it. Her, I mean. The pirates went off in her after they dumped us overboard. Cat and me, that is. Iduna jumped by herself. With the picnic hamper, bless her."

Helen filled in the gruesome tale while Peter could feel his hair, what was left of it, doing its best to stand on end. "So that's how we got here," she wound up. "Guthrie, could you tell us where Paraguay, Maine, is?"

He shook his head. "Don't ask me, Helen. I never heard of the place, and I've lived in Maine all my life, pretty much. You sure those guys said Paraguay, Mrs. Stott?"

Iduna shook her head. "No, I can't be sure and please call me Iduna. I couldn't actually overhear what they said, you know. I had to lip-read because the engine was so noisy. But it certainly looked like Paraguay to me. I assumed he meant the one in South America. Eustace was more inclined to think the men were talking about somewhere handy-by because

Maine has so many geographical place names, which makes a lot more sense. If they'd really been planning to go all that distance, it does seem they'd have had sense enough to steal themselves a more suitable boat. Wouldn't you think so, Peter?"

"Don't ask me, Iduna. I've never laid eyes on the *Ethelbert Nevin*. She's not a rum-runner by chance, is she, Guthrie? One of those James Bond contraptions with a couple of extra jet engines hidden under the lobster pots?"

Blushing slightly, Guthrie Fingal took his arm away from Catriona's shoulders and leaned forward to put another stick on the fire, which they didn't really need now that the sun was out and they'd already been located.

"Heck no, Pete. She's just an ordinary lobster boat like the rest of 'em. Bigger than some, which must be why the pirates picked her, but none too well maintained, which they probably wouldn't have realized. Eustace is no great shakes at doing any more work than he has to."

"She wasn't running all that smoothly yesterday," Catriona corroborated. "I doubt very much that those goons were able to get enough speed out of her to outrun that whale, though I didn't like to say so in front of Eustace."

"What whale, for God's sake?" Peter was feeling at sea himself by now.

"The whale they were shooting at to get it furious so it would charge and drown us. Or swallow us, as the case might have been. But it went after them instead, and I hope to heck it caught up with them. Not wishing my fellow man any hard luck, you understand, and I sure hope Eustace had plenty of insurance, but I'm having a rough time working up any charitable thoughts toward those who despitefully used us. I'm not quite rotter enough to wish them all drowned. However, I can't help thinking it would be a suitable climax to our adventure if that whale scared the pants off each and every one of those rotters, notably that smarmy bastard with the map."

"Who was he? Did you get any of their names?"

"I didn't," said Catriona. "Iduna, did you? Helen?"

Neither of her friends could help.

"Then what did they look like?" Peter entreated. "Can't you at least describe them?"

"Certainly I can. I can describe four of them all at once. They were either quadruplets or clones."

"Not quite," Helen contradicted. "One was shorter than the rest and one had a nick in his right nostril, as if his knife might have slipped while he was eating peas with it. I noticed while they were in the process of throwing us overboard. He was the one swinging you by the feet."

"Sons of bitches! By thunder, if that whale didn't drown them, they're going to wish it had." Oddly enough, it was Guthrie Fingal who roared the imprecation. He seemed rather embarrassed that he'd done so, and became brusquely matter-of-fact. "So all right, Cat, get on with it. What did they look like?"

"Black bears. You know. Short bandy legs, barrel bodies, bushy black hair, fuzzy black beards. Probably in their twenties, though the beards made them seem older. They all had big boots on and wore oddments of army fatigues and camouflage suits. Scruffy bunch, by and large. The fifth one—or perhaps I should say the first since he seemed to be in charge—was altogether different. He had brown hair cut close to his head, was clean shaven, had yellowish brown eyes and fairish skin. He was dressed like the others, only his pants and jacket matched, were clean, and looked as if they'd been pressed not long ago. He held himself very straight, like the little tin soldier. And when he came down to the boat he didn't run like the others. He marched."

"By George!" said Peter. "Did you see him throw anything?"

Catriona stared at him. "What an astonishing question. No, I didn't."

"I did," said Helen. "The bar he hit Eustace with. He chucked it overboard. Why, Peter?"

"Information received. Exactly how did he throw it, Helen? Can you demonstrate? Here, use this stick of driftwood."

"Darling, what an odd think to ask. Come to think of it, though, it was an odd way to throw. He'd struck Eustace with his left hand, I remember. When he threw the bar away, it sailed clear across the boat and over the port side. I was afraid for a second it was going to hit Iduna."

Helen shut her eyes for a second to aid reflection, then opened them, stared straight ahead, and flipped the stick sideways. "Like that, more or less. He'd been standing directly behind Eustace when he hit him, and kept looking straight at him as he fell."

"Bravo, my love. You may be gratified to learn that you've just proved Huntley Swope wasn't hallucinating. When we catch up with that murdering devil, I expect we'll find he's the man who chucked the grenade or whatever it was into the tallow vat and incinerated Caspar Flum. He comes from Clavaton and his name is Roland Childe."

"Cor stone the crows!" gasped Catriona. "I write this stuff, but I never dreamed it could happen in real life. How did you deduce all that from a mere flip of a stick?"

"It's those little gray cells in his brain," Helen answered for her husband. "Peter's awfully clever. Aren't you, dear?"

"M'well, my love, I can hardly deny your generous allegation considering the acumen I demonstrated by marrying you. I wonder whether the Coast Guard's located the *Ethelbert Nevin* yet."

"I'm wondering why in heck they don't come and get us out of here." Iduna the unflappable showed signs of beginning to flap. "I don't know about you folks, but if I don't get a hot bath and a cup of tea pretty soon, I'm going to be in serious trouble."

"Me too," said Catriona. "My hair's driving me crazy." She combed her fingers through the long red mane from which the last hairpin had long ago disappeared. "Ugh! It feels as if I'd shampooed it in mucilage."

"It doesn't look too bad," said Guthrie. "I kind of like it loose like that."

Catriona McBogle would have scorned to let one of her emancipated heroines favor a hero or even a beloved with a shy and winsome smile, Helen thought; yet she herself had seldom observed a shyer or winsomer one. Oh dear, were these two nice people going to get themselves involved in something that could turn out a good deal stickier than Cat's sea-soaked hair?

She wished to goodness the Coast Guard boat would come. Now that Peter was with her and she didn't have to keep a stiff upper lip any longer, she was about ready to drop in her tracks. How glorious it would be to get back to Cat's lovely old house! How much more glorious to go home to the Crescent, where there weren't any whales or pirates. After all, she'd done what she came for. Maybe she could talk Iduna into leaving first thing in the morning, as soon as they'd all had a good night's sleep. Peter looked exhausted, poor darling.

"I hope I got some good shots of your weather vane, Guthrie," she said, mainly to get her mind off the Coast Guard boat.

"Darn good thing you did," he told her. "It's gone now. So's the barn, just about."

"Oh, Guthrie, no! Not another snatch-and-burn!"

"Yeah, Pete was telling me. Looks as if we're just one more name on the list."

"Oh my stars," exclaimed Iduna. "Then it's your lumberjack they're taking to Paraguay."

"What? Mind backing up and coming at me again?"

"Not at all," Iduna replied politely. "You see, that's why they stole Eustace's boat. They have to deliver the stolen weather vanes to some millionaire in Paraguay who's going to buy them. So that's why they came to Maine. It did seem awfully strange that they'd driven all the way to Hocasquam just to steal a beat-up old lobster boat."

"What they were actually doing was completing the set," moaned Helen. "They must have had the soap-works weather vane right there in that van parked next to us at the rest stop in Kittery. If only we'd known!"

"It's a damn good thing you didn't," said Peter. "What could you have done?"

"Reported them to the highway patrol, of course. You don't think we'd have been stupid enough to tackle them by ourselves? From what Iduna lip-read, it appears they've actually been trailing me around, letting me lead them to the

Lumpkin weather vanes so they'd know which ones to steal. I feel like Typhoid Mary."

"Nonsense!" Peter certainly wasn't about to tell her he'd been suspecting that all along. "Don't fret yourself, my love. Those bastards are going to feel a hell of a lot worse before we're through with them. Ah, I believe we're about to get dismarooned."

There she was, a trim forty-footer flying the United States flag and the Coast Guard ensign. Helen felt tears beginning to smart as the boat hove to at a safe distance from the rocks and lowered a rubber dinghy to take them aboard.

Eustace Tilkey and Wedgwood Munce were not in sight. The castaways were told that Tilkey and Munce had escorted the Coast Guard boat just far enough to make sure she was on the right course, then turned around and headed back to Hocasquam. Mr. Munce hadn't objected to doing his duty, but he'd seen no reason to burn extra gas.

"We're going to get you back to Hocasquam as fast as we can," Ensign Blaise, the officer in command, told them once they were safely on board, "but we've got a little complication. Our helicopter spotter's just radioed that he's spotted another set of castaways and the remains of a wrecked boat not too far from here. We'll have to run over there and find out what that's all about. In the meantime, I expect you'd like to wash up and get comfortable. Seaman Willett will show you below."

The three women gratefully followed Seaman Willett to where, God willing, they might find soap, towels, and hot water. Peter and Guthrie stayed on deck.

"Those other castaways," Peter began, "they're not by any chance five youngish men in army fatigues?"

"We hope so. Eustace Tilkey told us about the *Ethelbert Nevin* hijackers. We'd like you two and the ladies to keep out of the way when we go to pick them up. Mr. Tilkey claims they're a pretty rough bunch. He thinks there might be shooting. We don't know whether to believe him or not. He told a pretty strange yarn, and he did say he'd been hit on the head."

"You can believe him, Ensign. My wife and her friend

Miss McBogle had gone into the cabin for—er—personal reasons. My wife was just coming out when she saw the man who appears to be the leader of the group knock Tilkey down with some kind of club. One of his henchmen helped him throw Tilkey overboard while another took Tilkey's place at the wheel. The men then overpowered my wife and Miss McBogle and chucked them after Tilkey. Mrs. Stott jumped of her own accord."

"Mrs. Stott's the big blond lady?"

"M'yes. A wonderful woman. She even remembered to take the picnic hamper with her."

"No kidding! I wouldn't mind getting shipwrecked with her. Can we offer you anything, gentlemen? A cup of coffee to warm you up?"

"Mrs. Stott was talking wistfully of tea."

"We'll make sure she gets it. See anything yet, Higgins?"

"Not yet, sir." The lookout didn't turn his head.

"According to the helicopter pilot's bearings, we shouldn't be much longer. If this bunch are your pirates, they didn't get far. They probably tried to go too fast in the fog."

"My wife says they were trying to outrun an irritated whale. They'd fired at the creature, apparently to stir it up so it would go after their victims in the water and finish them off. Instead, the whale started chasing the boat."

"Whales are a darn sight smarter than some people, if you ask me."

After that, nobody said much until the lookout reported, "Coming up on the starboard bow, sir."

"Can you make out any details?"

"I can see the boat. Her bow's stove in. Looks as if they ran her on the rocks at high speed."

"Any people?"

"One man. I think it's a man. And four black bears in camouflage suits, looks like."

"Those are the guys," said Guthrie Fingal. "Cat told us they looked like bears. So now what do we do?"

"So now you go below," Ensign Blaise told him. "And you stay in the cabin until I send for you to come on deck. Not to be rude, gentlemen, but that's an order."

Peter was not loath to obey. He hadn't cared for the idea of being shot at in the darkening woods night before last, and he was reasonably sure he'd like it even less on an open deck in bright sunshine. Besides, he was getting hungry. That bite of jam tart hadn't been particularly sustaining. Guthrie followed Peter without demur. Perhaps he didn't care for being shot at, either; or perhaps the sea air was sharpening his appetite, too.

They found the three women lunching at a table in the main cabin, showered and shampooed and dressed in dry lendings. Garments would be too specific a term, Peter decided, though Catriona did look handsome and even chic in Ensign Blaise's dress uniform. She'd washed her hair and tied it back with what appeared to be somebody's spare shoelace; drying tendrils softened the somewhat too well defined lines of jaw and cheekbone.

Helen, on the other hand, reminded her husband of a chicken trying to struggle out of the egg. She was engulfed in a navy blue pullover that might have fitted better on Guthrie, and somebody's work pants with the legs rolled up into tire-sized lumps so they wouldn't drag on the floor.

When it came to outfitting Iduna, the crew had obviously not even tried. She'd fashioned herself a caftan out of two government-issue blankets and a great many safety pins. The two men at the table with her were too busy gazing at her with gleams in their eyes and no doubt lust in their hearts to keep their minds on their food.

Peter himself was inured to those wheat-colored curls, those innocent blue eyes, those blush-suffused cheeks, that sweet-cream complexion, that cupid's-bow mouth with the dimples at the corners, those voluptuous arms tapering into dainty hands and rose-tipped fingers. To men who had to cruise around day after day with nothing but an occasional whale to look at, though, the effect of that much woman all at once must naturally be fairly overwhelming. He hoped they wouldn't decide to shanghai her and spoil Dan Stott's homecoming banquet.

He'd intended to sit next to Helen, but the engineer had beaten him to her. He'd expected to find fish on the menu, but it appeared the doughty lads and lasses of the Coast Guard preferred pasta primavera. No matter, it was good. He ate with one ear cocked for sounds of gunfire and commotion on deck. He didn't hear any. He ate his piece of lemon pie and drank his coffee. He was wiping his lips when the crewman who'd acted as lookout entered the messroom and requested that Mrs. Shandy, Mrs. Stott, and Miss McBogle please go up on deck. He didn't invite Professor Shandy and Fingal, but he'd have had a hard time trying to keep them from going.

FIFTEEN

Helen wished she hadn't eaten. She should have realized what could happen to a woman's stomach when she had to stand facing a group of men who, until a moment ago, had been comfortably sure they'd put her and her friends safely away in Davy Jones's locker.

She'd peeked out at them a moment ago from the companionway, just as she'd done aboard the *Ethelbert Nevin*. They'd been relaxed enough then, laughing and chatting with the crewmen on deck. Now the four bears were lined up shoulder to shoulder, their faces fish white above their beards, their eyes popping from under their fright wig hair, their mouths making red O's among the wild black fuzz as if they all wanted to say something and couldn't make the words come out. Helen felt an unwanted pang of sympathy for them. She wouldn't be able to speak, either.

But she'd have to. Lieutenant Blaise was saying in a no-nonsense way, "Mrs. Shandy, can you help us identify these men?"

It was the calm self-assurance on Crewcut's face that loosened her tongue.

"I certainly can. That beardless man who's so obviously engaged in trying to think up a plausible lie is the one who thought he'd killed Eustace Tilkey. The man second from him, with the nick in his left nostril, picked up Eustace's feet and helped to throw him overboard while that tall one in the middle took over the wheel."

"You watched this from the cabin, you said?"

"Yes. I'm quite sure they didn't notice me watching. The cabin windows were so dirty it would have been hard for them to see in. I didn't know what else to do, so I thought I'd better just go out and take my seat as if nothing had happened. They didn't interfere. But then Cat—Miss McBogle—came out. She was naturally surprised to see one of the passengers at the wheel and asked him where Eustace was. I couldn't actually hear above the noise of the engine, but I assume that's what she said. He answered, but I couldn't see his lips on account of the beard. Cat said something else, then the first murderer—my husband says his name is Roland Childe—"

That rocked him. He lost his self-satisfied smirk for only a second, but that was long enough. The bears quit staring at Helen and stared at their leader, then at each other, clearly jolted.

Ensign Blaise was interested. "Then you know this man, Mr. Shandy?"

"No, but I met a relative of his who told me enough about him to make a positive identification. There's a strong family resemblance between them, though I'll have to apologize to the relative for saying so. Childe comes from Clavaton, Massachusetts, and is wanted in Balaclava County for arson, grand larceny, and manslaughter. Not to usurp your authority, Ensign Blaise, but if you happen to have any manacles and leg irons kicking around the brig, this might be an opportune time to trot them out. Er—sorry to interrupt your testimony, my dear."

"Not at all, Peter. While we're on the subject, I trust these men were all searched for weapons before they were brought aboard."

"Not to worry, Mrs. Shandy," Blaise assured her. "We explained the regulations about unauthorized weapons aboard a U.S. Coast Guard vessel and impounded four knives, two sidearms, a rifle, and a hand grenade Mr. Childe was carrying. He explained it as a souvenir of his wartime experiences."

"How sentimental of him."

Helen was relieved to see that the crewmen who'd appeared to be standing idly by were now closing in on the five men. She hadn't realized belaying pins were still issued, although she was well aware of the Coast Guard's venerable tradition. In 1790, George Washington had approved the revenue cutter service that predated the United States Navy. A Coast Guard cutter had captured the first American prize in the War of 1812. Another cutter, the *Harriet Lane*, had been attached to a squadron of naval vessels sent to Paraguay in 1858.

And that was what had been nagging at her all this time about Guthrie Fingal's wife. Almost the last professional act Helen had performed before she'd left California to come back east and marry Peter, though that hadn't been on her agenda at the time, had been to assist a student researching a paper on Francisco Solano Lopez.

To Helen, the most interesting part of the search had been finding out about Lopez's beautiful, intelligent, almost but not quite indomitable mistress. Irish-born, French-educated Ella Lynch had been christened Elisa Alicia, married at fifteen to a French army officer named Xavier Quatrefages, handed over by Xavier to his commanding officer three years later.

Ella had had a brief romance with a Russian who set her up in Paris as a courtesan of the highest rank, been annexed at nineteen by the Paraguayan general who intended to become an emperor, and was reputed to have been the undeclared ruler of both Francisco and Paraguay until he fought his last losing battle against the Brazilians in 1870.

She had buried her lover with her own hands under the mocking eyes of Brazilian soldiery. Ella had been thirty-seven then. It had taken her almost another twenty years to die, starved and penniless, on a thin, dirty mattress in a Paris lodging house.

Ella had borne four sons to Francisco. Pancho, the eldest, had been stabbed at her side by a Brazilian corporal. She'd scraped out his grave with her bare hands, too. Helen didn't know what had happened to two of the four, but she knew biographer William E. Barrett had talked with a lady who'd been married to a third and had borne him two daughters. There might be other grandchildren, even great-grand-children. Ella had also reared as her own a daughter of Francisco's born to another woman. Legally, she'd been forced to remain Elisa Alicia Quatrefages until the day she died, even though by some legal sleight her long-ago husband had been able to divorce himself from her, without divorcing her from him.

And what a time to be remembering all this! Now fully in command of herself, Helen gave the young ensign a smile and a nod.

"Thank you, that's most reassuring. As I'd started to say, Mr. Childe and his accomplice picked up Miss McBogle by the wrists and ankles."

"They didn't knock her out first?"

"No. Mr. Childe had tossed overboard the bludgeon he'd used on Eustace. I expect he was confident he and his four trained bears would be able to overcome three defenseless women without it. Needless to say, he was right. When I tried to make them let go of Miss McBogle, the two men who hadn't yet taken any part in the fracas—those two on the end—grabbed me by the wrists and ankles, too. The four of them started swinging us both back and forth. They counted one . . . two . . . three, then they chucked us as far as they could."

Ensign Blaise winced. "Did the man at the wheel take any part in these attempted murders?"

"Objection, Ensign." Roland Childe was getting his aplomb

back. "Attempted murders strikes me as pretty strong language to describe what was nothing more than a little maybe ill-judged horseplay. We'd have pulled the ladies right out again, but this big whale came up behind us and started chasing the boat. The stout lady there got hysterical and jumped overboard, then our man at the wheel panicked and shoved the engine full speed ahead before I could stop him."

The only way to handle so blatantly stupid a liar was ignore him. Helen went on as if she hadn't heard. "To answer your question, Ensign Blaise, the man at the wheel did not participate in the attempted murders."

"Did he make any effort to stop those who did?"

"Not so you'd notice it. He stood there laughing his head off. They were all laughing."

"What about you, Miss McBogle? Do you agree with Mrs. Shandy's account of what happened?" ·

"I agree with as much of it as I'm in a position to agree with," Catriona replied. "I didn't see the attack on Eustace Tilkey. As Mrs. Shandy explained, I was still below when that happened. When I saw the bear at the wheel, I asked him where Eustace was, and he said he'd gone up front to look for whales. That didn't make sense to me. I could see Eustace wasn't on the cabin roof and you know how big the foredeck of a lobster boat is. Besides, the *Ethelbert Nevin*'s was all cluttered up with luggage they'd brought on board with them."

Catriona hesitated, then went on with her tale. "I sung out but Eustace didn't answer. Then I guess I said something like, 'I don't see him.' Smiley here said, 'Go look for him,' or words to that effect. He grabbed my wrists from behind and somebody else got me by the ankles. I was too busy trying to bite Smiley's arm to notice which bear that was, but you can trust Mrs. Shandy for the facts. She's a librarian and never gets anything wrong. Iduna, you're the one who saw everything. Tell him."

So Iduna told. It would have been impossible for anybody not to believe her. As she repeated what she'd gleaned from her lipreading, the stink of fear off the four bears became almost nauseating. Even Roland Childe was looking the way somebody might if a cuddly pet guinea pig made a sudden savage leap for his jugular.

"And I certainly hope you brought those suitcases Cat mentioned back with you, or Helen's going to raise the roof."

"Suitcases?" Ensign Blaise turned to the man next to him. "Pulsifer, did you see any suitcases when we picked them up?"

"No, sir."

"How about a big fishing creel, a camera case, and a tackle box?" Helen's mouth was so dry she could barely articulate.

"Sorry, ma'am."

"But the *Ethelbert Nevin* doesn't look to be all that badly wrecked. Didn't you find anything whatever on board?"

"Yes, ma'am, we found stuff you might expect to find— spare gas cans, bait buckets, foghorn, you know. There's a big hole in the forward hull where she ran aground, but otherwise the boat's pretty much intact. Where would the suitcases have been, ma'am?"

"Lashed to the foredeck. Quite securely, I should have thought. We'd been cruising most of the morning since Eustace tied them down, and they were still there the last I saw of the boat. The creel and other things were tucked under the bench in the cockpit where they should have been safe enough. How could you have missed them?"

"We couldn't have, ma'am. These guys must have thrown them overboard before they crashed."

"But why? They couldn't have known they were going to crash until it happened. The whole point of stealing the boat was to transport the stuff they were carrying to the buyer. They must have cached it somewhere on the island for fear you'd open the cases and see the stolen goods inside."

"And what would this stolen cargo have been, Mrs. Shandy?" Ensign Blaise wanted to know.

"Weather vanes."

"Huh?"

"Antique weather vanes," Helen explained, "worth a great deal of money."

"Like how much, if you don't mind me asking?"

"Well, Chief Mashamoquet of the Nipmuck Indians sold for $85,000 in 1986 at a legitimate public auction. We don't know what sort of prices have been paid under the table by private collectors for stolen ones. Stealing antique weather vanes has become a highly lucrative racket, in case you didn't know. And these are Praxiteles Lumpkin weather vanes."

"They're pretty special, are they?"

"Very special indeed, Ensign. Special enough for this man Childe to have burned down several barns and the Lumpkinton soap factory in order to conceal the fact that he and his friends were stealing them. The fact that he killed an innocent man and put a whole village out of work by destroying the factory doesn't seem to have cut any ice with him."

"Why should it?" said Childe calmly. "I didn't do it."

"Nonsense," said Peter, "of course you did. We have an eyewitness who described you beyond any doubt. He's in the hospital recovering from third-degree burns, by the way, which he received trying to rescue the chap who was in the tallow room when you threw the grenade into the tank with your famous sideways flick."

"What are you talking about? Ensign, this is obviously a case of mistaken identity. I don't know why these people are telling such totally ridiculous lies about me, but I'm not going to stand here and take it."

"Oh, I think you are, Mr. Childe," said Ensign Blaise. "You really have nowhere else to go, do you? Don't worry, you'll be given every opportunity to defend yourself when the time comes. Right now, I'd like to get this business of the weather vanes straightened out. Where would they have been taking them, Mrs. Shandy? Have you any idea?"

"Mr. Childe evidently has a rich buyer all lined up, but we're not yet clear on whether he was taking the weather vanes there or to an intermediary. Do you happen to know where Paraguay, Maine, is?"

"No, but we can look it up. Do we have a Maine atlas aboard, Pulsifer?"

"Yes, sir. But I can tell you right now there's no Paraguay

in Maine, unless it's the name of somebody's private camp or something. I studied up on all the place names when I got picked to be on 'So You Think You Know Maine' last February."

"That's a television quiz show," Catriona McBogle explained to the folks from away. "Did you win, Mr. Pulsifer?"

"Yes, ma'am."

"In that case," said Helen, "perhaps we ought to scratch Paraguay as a real place and start thinking of it as a code name. That man who piled up the *Ethelbert Nevin* might care to enlighten us, since he's the only one of the five who stands a realistic chance of gaining clemency by turning state's evidence. Who's Paraguay, Mr. Bear?"

"I damn well know who this guy is," Guthrie interrupted. "Or at least I know the name that's on our enrollment books. He's John Doe Buck, he's a first-term student, and he's flunking dendrology. What are you doing in this crowd, Buck? Come on, make it easier on yourself. Who's Paraguay?"

"I don't know what you're talking about," the man who'd been at the wheel mumbled.

"Nonsense, of course you do," Helen prodded. "What's your own code name?"

"Don't answer," shouted Roland Childe, but he was too late. The man had already muttered "Peru."

"Thank you, Mr. Buck, or Peru, if you prefer. And Mr. Childe's is, of course, Brazil."

Peru was by now completely rattled, and so were the other three bears. "How did she know that?" they whispered to each other.

"Because it's where the nuts come from," she answered sweetly. "Now what about those weather vanes, Peru?"

"Shut up, all of you!" Childe was sweating like the rest of them now. "Death before disclosure. Men, remember your oath!"

With a lightning-quick gesture, he reached into the breast pocket of his fatigue jacket, pulled out something tiny, and popped it into his mouth. His accomplices, drilled to follow orders, did the same.

"Great Scott," cried Peter, "they've got cyanide capsules!"

"And we'll use them if we have to," said Childe, articulating with the greatest care. "Don't push us."

"You're a pack of fools. Spit those things out," Ensign Blaise ordered.

They faced him, not moving. It was Iduna who coped. Stepping up to Peru, she held out her hand, palm up.

"Come on, John Doe. Spit it out like a good boy."

The shaggy creature stared wildly into those commanding blue eyes. Then, with something like a sob, he spat.

"There you are, all better. Good boy."

He might have been a pet sheepdog. Iduna gave him a quick pat on the beard and went on to the next. And the next, and the next. Four awesome white pellets lay, spit-soaked, in her soft, rosy palm. She faced Roland Childe.

"Give it up, Roland."

He spoke through clenched teeth. "I stand on my oath."

"You'll do as you're told."

Iduna reached around and fetched him a sound buffet between the shoulder blades. His mouth snapped open, the object he'd been nursing in his cheek flew out. She caught it on the fly.

"A lemon jellybean!"

Iduna passed it around for all to see. "You four-flushing little snotnose! You'd have let those four young idiots kill themselves so you could lie your way out without having them around to contradict you. I declare to goodness, if I had a Bjorklund buggy whip with me right now, I'd sure as heck use it to take a few strips off your good-for-nothing hide."

SIXTEEN

After that, they had no trouble getting the four bears to talk. The trouble was, neither Peru, Argentina, Colombia, nor Venezuela had anything much to say. Peru admitted he'd enrolled in the school under Paraguay's orders, filtered through Roland Childe, known to them as Brazil. They all admitted Paraguay was a person, not a place. They took it for granted Paraguay was a man instead of a woman because they were the sort who naturally would. They had a general idea that the rendezvous was supposed to take place in or around New Haven, Connecticut, because Brazil had shown them on the chart what route they were intended to take. However, they didn't know whether or not Brazil had been telling the truth. That lemon jellybean had left them all pretty shaken.

As for the weather vanes, those had been unloaded from the *Ethelbert Nevin* as soon as she crashed. A cache had been dug out with knives and hands in the only patch of diggable soil they'd been able to find on the islet. Peru showed Iduna his blisters, perhaps in the hope of getting another pat on the cheek. Instead, she took the heartless position that it served him right and he ought to have known better than to get mixed up with a nasty creature like Brazil in the first place.

By the time they'd got through the interrogations, the Coast Guard boat had been coming up to Hocasquam. Ensign Blaise had radioed the local sheriff that he had a gang of pirates aboard in custody; so when they docked, they were met by quite a posse. The prisoners were being taken to Thomaston State Prison for safekeeping until charges could be properly filed.

Catriona rather hated to leave the scene of action, but she was anxious about her cats. She changed back into her still-clammy running pants and sweatshirt, thanked Ensign Blaise for the loan of his dress uniform, and disembarked with Guthrie Fingal, who'd grown deeply concerned about his barn as soon as he learned Miss McBogle was going home. Iduna and her picnic hamper, to the regret of the engineer and the quartermaster, went along with them.

Helen was not to be budged. "I'm sorry, Cat," she said, "but I can't possibly leave this boat until we've gone back and collected those weather vanes."

"And I'm not leaving Helen," Peter added. "I hope you don't mind putting up with us a while longer, Ensign Blaise."

"Not at all, Mr. Shandy. Happy to have you aboard."

Catriona didn't try to argue the Shandys into quitting the chase before it was over. "Then you'd better take my car keys. Iduna and I can ride home with Guthrie. You're sure you know your way back from here?"

"We'll find you," Peter assured her. "You'd better not wait supper for us."

As it happened, though, the Shandys had their traveling time shortened considerably. They'd barely pulled away from Hocasquam Head when Ensign Blaise got an SOS about some fighting lobstermen and had to rush off in a different direction. So Helen and Peter had the thrill of being picked off the deck by helicopter and airlifted back to where *Ethelbert Nevin* had been wrecked.

The cache was a cinch to locate; they easily spotted the disturbed soil over which a few slabs of rock had been unconvincingly arranged. The two suitcases, the creel, the tackle box, and the camera case turned up only inches below the surface.

"Didn't kill themselves digging," Peter grunted.

"They thought they'd be back to pick up the loot as soon as they could steal another boat," said Helen. "Beasts! Well, come on, Peter. Open the cases and let's see what we've got. I'm almost afraid to look."

She needn't have been. All three of the most recently stolen weather vanes were there, neatly wrapped in the *Balaclava County Fane and Pennon*. "Too bad Swope isn't here to take a picture," Peter remarked, but Helen didn't pay any attention. She was busy checking Praxiteles Lumpkin's masterpieces for possible damage.

The man in the tub had sustained a slight bend in his brush, but that could easily be put to rights. The cow kicking over the bucket must have suffered rough handling; the bucket was going to need a bit of restoration. Guthrie Fingal's lumberjack was in A-one condition. Helen gloated.

"Look, Peter, he's got a squirrel sitting on his head. When I took the photographs, I thought it was just some kind of funny hat."

"Wearing a squirrel for a hat is probably an old Maine custom. What's this stuff in the fishing creel? By George, Helen, look at this. They were planning to disguise the *Ethelbert Nevin*."

Peter unrolled the piece of painted canvas he'd found and spread it out on the ground. It had been cut to fit the boat's upper transom and bore the artfully worn and battered letters:

GUY LOMBARDO
ROCK

Which "Rock" had been tastefully obliterated.

"Clever," Helen remarked. "There are plenty of 'Rocks' around. Its home port could be anywhere. And here's another strip of canvas in the tackle box with a lot of numbers on it, to cover up the real registration. And a pot of glue in the camera case. I suppose they thought they were being too clever for words."

Peter held the strip of numbers up against the side of the boat. "Made to order, antiqued to match the rest of the hull. These weren't done in a minute, my love. I wonder how they got the pieces to fit so perfectly."

"They had someone measure the boat and take pictures."

Helen could have explained about Elisa Alicia Quatrefages then and there—and perhaps she should have—but the helicopter pilot was anxious to get them back to Hocasquam. He'd radioed for another detail of police to be at the landing place to receive the contents of the cache, which would have to be impounded as evidence. She'd have to tell then, but she needed to talk to Peter first. Guthrie Fingal was, after all, a very old friend of his.

"Too bad you've got a car to pick up," the pilot said hospitably as they were setting down. "I could have delivered you right to your own back yard."

"Oh, that's all right," said Peter. "We'll take a rain check."

"And hope to God we never have to use it," he added after they'd got away from the helicopter.

They handed over the two suitcases, the creel, the tackle box, and the camera case and got a receipt. Helen impressed the policemen with the importance and value of that which was being intrusted to them. They promised to take extra good care of the cow and the bucket, the man in the tub, and the lumberjack with the squirrel on his head. Somewhat relieved, she got into the car.

"Shall I drive, dear? You must be sick of it after coming all the way from home and then having to rescue us and the weather vanes."

"You've been through more than I have, my love. Allow me to handle the chest thumping this time around."

After the usual preliminary fumbling in a strange car, Peter got the key into the ignition right side up and they started. This time he took it slowly. He needed to be alone for a while with Helen just as badly as she wanted time with him. They wound up pulling off the road into a lay-by and winding their arms around each other like a pair of amorous teenagers.

"So, Peter, what have you been up to?" Helen spoke a little bit breathlessly, as well she might, all things considered. Peter cleared his throat.

"M'well, my dear, I spent last night in the company of another woman."

"How nice for her," Helen replied politely. "Would you care to elucidate?"

"It would give me the greatest pleasure to do so."

Leaving out some of the hairier bits about bullets and bogs, Peter told his tale. He had not expected Helen to be other than appalled, and appalled she dutifully was. Naturally, she was also intrigued.

"What a remarkable woman! Is there any hope of my ever getting to know her, do you think?"

"Time will tell, my love. I have a hunch Miss Binks may not be so unsociable as she claims to be, but she'll require careful stalking. Books, I think, would be the most useful bait. You might try laying a trail of Turgenev, Tennyson, and Trollope and sneak up on her when she gets to *Barchester Towers*. And now, my love, what is it you've been keeping back from me about your own adventures?"

"I thought you'd probably notice. It's something I don't think you're going to like much. You did know Guthrie Fingal's married?"

"I'd had a general impression to that effect. But—er— recent developments had led me to believe I may have been mistaken."

"You noticed that too, did you? Peter, I'm dreadfully worried. Cat was totally desolate when Ben died. That was about fifteen years ago and she's never looked at anybody since, as far as I know. Or hadn't, evidently, until she moved to Sasquamahoc."

"What prompted her to come here?"

"The old upstream syndrome, I suppose. All things come home at eventide. Cat was born around here somewhere. In a smelt shack during the February freeze, she claims, but I suspect that's hyperbole. Anyway, Cat's only peripherally involved as far as Guthrie's wife is concerned. The big thing right now is that Mrs. Fingal calls herself Elisa Alicia Quatrefages."

"Am I supposed to clutch my brow and swoon? No doubt the name Elisa Alicia Quatrefages is fraught with dire import, and no doubt I ought to know what it imports, but I'm damned if I do."

"The only import I know is that it was the married name of a woman better known as Ella Lynch, who played a key role in Paraguayan history around the eighteen sixties. Paraguay appears to be the code name of the person to whom Roland Childe and his crew are supposed to deliver the weather vanes."

"But drat it, Helen, that doesn't necessarily mean the two are connected."

"Then consider the fact that Eustace Tilkey told us Guthrie Fingal's wife had been hanging around Hocasquam Cove recently, taking photographs of the *Ethelbert Nevin*. According to Cat, she's an artsy-craftsy type who makes doodads and whatnots for the New York boutiques and goes off by herself for a good part of every month, ostensibly to peddle her wares. Would you care to make the connection yourself, or shall I make it for you?"

"Spare yourself the effort, mine own. However humble my powers of ratiocination, the effort is not outside their compass. The question now arises, how the flaming perdition are we going to tell Guthrie?"

"I should say the larger question is whether Guthrie already knows."

"Impossible! Guthrie Fingal's a decent man."

"Whom you haven't been in close contact with for umpty-seven years."

"So what if I haven't? Can a leopard change its spots?"

"Is Guthrie a leopard? I said you weren't going to like it, Peter."

"And you've never been more right. I don't like it, not one damn blasted bit. Why should Guthrie have burned down his own barn in order to steal his own weather vane?"

"Not to be contentious, darling, but the barn was only damaged, not destroyed. Moreover, we have to address the question whether the barn and the weather vane do in fact belong to Guthrie or whether they're the property of an independent institution controlled by a board of trustees. Do you honestly believe Guthrie could simply have climbed up and got that weather vane, lugged it off and sold it to the hypothetical wealthy collector, and pocketed the proceeds for himself without exciting some kind of remark?"

"No, and I don't believe pigs can fly, either," Peter retorted sulkily. "I suppose I have to concede you the doodad maker, but I'll be eternally hornswoggled if I'm going to throw Guthrie in after her. So what do we do now?"

"Sit tight and see what develops, wouldn't you think?"

"How tight were you planning to sit? I've been hoping we might get back home tomorrow."

"So have I. When I said sit, I didn't necessarily mean sit here. Now that we've got the police involved, I don't see what we're likely to accomplish by hanging around Sasquamahoc, anyway."

"Did you tell that aggregation of fuzz about Elisa Alicia Quatrefages? I don't recall hearing you."

"I'd intended to," Helen admitted, "but the officer who was asking the questions never gave me a chance. You heard him. Whenever one of us tried to interject something he considered extraneous, he'd start yelping 'Just give me the facts, ma'am,' like an old Jack Webb rerun. So I decided I might as well not try. It did seem awfully tenebrous trying to pin a rap on a woman I've never met, just because she happens to use an unusual name."

"And even more tenebrous to pounce on the woman's husband just because he happens to have part of his barn left," Peter made the mistake of pointing out.

Helen gave him a weary look. "If you say so, dear. Let's go."

They found their way back to Sasquamahoc with no trouble. Catriona, Iduna, and Guthrie were all three sprawled in deck chairs on the side lawn, each with a tall glass full of ice, lime, and no doubt one or two other things. They hailed the Shandys with delight.

"Did you find your windmills?" Cat shouted.

"Weather vanes," Helen corrected.

"Whatever. Did you? Where are they?"

"We did. They've been impounded as evidence by the constabulary or the horse marines or whoever those seventy-three authoritarian figures were who met us at the dock. We got helicoptered, by the way. Ensign Blaise had to go and break up a lobster war. Don't ask me what the lobsters were fighting about because I haven't the faintest notion."

"Unworthy of you, Marsh. Want a drink?"

"Yes, but I'm going to get bathed and changed first. Peter can stay and fill you in on the details. He hasn't had the chance to do any proper visiting yet, poor dear."

Helen dropped a kiss where her husband's bald spot was soon going to be and went along into the house. Peter fell gratefully into the lawn chair Catriona hauled up for him, and waited for Guthrie to bring him his drink.

Whoever built this grand old house had known how to pick a site. Peter enjoyed its simple squareness, and he liked the way it sat. After all that choppy water, he found it refreshing to look at rolling hills and open meadow. So many black-eyed Susans told him Catriona McBogle's fields would be the better for a few loads of top dressing, but he had to admit their bold orange-yellow stars struck a cheerful note of contrast among the demure white oxeye daisies and the blue-purple cow vetch.

He obliged with the details, got his drink, took a few sips, and set the glass down beside him on the grass. Raising it to his lips was getting to be too much of an effort. So was holding up his eyelids. When Helen came out, clean and colorful in a flowered print sun dress, she found her husband asleep and the other three close to it.

"Well, this is a lively party, I must say. No, Guthrie, don't get up. I'll finish Peter's drink. Half is plenty for me anyway, or I'll be dropping off like the rest of you. Cat, what about letting Peter and me take us all out to supper? Is there a halfway decent restaurant anywhere handy?"

"No, there isn't and, no, you can't. We'll scare up something in the kitchen. You'll stay, won't you, Guthrie?"

"Thanks, Cat, but I've been gone quite a while already. I'd better be moseying along, they'll be expecting me back at the school. Helen, you and Pete won't take off in the morning without giving me a chance to say good-bye, I hope?"

"We wouldn't think of it," she assured him. "I shouldn't be surprised if Peter dropped over for a little visit later on, assuming we can get him awake to eat his supper. You'll be around, won't you?"

"Oh sure, I'll be there. I don't stray far from home base, as a general rule."

"His wife's the traveler in the family." Catriona must be annoyed because Guthrie wouldn't stay to supper, Helen decided; otherwise, she wouldn't have brought up a tender subject. "Where's she off to this trip, Guth?"

He shrugged. "Who knows? New York, I guess. I quit trying to keep track of her long ago. Well, see you later, folks. Thanks for the drink."

SEVENTEEN

Iduna gave her silver gilt curls a compassionate shake. "If that's women's liberation, I'll take raspberry. Imagine a wife having no more consideration than to go off for weeks at a time and not even tell her husband where she's going. I'd no more do that to Daniel than I'd order him to get up and cook my breakfast for me."

"Peter usually fixes mine," Helen admitted, "but I know what you mean, Iduna. I wouldn't do a disappearing act either, if I could help it, and I certainly wouldn't want Peter to do it to me. Not to criticize your friends, Cat, but the Fingals must have rather a strange marriage."

They were all in the huge kitchen now, watching their hostess pull food out of the air with the practiced ease of all hostesses who live in country places and have scads of visitors in the summertime. Catriona probably didn't mean to set the platter of cold roast chicken down on the table with quite so hard a thump.

"Don't pussyfoot on my account, Marsh. Not that it's any of my business how Guthrie and Elisa Alicia run their lives."

"Nonsense, my dear. I've never yet been in an academic community where everybody's business wasn't everybody else's business. I can't imagine it's not the same up here. Or do I mean 'down'?"

" 'Down East' properly refers only to Lubec and Eastport, not that anybody seems to give a damn nowadays except the guys who give the weather reports. Okay, everybody, haul up and set. Supper's ready, such as it is."

She had fresh asparagus, boiled just enough to take out the rawness without spoiling the crunch, fresh leaf lettuce from the patch beside the bulkhead, fresh bread baked by the lady down the road who'd put a little fresh dill in the batter. There'd be fresh-picked strawberries for dessert.

"I roasted this chicken as soon as you called up and said you were coming, just in case. I get them from Harriet McComb's poultry farm over at Squamasas. She pinfeathers them all in person."

Catriona rambled on about the chicken until Helen took the bull by the horns. "Cat, listen to me. The Fingals are your business and they're ours as well. Guthrie was Peter's friend long before you ever knew him, and we have reason to believe he may be in serious trouble. If he means anything to you at all, you'd better tell us right now everything you know about Elisa Alicia Quatrefages. And if you want the reason, it's because I have a very strong hunch she may be our link with Paraguay."

Catriona had just picked up a spear of asparagus. She began whipping it to and fro with nervous jerks of her hand. "Would you care to explain why?"

"Would you kindly stop waving that asparagus around first, before it starts coming apart all over the tablecloth?"

"Oh, sorry." Catriona examined the spear for possible damage, bit off the tip, and began to chew. "Carry on, old scout."

Helen carried. If she'd expected to throw a bombshell, she was soon disabused of the notion. When she'd finished her explanation, Catriona merely nodded.

"Okay, Marsh. What do you want to know?"

Helen wasn't prepared for immediate capitulation. She threw a helpless glance at Peter. "Darling, what do we want to know?"

"M'well, for starters, Cat, what does Elisa Alicia look like?"

"Like a pea-brained twit who'd get a kick out of playing Anna the Adventuress. Long black hair worn in artful dishevelment, slinky black jumpsuits unbuttoned to the bellybutton or thereabout, lots of jingly chains and clanking bracelets, earrings dragging on her collarbones, fourteen different shades of eye goop—"

"What color eyes?" Peter interrupted.

"What color happens to be in fashion at the moment? To tell you the truth, I've never taken the trouble to grope my way through the layers of false eyelashes far enough to notice. Sultry brown, one would assume."

"The original Elisa Alicia was a blonde with blue gray eyes," said Helen, "though I suppose if this one is really a descendant of Francisco Lopez, she'd be a brunette."

"If she's a Lopez, why would she be calling herself Quatrefages?" Iduna wanted to know.

"Because it sounds classier, perhaps?" Catriona suggested. "She was bending my ear a while back about changing my name to Clarissa Armitage."

"Whatever would you want to do that for?" Iduna helped herself to more asparagus. "My, this is a real treat. Do you see much of Elisa Alicia when she's around, Cat?"

"Oh, I try to be sociable for Guthrie's sake, but it's an uphill struggle. I suppose what you're mostly concerned about, Peter, is where she goes on those trips of hers. The only places I've heard her mention are New York and Boston. I don't recall the names of any specific shops, not that they'd mean anything to me if I did because I wouldn't go shopping in New York if you dragged me by the boot heels through

Macy's basement. According to what she says, every high-class boutique operator on the East Coast is clamoring for her wares."

"She must really be making money out of them, then."

"She claims she does. I asked her once if it was because she makes those herb wreaths of hers out of hashish. She pretended to think I was being funny."

"Does she in fact show any sign of untoward affluence? For instance, does she dress better than a pedagogue's wife normally would? I'm assuming Guthrie doesn't find money growing on those trees he's raising."

"No, I don't think he's getting rich in a hurry. As far as Elisa Alicia's clothes are concerned, better is hardly the *mot juste* since she appears to take a perverse pride in dressing as unsuitably as possible. She buys expensive stuff, though, and her so-called costume jewelry looks to me like the genuine article. Guthrie wouldn't know the difference, poor clod. I can't tell you whether he really believes everything she tells him or if he's simply quit listening. She did rattle his socks a bit the time she drove off in his old brown Toyota and came back in a brand-new bright green Cadillac Sedan de Ville."

"My God!" Peter ejaculated. "Did she offer any explanation?"

"She told him the Toyota didn't adequately express her personality and besides she needed more trunk space for her merchandise. She'd paid cash for the Caddie except for whatever allowance she got on the Toyota, so there wasn't a great deal Guthrie could do about it except fume. He's never once set foot in the new car."

"She goes on these trips all by herself, then?"

"To the best of my knowledge. She always has so much fragile junk to carry that it's really the most practical way for her to go. She claims to enjoy the driving and she has nothing else to do so an extra couple of days' travel time doesn't bother her."

"She just packs up and leaves whenever she feels like it, then?"

"That's what she does. And never tells Guthrie where

she's going, when she'll be back, or how to reach her in the meantime, assuming he'd ever want to. She may spend the whole time peddling her wares or she may be doing God knows what. She actually does make all the things she takes because I've seen her working on them. They're not the sort I personally go for, but they're cleverly done. She's good at decorative painting, and could certainly have concocted that Guy Lombardo camouflage for the *Ethelbert Nevin*. And that's about all I can tell you, Peter. I don't know whether Guthrie could add a great deal more, but there's only one way to find out. Want some cream for your strawberries?"

Peter accepted the cream and ate his strawberries in a state of perturbation, which he regretted because they were excellent and deserved his full and undivided attention. He then made his excuses to the ladies and went to call on his old schoolmate. He found Guthrie gazing in melancholy absorption into the lush foliage of a horse-chestnut tree that would have been just the ticket for Miss Binks to nest in.

"What's up there, Guth?"

"Oh, hi, Pete. Nothing in particular. I was just sort of musing. Had your supper?"

"Yes. You should have stayed. Catriona's a good provider."

"I know she is. I'd have liked to stay only— Oh, hell, Pete. Life's a bitch sometimes. Sorry, I didn't mean to sound grumpy. Come on, let me show you around the campus. It's not much like Balaclava, I don't suppose."

"Nothing's like Balaclava," Peter assured his friend. "Including at times Balaclava itself. I don't know whether you've ever met President Svenson?"

"I've heard about him." Guthrie quit looking sad and began to grin. "He must be hell on wheels to work for."

"Oh, I wouldn't say that. At least he's never dull."

They strolled around the school's grounds, swapping academic gossip. Guthrie showed Peter some work that was being done on tree development, which the visiting horticulturist found totally absorbing. Not until it got too dark to see what was happening in the experimental nurseries did he remember what it was he'd come for.

"Mosquitoes are beginning to bite," he observed with good cause, although in fact they'd already been biting for quite a while. "If you happen to have any thoughts about inviting me in for a drink, now might be a good time to voice them. Not hinting or anything, you understand."

"You always were a subtle cuss, Pete. Gosh, it's good to see you. Come on, then. That's my house right over there."

The president's dwelling at Sasquamahoc was no pillared mansion but just an ungainly two-story frame house built, Peter judged, during the ugly 1920s. Its clapboards were painted the most peculiar shade of yellow he'd ever seen. He suspected Elisa Alicia had chosen it. There was a useless little front porch; squares of pebble glass in garish red, blue, green, and amber framed the front door. A large wreath made of grapevines trimmed with artificial flowers, dried grasses, a good many guinea hen feathers, and a couple of plastic eggplants was no doubt intended to provide a welcoming note but didn't make Peter feel particularly welcome.

When Guthrie opened the door, Peter found himself confronted by a huge arrangement of gilded bulrushes, pampas grass, and peacock feathers in a lacquered brass cuspidor. Shying away nervously, he stumbled over a section of tree limb that had been mounted in plaster of paris to serve as a roosting place for a number of artificial birds. There were even a few nests artfully contrived from multicolored raffia and rolls of streamer confetti dipped in shellac.

Peter was horrified to notice real birds' eggs, blown of their contents, lying in the nests. Any doubt that Guthrie's peripatetic spouse could be linked up with that gang of evildoers he'd just had the pleasure of seeing off to the jug was dissipated. A woman with the kind of mind that could contrive this foyer would be capable of any atrocity.

"Come into my den," Guthrie urged. "It's the one place where Elisa doesn't put any homey touches. Does your wife go in for them?"

"She bakes me a pie now and then," Peter replied cautiously.

"Elisa makes pies, too. Out of papier-mâché with fake cherries on top."

Guthrie sank into gloomy silence for a moment, then blurted, "Honest to God, Pete, sometimes I wonder what the human race is coming to."

This was as good an opening as Peter was likely to get. He cleared his throat and took the leap. "How did you happen to meet her, Guthrie?"

"I was at a convention in New York and she happened along. She knew one of the guys I was talking to and a bunch of us wound up having drinks together. Then one thing led to another. You know how it is."

Guthrie shrugged. "It got so she'd fly to Portland for the weekend and I'd drive down to meet her. She was kind of . . . oh, exciting, I guess. She dressed different, smelled different, talked different. Did a few other things different, too, if you want to know. What the hell, Pete, I'd never been fifty miles from Sasquamahoc except when I went to college, and you know the kind of glamour girls we used to hang out with there. Great kids to muck out a stable with, but there's nothing romantic about rubber boots and a sweaty union suit."

"You might consider them homey touches," Peter murmured, but Guthrie was too steeped in woe to listen.

"So anyway, this went on for a few months, then I took a long weekend off and we went for a quickie tour of Costa Rica. I stayed drunk on planter's punches the whole time, and when I sobered up, I found out I was married. Sounds crazy, eh?"

What it sounded like to Peter was the old Bristol splice, but he thought perhaps this wasn't quite the time to say so. "What's her family like?"

"I don't know, I've never met any of 'em. They're all over in France, or so Elisa claims."

"Whereabouts in France?"

"Don't ask me. They never write, which doesn't surprise me any. She's not much of a one for keeping in touch, herself."

"What do you mean by that, Guthrie? Doesn't she phone you while she's away?"

"Heck, no. She just takes off whenever she feels like it and shows up here when she's run out of places to go. And when she is around, she might as well not be for all the good it does me. Not that I give a damn, if you want the truth."

Guthrie started to pour himself a little more Old Smuggler, then changed his mind. "Help yourself if you want to, Pete. I don't drink much any more. Look where it got me that other time. Not that I'm blaming Elisa. She's what she is and I'm what I am and I was a damn fool to think we could make a go of it in the first place. I could be worse off, I suppose. We don't fight or anything. She's got her craft business and I've got the school. It's easy enough to stay out of each other's hair even when she's around. It's just that—well, damn it, seeing how it is with you and Helen—"

"I know what you mean, Guthrie." Drat it, this could get embarrassing. "Then according to what you've just told me, you don't actually know one damned thing about your wife except that she puts fake cherries in her pies and knows how to gild the bulrush. Furthermore, you've reached the point where you don't care."

"That's about the size of it, Pete. I've mentioned divorce once or twice, but she just laughs in my face. Elisa claims she doesn't see anything wrong with the way we're living now, and if I think I can divorce her, I might as well forget it."

Peter could think of one perfectly good reason why a divorce would be impossible, but he didn't feel this was quite the time to bring it up.

"In view of what you've been telling me, Guthrie, perhaps it won't offend you too much if I get on to asking what I've been trying to work up nerve enough for."

"Such as what?"

"M'well, for instance, does the name Elisa Alicia Quatref-ages mean anything to you, other than that your wife insists on being called by it?"

Guthrie stared at him. "Isn't that enough? What the hell are you driving at? Why should it mean anything else?"

Instead of answering, Peter put another question. "Does the word Paraguay mean anything to you personally?"

"Hardwoods, mostly. Their principal export used to be a tanning agent made from the quebracho tree. Maybe it still is, I couldn't say. God knows what's happened to their economy in recent years, with all this clearing of rain forests. Unless they're smarter than some of their neighbors."

"That wasn't quite what I had in mind, Guthrie. When I said personally, I meant—er—personally. For instance, have you ever heard the word used with regard to your wife?"

Guthrie slammed down his glass and sat up straight. "No, by God, but I heard your wife use it with regard to those bastards who tried to drown her and Cat. Pete, are you trying to tell me Elisa's involved in that weather vane racket?"

"I'd like to be reassured that she isn't."

"So would I. What makes you think she might be?"

Peter finally got around to explaining. Guthrie didn't interrupt once. When his friend got through talking, all he said was, "So now what happens?"

"So now, if you'll forgive me, I want to search through your wife's personal effects and see whether we can find something that either clears her of suspicion or—"

"Lands her in the soup," Guthrie finished for him. "And me with her, I suppose. Okay, Pete. If it has to be done, now's as good a time as any."

EIGHTEEN

Whatever else Elisa Alicia Quatrefages might be, she was indubitably a dedicated bulrush gilder. Except for one bedroom that Guthrie had staked out for his own, she'd managed to fill the entire second floor with the raw materials of her craft. She had stocks of dried grapevines, dried milkweed, dried vegetable matter of all descriptions and some that even Peter found downright indescribable. She had Styrofoam in sheets, chunks, cones, spheres, rhomboids, and dodecahedrons. She had plastic flora and fauna; she had whimsical elves, gnomes, sprites, witches, pookas, and banshees. She had plywood cutouts of roosters, fish, pigs, sheep, cats, dogs, emus, wildebeests, apples, pears, papayas, cauliflower, Swiss chard, potatoes, tomatoes, kohlrabi, pomegranates, mangoes, and spaghetti squash.

"But yes, we have no bananas," Peter murmured. What anybody would want of all this stuff was beyond his comprehension.

From the looks of her ledgers, though, Elisa Alicia knew what she was doing. Peter blinked when he looked at her profit column.

"By George, Ms. Quatrefages has quite an enterprise going here."

Guthrie shrugged. "Does she? I keep my nose out of her affairs."

"You wouldn't know whether she—er—farms out work to housewives in the area, or anything of the sort?"

"No, Pete, she doesn't. That's one thing I would know, because I hoped when she first started doing this stuff that she might develop it into a sort of local cottage industry. Lots of folks around here would welcome a chance to earn a few extra dollars to help tide them over the winters. I suggested it once or twice when she was moaning about how she'd never be able to fill all the orders she was getting, but she got sore at me for thinking anybody else could ever meet her standards of artistry. What are you making faces at?"

"Take a look at these figures for her various accounts. Most of her total sales per store have run anywhere from a couple of hundred to a thousand dollars. I'd say that in itself was darned good money for one person working alone to earn from items that probably don't sell for more than thirty or forty dollars maximum at retail. But here's this Brasilia Boutique account. She appears to have raked in over twenty thousand so far this year from this one shop. How the flaming perdition does she do it? Can you tell me that?"

Guthrie rubbed his Lincolnesque jaw. "Damn good question. And I don't suppose we ought to overlook the coincidence between the shop's name being Brasilia and Childe's code name being Brazil. Jesus, Pete, what am I going to do?"

"Just keep on looking, Guthrie. There's got to be something more than this."

It took them another hour to find it, but there it was, inside a hollowed-out block of Styrofoam bedecked with purple velvet ribbons and plastic passion flowers hung on Elisa Alicia's bedroom wall. Elisa Alicia had kept a diary, covered in purple satin, written in purple ink. In code.

"What the hell is this?" Guthrie turned the pages in helpless wonderment. "Can you make any sense of it, Pete?"

"I don't know yet. Where's a mirror with a good light over it?"

"In the bathroom. Over here. Sheesh! Is that all she did?"

As the two men studied the characters, it became clear enough that Elisa Alicia had simply taken her inspiration from Leonardo da Vinci and formed her letters backward. The only hitch was, she hadn't written in English.

"I can't make head nor tail of it," Guthrie fretted. "Is it Latin or something?"

"Either French or Spanish, I'd say. Some kind of dialect, maybe. I'm no good at languages, but my wife is. Would you mind if we asked her to come over here and see what she can make of it?"

"I wouldn't mind, but Helen might. Maybe you don't realize what time it is, Pete. They're probably all in bed over there by now."

"Drat! No, I hadn't realized. And none of them got any sleep to speak of last night on that damned lump of rock. I suppose in common humanity we ought to wait till morning. On the other hand, they may still be sitting up talking things over. I tell you what, Guthrie, let's take this diary over to Catriona's and see what's happening. Is that okay with you?"

"I guess so." Guthrie didn't sound any too sure. "The only

thing is, if Helen can make out this gobbledygook, I'd just as soon she didn't read it out loud in front of everybody. God knows what Elisa may have written. I'm not even sure I want to hear it myself."

"Of course, Guthrie, I understand how you feel. Then why don't I just take it with me and go by myself? If Helen's asleep, I'll wait and show her the diary first thing in the morning. Your wife's not likely to come back and start looking for it tonight, is she?"

"God knows what she might do. Ah, go ahead and take the damn thing. If Elisa shows up, I'll distract her one way or another. Want me to walk over with you?"

"If you feel like it, sure."

They didn't talk much on the way to Catriona's. Peter was realizing how unspeakably tired he was. He hated to think about what was in Guthrie Fingal's mind just now. Well, maybe this diary would clear matters up between husband and wife, if in fact they were lawfully espoused. He had no reason to suppose it would.

Catriona had left the light on over the side door and a lamp burning in the kitchen. It was plain to see, however, that she and her two old friends were all tucked up for the night. Guthrie turned to go back to the school and Peter let himself in as silently as possible, considering how creaky the aged pine floor was.

The lady of the house had thoughtfully set out the whiskey bottle, a clean tumbler, and a plate of crackers on the kitchen table. In view of the exhausting evening he'd spent among the arts and crafts, Peter decided he'd earned a modest nightcap. He was sitting at the table with the untasted drink in front of him, nibbling on a cracker and poring over the diary in hope of finding some word he could recognize, when Helen slipped into the room and shut the door to the upstairs behind her.

"Peter, whatever are you sitting here for at this hour? You must be ready to drop. Come on up to bed."

"Yes, my love. Take a look at this, will you?"

"Purple satin? Heavens to Betsy, what is it? Somebody's diary?"

"I think so, but I can't read the plaguey thing. As far as I can tell, it's written backwards in Paraguayan."

"By Elisa Alicia Quatrefages, I gather. She sounds to me like just the type."

Helen picked up the small bound notebook and held it under the light. "Arcade writing and tightly closed small letters. I knew she had to be up to something. It seems to be a mixture of bad Spanish and worse French, with every third word misspelled. But oh, my! She's fluent enough in some areas. I hope Guthrie doesn't understand Spanish."

"Not a word, he thought it was Latin. Why? What does she say?"

"I'd blush to tell you, but it's not about Guthrie. Elisa Alicia has a boyfriend."

"Does she say who the guy is?"

"I don't know. So far it's just '*me amoor*.' I think she means '*mi amor*.' Or possibly '*mon amour*.' Make us some coffee, why don't you? and hand me that pad and pencil by the telephone."

"Drat it, Helen," Peter expostulated, "I didn't intend for you to sit up all night translating that thing. Er—wouldn't it be easier to read if you held the text up to a mirror?"

"I suppose it would."

She made no move to do so. Peter sighed and filled the teakettle. Catriona had left a jar of instant decaffeinated on the counter by the electric stove, he noticed. That would do well enough. He was suffering qualms of conscience about having shown Helen the book; at the same time he was itching to know what she was finding out. He wished his mind would make itself up. He spooned out coffee into two mugs, poured hot water over it, brought the mugs over to the table. That done, he sat down, trying not to fidget while she went on poring over the text and jotting down notes on Catriona's telephone pad in her small, precise librarian's handwriting.

Apparently he fidgeted, after all. Helen looked up from her work with just a shade of impatience. "Darling, why don't you go to bed and get some rest? You'll be doing most of the driving tomorrow, I expect, and I need time on this."

"You don't have to translate the whole damned thing tonight!"

"Of course I do. You don't think I could quit now, do you? Besides, Guthrie had better sneak the diary back first thing in the morning in case she comes bouncing home to write a new chapter. She's flaky enough to do anything, I should say from what I'm reading here. Give me a kiss and go tuck yourself in. I'll tell you all about it when I come up."

Exactly when Helen did come to bed was something Peter never knew. He woke in broad daylight to find her sound asleep by his side and a large orange cat with long sideburns purring on his chest. The cat seemed indisposed to move and Peter didn't hear anybody stirring or smell any breakfast being prepared, so he shut his eyes again.

When he woke again, the cat was gone and so was Helen. He bounded out of bed and started down the stairs. Then he remembered he'd slept in his underwear because he'd forgotten to pack pajamas, much less a robe. He scooted back to the guest room he'd shared with his wife, pulled on his rumpled trousers and that green blouse of Miss Binks's aunt, which he was getting awfully sick of wearing, and went downstairs.

"Ah, here's the sleeping beauty now."

Catriona, wearing a turquoise blue terry-cloth robe that appeared to function also as a scratching post for the marmalade coon cat and whatever other feline residents there might be, got up from the kitchen table and went to pour him a cup of coffee. Helen and Iduna were sitting there, the former in a trim pink seersucker housecoat and the latter in a confection of lace and baby blue ruffles straight out of *Godey's Lady's Book* that would have looked absurd on anybody else. Peter wasn't at all surprised to find Guthrie Fingal at the table, too.

"Drat it, Guthrie, if I'd known you were coming I'd have asked you to lend me a shirt. I was in such a dither to get away yesterday that I forgot to bring any clothes."

"That's some shirt you have on now, old buddy. Left over from Saint Patrick's Day, was it?"

"Actually it's a blouse which was purchased by the aunt of

a woman I met while Helen was away. The aunt died before she had a chance to wear the thing, so I'm helping my new acquaintance get some good out of it. Er—Helen, have you—"

"Yes, dear. We've all had our orange juice. Want some?"

"Why not? What happened to the cat?"

"Which cat?"

"The one who was using my chest for a chaise longue a while back when you were still rapt in slumber. A large, ruddy animal with peach-colored whiskers and a thoughtful expression. He reminded me a little of Rutherford B. Hayes."

"Oh, that must have been Thomas Carlyle," said Catriona. "I let him out when I came downstairs. He'll probably be back when he smells the bacon frying, which I suppose I ought to get on with. Carlyle never goes far."

"Unlike some people we could mention," said Guthrie with a wry twist to his mouth. "Pete, did you get a chance to—"

Peter looked at Helen. She nodded. "Whenever you say, dear." He then raised his eyebrows at Guthrie, who also nodded. Thereupon, Helen set down her coffee cup and cleared her throat.

"You know the things I've been saying about Elisa Alicia Quatrefages the First, so I needn't go into details about why Peter and Guthrie decided last night to make a search for more information about her namesake. They found a diary and brought it to me for translation since it's written backwards in a kind of multilingual hash. There are some words I haven't been able to figure out at all, I'm inclined to think she may have made them up. The gist, however, is that as we've suspected, the current Elisa Alicia is involved with Roland Childe and his gang."

Catriona reached across the table and laid her hand on her neighbor's. "Oh, Guthrie, I'm so sorry. Are you sure you want us to hear all this stuff?"

He made an odd little sound through his nose. "You'll hear it sooner or later anyway. Go on, Helen."

"What it boils down to is that Elisa Alicia is their superior officer. She's been giving Roland his orders, using that fellow John Buck who's been posing as a student here as a go-between. She's also been playing a very active part in organizing the thefts they've been pulling."

Peter interrupted, "Am I right in assuming the weather vane robberies are only the current phase?"

"I don't know, dear, but I should think it likely. Anyway, it was she who hatched that ridiculous plot of hijacking the *Ethelbert Nevin* to get the weather vanes away. She's supposed to be meeting the boat in New Haven today, you may be interested to know. Her part is to drive the weather vanes to New York and turn them over to somebody named B.B."

"B.B. probably stands for Brasilia Boutique," said Peter. "If she's using the shop to fence stolen goods, that would explain what we found in the ledger, Guthrie."

"Yeah, Pete. I've been wondering about Elisa's ledger. I'm surprised she'd bother to account for her share of the money like that. Why doesn't she just pretend she never got any?"

"She's smarter to account for what she collects than try to get away with not declaring it," said Catriona. "Income tax evasion has jailed plenty of racketeers who couldn't be caught any other way. Besides, she needs some plausible way to account for all the money she's been throwing around on jewelry and Cadillacs. Helen, you're not trying to tell us Elisa Alicia is actually the brains behind this weather vane ring?"

"No. She's second in command, I gather. Paraguay's the leader, not the buyer. He's head of what seems to be a fairly large and varied operation and also—I'm sorry, Guthrie—her lover."

"What's his real name?" Guthrie didn't sound particularly interested.

"She never says. She does mention that he's behind that crowd at Woeful Ridge. Elisa Alicia appears to be under the delusion that they're all working together on behalf of some noble and glorious cause."

"What cause?"

"She doesn't say that, either. I'm not sure she's any too clear, herself. What she writes doesn't always make a great deal of sense to me. My translation may be terribly faulty, of course."

"I doubt that," Guthrie grunted. "Elisa's never made a hell of a lot of sense to me, either. So that's the story?"

"That's the part that counts. The diary isn't very long, actually. She hasn't written in it every day—only when the spirit moves her, I gather. A good deal of it's about her personal feelings and so forth, which you probably wouldn't be interested in hearing. I didn't bother to translate much of that."

Liar, thought Peter fondly. "Did you get any clue to whether Elisa Alicia Quatrefages is her real name?"

"I'm fairly sure it isn't. Apparently her true identity came to her in a great psychic revelation while she was in Rio de Janeiro drinking a rum swizzle. She believes herself to be the reincarnation of Ella Lynch."

"Then why doesn't she call herself Ella Lynch?"

"I couldn't tell you, dear. Perhaps it's all part of the cloak and dagger thing, or perhaps her real name actually is Ella Lynch and she found that too prosaic."

"Nobody names a girl Ella these days," Catriona objected. "It's more likely Alice or Lisa, wouldn't you think?"

"Ah, what difference does it make?" Guthrie growled.

"It could make a hell of a lot of difference if she married you under an alias," said Peter.

"It could make even more difference if she never married you at all," Helen added. "There's something in the diary about divorce that puzzles me, Guthrie. She said you'd asked her for one and she couldn't help laughing to think why she'd never be able to give it to you."

"Well, I'll be damned!" said Guthrie. "That's something to think about, all right. Want a hand with that bacon, Cat?"

NINETEEN

"All's well that ends well," said Helen.

In fact, nothing had ended yet, and Helen knew it perfectly well. She and Peter were alone in their own car. Guthrie Fingal had turned over to his assistants the reins of office, which he said were pretty slack just now anyway, and offered to drive Iduna and her car back to Balaclava Junction. Catriona had turned over the cat feeding to Andrew, who was still only a surly muttering at the back door as far as the Shandys had been able to discover, and come along with Guthrie and Iduna because she wasn't about to be left out of whatever was going to happen next.

"I expect my next move is to get on with the translation," Helen added. "I promised the sheriff I'd send him one as quickly as possible."

They'd decided at the breakfast table that they'd be crazy to put Elisa Alicia's diary back where they'd found it and risk having so vital a clue destroyed. They'd attempted to turn their find over to the Hocasquam sheriff, since according to protocol he seemed the likeliest person. However, the sheriff said he'd had trouble enough with the prisoners yesterday and why didn't Helen just hang onto the diary until she'd got it all figured out? By that time they'd know who was handling the case and it would be somebody else's headache instead of his.

That made sense. Furthermore, Helen was eager to sit

down with her dictionaries and work out a complete translation along with a short biographical sketch of the original
Elisa Alicia.

"Sounds like a good idea to me," said Peter. "Mine is to
get hold of Swope and find out what's going on. I tried to
phone him from Catriona's but he wasn't around. I left a
message that we'd be home early this afternoon, so with any
luck he'll be perched on the doorstep waiting for us."

"Does he know his brother is off the hook?"

"I expect so by now. After we got to Catriona's yesterday,
I called the *Fane and Pennon* to let them know the weather
vanes stolen from the soap factory and Gabe Fescue's barn
have been recovered, and five suspects taken into custody. I
asked for Swope, but he wasn't around and they didn't seem
to know where he was. He's probably trying to call Catriona's house now and having kitten fits because nobody's
answering. I can't imagine why he never phoned me last
night, though. I left her number with the woman at the news
desk. He could have got it from the Enderbles anyway. I just
hope to Christ Swope hasn't gone scouting off on his own and
got into trouble again."

"Surely Cronkite wouldn't have gone back to Woeful
Ridge," Helen protested.

"If he did, he ought to have his head examined. Unless he
took Miss Binks with him. That woman's a whole team and
the dog under the wagon all by herself. Damn, this is a long
ride. I wish we had that helicopter back."

"Peter dear, Balaclava County managed to get along
without you all day yesterday. I expect they can manage for
another few hours. You'd better either slow down or let me
drive before we wind up either in the hoosegow or in the
hospital."

"Oh, sorry." He let up a little on the gas pedal. "You've
got those snapshots Catriona found of Guthrie's wife. Or
nonwife, as I fervently hope the case may be. We've got to
get them down to the New Haven police some way or other.
Maybe Roy Ames will take them, if he's around. He's the
next best thing to a helicopter any day."

"Yes, dear." Helen was back at the purple diary. Peter left

her to it and concentrated on his driving. He didn't quite know what else to concentrate on.

"Drat, I wish she'd left some kind of clue as to who this mastermind may be or at least what he looks like."

"He's short, fat, bowlegged, and given to wearing fancy uniforms," Helen replied absently.

"Where does it say that?"

"*Woman on Horseback*, William E. Barrett, Doubleday, 1952. Though there may have been an earlier printing in 1938. I must verify the reference."

"Don't bother on my account. Your thesis being, I gather, that since Elisa Alicia considers herself a reincarnation of Ella Lynch, she'd naturally choose a paramour who's a reincarnation of Francisco Lopez?"

"Well, of course. Wouldn't you? I can't imagine what she ever saw in Guthrie. He's too tall, too thin, too unpretentious, and much too good-looking."

"It's obvious to me what she saw in him," Peter replied waspishly. "Namely and to wit, a sucker. Guthrie was able to provide her with a respectable identity and a base of operations which has no doubt doubled as a hideout whenever she's needed one, as I can't imagine she hasn't. God, I'll be glad when he's rid of that harpy."

"Yes, darling." Helen had her nose in the diary again. "I wish I knew more Spanish obscenity. Those night classes I attended in California didn't equip me for this sort of translation."

" 'Dash dash dash you, Harold Ramorez, what did you bite me for?' " murmured Peter.

"I hope the sheriff in Hocasquam can interpret dashes," Helen retorted.

"He dashed well better had, though I'm sure he won't be the final arbiter of this case."

"Who will?"

"*Quién sabe?* I expect Maine and Massachusetts will just keep passing the buck from echelon to echelon until somebody sees the chance for juicy headlines and grabs it by the horns. Want to make a pit stop? Speak now or forever hold your—"

"Peter. I'm getting enough scatology from Elisa Alicia. Yes, I'd like to stop. I feel like doing something mad and reckless, like buying a Pepsi-Cola and a bag of potato chips."

"Gad, woman! Turn you loose in the wilds of Maine and you come out a reincarnation of Pearl White. Very well, my love, I'll stand you a Pepsi, but I'm damned if I'll help you drink it."

"I wouldn't let you anyway. You're driving, don't forget."

Guthrie, who'd been tagging Peter all the way from Sasquamahoc, pulled in directly after them. Somehow or other, the entire party wound up sitting at the counter eating banana splits. There was, Iduna reminded them, a lot of potassium in a banana.

Thus fortified, they proceeded southward into Massachusetts and westward to Balaclava Junction. Iduna wanted to go straight home in order to get in a few preliminary cooking licks toward Daniel's homecoming feast, so Catriona and Guthrie delivered her and her car to Valhalla, then walked across campus to the Crescent.

By the time they got to the Shandys', Helen and Peter had made their peace with Jane Austen, who was not a cat to hold a grudge beyond reasonable limits. Helen was opening the mail, which Mary Enderble had been scrupulously fetching from the mailbox and stacking on the dining room table. Peter was on the phone to the *Balaclava County Fane and Pennon*.

"When did you last— That long, eh? Well, as soon as he calls in, please tell him Professor Shandy's back home and wants very much to get in touch with him. He knows my number."

Peter gave it anyway and came back to join his wife and friends, considerably disgruntled. "Drat the fellow, why can't he stay put once in a while? Even Swope's editor doesn't know where he's gone or what he's up to. The old coot sounds pretty teed off about it, I may add. Which reminds me, Catriona, you may feel a tad miffed when you get your phone bill. I owe you for a couple of long-distance calls."

He moved to take out his wallet, but Catriona stopped him. "Not to worry, Peter. I'll take them off my expense account."

"Would it be unsporting of me to ask on what grounds?"

"Research, naturally. You don't think for one moment I'm going to let a plot like this go to waste, do you? I won't tell it quite the way it happened and none of you will recognize yourselves by the time I get through, but you'll be there in spirit. I think I'll have a beautiful red-haired heroine with skinny hips and a perfectly flat stomach. The type who can eat a banana split without experiencing instantaneous tightening of the waistband."

"Yes, why don't you?" said Helen. "She'll be an inspiration to us all. I'm going to make some tea and find out whether there's anything to eat in the house. Unless you'd prefer to try the faculty dining room?"

"You three go ahead over there if you're hungry," said Peter. "I've got to wait here in case Swope calls back."

Nobody wanted to leave him alone, so they all four crowded into the small kitchen and ate fried egg sandwiches, which Guthrie had suggested as the most incongruous follow-up to a banana split appetizer that he could think of. Helen was breaking out her emergency stock of ginger snaps to go with the tea when Cronkite Swope finally telephoned.

"Gosh, Professor, I'm glad I caught you. Can you meet me in front of the soap works in fifteen minutes?"

"Has it quit sudsing?"

"Pretty much, but you'd better wear your old clothes."

"Why? What's happening?"

"I can't tell you on the phone. Top secret maneuvers."

"How long is the secret going to take? We have out-of-town guests."

"I can't tell you that, either. Maybe quite a while. I just don't know. But you've got to come, Professor. We really need you. Besides, you'll hate yourself if you don't."

"I'll be there."

What else could he say? But drat it, why now? Peter wouldn't have minded a short rest after that long drive, and a chance to catch up on his cat patting. Helen was looking a trifle pinched around the mouth as he hung up the phone.

"What was that about?"

"Swope wants me to meet him over at Lumpkin Upper Mills right away. I'm sorry, everybody, but he's all wrought up about something and he wouldn't tell me what. I asked how long we'd be, but he doesn't seem to know. Excuse me, everybody, I've go to run upstairs and change out of this dratted green shirt."

"Sure, Pete," said Guthrie. "Say, is there any place around here where Cat and I can rent a car? She and I decided on the way down that we ought to be the ones to go to New Haven and see if we can spot Elisa. We'd stand a better chance than the police would of recognizing her, specially if Elisa's in disguise, which I wouldn't put past her. Besides, I've got a few things I want to say to that dame before they lug her off."

"You'd better be careful how you approach her," Peter warned. "She might have a gun on her by now."

Guthrie snorted. "She wears her clothes so cussed tight a gun would stick out like a sore thumb. Don't fret yourself about me, Pete. I'm not aiming to put Cat in any danger, nor myself either. What about that car?"

Helen was already on the phone. "Charlie Ross has one he'll rent you, but you'll have to bring it back here," she reported. "That will be fine, because then we'll get to see you again. Peter will take you to Charlie's. I'd go, but I have to prepare that written translation of the diary, which will take me the rest of the day, at least. Do be careful, all of you."

"Never mind us," Peter retorted. "You be careful. I don't like leaving you alone here with that passionate purple time bomb. I'm going to call Fred Ottermole to come and sit with you till we get back."

"Peter, that's ridiculous. Elisa Alicia doesn't know we have her diary, and I doubt if Paraguay knows it exists. Oh, all right, if it will make you feel any better. Fred can keep Jane company. He's good with cats."

Peter made sure Fred Ottermole was available, then he ran upstairs, changed the green shirt for a sober gray and brown plaid, kissed his wife, tickled Jane's whiskers, and steered his friends to Charlie Ross's garage. Charlie had the rental car all gassed up and ready to go. While he was refilling the

Shandy vehicle's depleted tank, Peter bought a couple of peanut bars from the slot machine. He was not about to be caught foodless again in the midst of whatever escapade Cronkite Swope might be about to lead him into. Thus prepared, he told Charlie to put the gas on his monthly bill, and took off hell-for-leather toward Lumpkinton.

From a distance, the soap factory's ruins in their nest of grimy suds looked like a mouthful of neglected teeth with pyorrhea around the gums. Up close, they probably looked a good deal worse, but Peter didn't stop to notice. Cronkite Swope had been standing right where he'd said he'd be. When he saw Peter's car, he came running up the street, his camera on its strap thumping against his chest with every step. Profiting from sad experience, he'd eschewed his usual natty garb in favor of blue jeans and a plain gray sweatshirt that might actually have been Miss Binks's. Peter pulled over to the curb. Cronkite leaped in beside him and fastened his seat belt.

"Hi, Professor! Gosh, I'm glad you could make it. You're just in the nick of time."

"For what?"

"The invasion of Woeful Ridge. That's what I couldn't tell you on the phone. It's top secret. The National Guard are moving in and the SWAT team are set to attack in precisely"—he glanced at his watch—"thirty-seven minutes. We'd better step on it. Cut through South Plum Street, why don't you? I know a shortcut."

"My God!"

That was all Peter had time to say until Cronkite had finished directing him through a spiderweb of back streets and out to the highway they had traversed together such an amazingly short time ago. Something in the vicinity of fifty years would have been a more reasonable lapse, Peter felt.

Once they were on a straight road, he could relax enough to talk. "What are you talking about, Swope? Who organized this brouhaha? You make it sound like a full-scale military operation."

"It is one."

Cronkite was checking his camera as thoroughly as a

mother cat washes her kitten's ears. He'd got some memorable news photographs in the past; but this, he clearly felt, would be an opportunity to surpass them all.

"What's going to happen, Professor, is, first the National Guard unit cordons off Woeful Ridge. Then the Lumpkinton SWAT team moves up behind the ridge under riot shields. Then Chief Olson rides up in an armored car with a bullhorn on it and yells to the survivalists to surrender."

"Chief Olson? How in Sam Hill did that tub of lard get in on an operation like this?"

"He had to be. I went over and talked to Mrs. Wetzel, the county district attorney, as you told me to. Mrs. Wetzel said we had to refer the case back to Chief Olson because that's how the system works. But Olson's been terrific. Honest, Professor, I wouldn't have thought he had it in him."

"Don't tell me he was the one who thought of getting the National Guard involved."

"He sure did. Or maybe it was his wife. One of Mrs. Olson's cousins is the local commandant over at Clavaton Armory. But it was Olson himself who thought of organizing a SWAT team. He got a couple of experts out from Boston to show them how and they've been secretly drilling ever since Tuesday afternoon. They're only going to shoot rubber bullets. Olson doesn't want any of the survivalists to get killed because he's afraid they might turn out to be some of Mrs. Olson's cousins."

"A point to consider," said Peter. "And where do you and I fit into the scheme of things?"

"Well, naturally, Chief Olson wants a representative of the press along to cover the story and I'm the only one who's in on the secret. And he wants you because you were with me the first time. We have to show them exactly where the ammo dump is. That's what Chief Olson calls it."

"Do we go in shooting rubber bullets?"

"Oh, no. We ride in the armored car with Chief Olson and his driver. The only thing is, I don't know whether I'll be able to take any decent photographs through that bullet-proof glass. Do you think I'll be allowed to roll the window down a little?"

He damned well wouldn't if Peter Shandy had anything to say about it. Peter was wondering what made Olson think he could drive his armored car all the way in to the cache, and just how effective those riot shields might be against real bullets,

Cronkite must have noticed that Peter wasn't sharing his enthusiasm. "What's the matter, Professor? You're not worried, are you?"

"I admit to being a trifle concerned about what President Svenson's going to say when he gets back from Sweden and learns we participated in a fracas of this magnitude without letting him in on it." Better a liar than a branded poltroon, Peter thought—though in fact it wasn't a lie at all because Svenson would be apoplectic.

"Yeah, but if he were here they wouldn't need the National Guard or the SWAT team," Cronkite replied, also with perfect truth. "Then the raid wouldn't have the same dramatic visual impact. I'm hoping to get some really good shots."

"I just hope you don't intercept any good shots," Peter retorted. "And myself likewise."

"Oh, they've probably got extra bulletproof vests and stuff we can use." Cronkite was beginning to sound a shade less ebullient. "I know what you mean, though. It wasn't much fun out there in the swamp, was it? Gosh, I hope Miss Binks is safely under cover. I couldn't tell Olson about her, of course. I did sneak over last night and hide a note under her bicycle. I don't suppose she goes there all that often, but I didn't know what else to do. I knew I'd never find any of her rabbit holes, she's got them so well hidden. Anyway, it seemed sort of intrusive even to try."

"Furthermore, you'd have been a damned fool to go prowling around those woods at night by yourself," Peter growled. "Not to change the subject, but has Sam Snell come to any decision yet about reopening the soap factory?"

"Yes, he's decided to go off on his yacht and think it over. I tried to get an interview with him yesterday morning, but he was in a tearing hurry to get away and wouldn't talk to me."

"His yacht. Where in Sam Hill does Snell keep a yacht?" Balaclava County was rather noticeably short on navigable waterways.

"Oh, he belongs to a yacht club somewhere down around New Haven so he can hobnob with the rich Connecticut and New York bunch. He was yammering about having to meet some friends, and it must be well over a two-hour drive from here, I should think. I've never done it myself. Neither has he, of course. His chauffeur takes him." Cronkite got enough venom into the word "chauffeur" to supply a colony of vipers.

"M'yes," said Peter thoughtfully. "And what's happening in your family situation?"

"It ought to be starting to perk up about now." Cronkite reached under his sweatshirt and pulled out a copy of the *Balaclava County Fane and Pennon*, still smelling of fresh printer's ink. "We're an afternoon paper, you know, and we've just begun to hit the streets with the story you called in. How does that headline grab you?"

Peter glanced over at the paper. " 'Arson Suspects Caught in Maine. Priceless Lumpkin Weather Vane Recovered in Wreck of Pirate Ship.' Great Scott, what does it say?"

" 'According to a reliable informant'—that's you, Professor—'a Clavaton man apprehended in Maine on a charge of attempted murder is also the arsonist who set fire to the Lumpkin Soap Works, in an attempt to cover up the theft of the Praxiteles Lumpkin weather vane that has been a Lumpkinton landmark for the past century and a half. He and four accomplices were attempting to deliver the weather vanes to an undisclosed destination in a stolen boat when they were picked up by the U.S. Coast Guard working in cooperation with the Hocasquam police. The five are now in custody awaiting arraignment, and the famous old man in the tub, along with two other Lumpkin masterpieces valued at upward of $100,000 apiece, are being held as evidence. More details will be reported as soon as they are available.' "

Cronkite tossed the paper into the backseat. "I'm sure grateful to you for calling in the story. It would have been nice if we'd got in a few more details, but at least this ought to keep Brink from being tarred and feathered. Do you honestly think they've got the right guy?"

"I know it for a positive fact. His name is Roland Childe and he comes from Clavaton. He answers Huntley's description and he did exactly what your brother described him as doing. I expect we're going to learn that one of the other four men had been planted in the factory as a workman. This man, whose code name is probably Argentina, Colombia, or Venezuela, most likely sneaked up to the roof under cover of darkness, detached the weather vane from its base, and lowered it over the side of the building to a confederate waiting below, who was either Childe or one of the other three. The four accomplices were all ratting like mad when I last saw them, so we'll probably have the complete facts very soon."

"You were in on the pinch?"

"I was, yes. So were my wife and Iduna Stott, whom you know, along with an old friend of theirs named Catriona McBogle and my college roommate, Guthrie Fingal, who also had his weather vane stolen. I'll give you a complete eyewitness account as soon as you have time to write it down. By that time, if I'm not grievously mistaken, you'll be able to write the final chapter for yourself."

TWENTY

The first things Peter and Cronkite saw when they pulled off the highway were half a dozen National Guard trucks parked as far off the dirt road into Woeful Ridge as they could get, which wasn't quite far enough. Peter barely managed to squeak by.

"How far in do you think we ought to go, Swope? I'd as soon not get my car trashed in the fracas."

"I can't blame you for that, Professor, after what happened to mine. Look, there's another bunch of transport trucks up ahead. They must have brought a whole battalion. Why don't you pull in just behind them? We can walk the rest of the way. It's not more than half a mile from here."

"One might have thought they'd send an armored car for us," Peter joked.

As it turned out, they had. Peter and Cronkite hadn't gone more than a couple of hundred yards when Chief Olson pulled up beside them in an impressive vehicle he must have borrowed from somewhere. Olson was in police uniform and so was the driver.

"The very guys I was looking for!" the police chief called out. "Hop in the back seat, quick. Glad you could make it, Professor. I had my people try to call your house a couple of times, but couldn't get an answer."

"I was called out of town unexpectedly," Peter explained. "Naturally, I had no idea all this was going on. I just got back an hour or so ago."

"Well, better late than never."

Chief Olson appeared to be in a remarkably chipper mood. Peter couldn't recall having seen the man smile before, not that he ever saw much of him anyway. He wondered whether Olson's uniform was always this well pressed, and if the brass buttons always glittered like nuggets in a well-salted mine.

Now that he'd noticed, Peter wondered why the buttons were brass. He'd thought that sort of button was supplanted long ago by utilitarian chrome. Fred Ottermole, Balaclava Junction's police chief, had silver-colored buttons on his uniform jacket, not that Fred ever wore it much. On a warm day like this, he'd be in blue shirt sleeves—clean ones, to be sure, for Fred's wife Edna Mae was most particular about maintaining the dignity of his rank even if Fred wasn't. Too bad he couldn't be here, Peter thought. Ottermole liked a good scrap almost as much as Thorkjeld Svenson did.

And now Olson was showing himself pugnacious where Peter had always assumed him merely cantankerous. "We have to wait just below the ridge till the SWAT team moves up," he was explaining, "then I take charge. I yell through this mouthpiece here, and it comes out good and loud through that bullhorn mounted on the roof. If they don't surrender right away, the SWAT team proceeds forward and the National Guard guys start moving up on Woeful Ridge till they've got it completely encircled. Everybody holds their fire till I give the signal."

"Glad to hear it," said Peter. "Er—if the troops are in a circle, wouldn't they be firing at each other if they did let fly?"

"Of course they wouldn't!" That was the Olson he knew, mad as a wet hen at the merest hint of criticism. "What the hell do you think we are, a bunch of incompetent jackasses?"

"On the contrary," Peter hastened to assure him, "this looks to me like a thoroughly professional operation. I marvel that you've been able to get it together in so short a time."

Olson puffed himself up like a toad swallowing air, which in fact he somewhat resembled. "It took one hell of a lot of organization, let me tell you. So anyway, once we've got 'em trapped, you, Swope, and I move up with the SWAT team and you show us where that ammo dump is. Don't worry, Professor, we'll make sure you're well protected."

"That's heartening news, Chief Olson. I'm sure we'll be—er—perfectly safe in your competent hands."

That was hyperbole of the first water. The only thing Peter was sure of was that he wished he hadn't been in such an all-fired hurry to leave Maine. However, he was too near the end of the tunnel to start backing up now. As they neared the ridge, he found himself experiencing the kind of euphoria Cronkite Swope had been showing a while back, but was failing to exhibit now.

"Er—Swope, why don't you try a close-up shot of Chief Olson here in the armored car?" he suggested. "Can you do that?"

Cronkite brightened up a little. "I could try, though it's kind of close quarters. I'll have to use the flash."

"No flash," Olson barked. "We can't risk alerting the enemy prematurely."

The enemy, no less! If twelve truckloads of National Guardsmen and a dratted great big armored car hadn't already alerted that handful of thugs, Peter hardly thought one tiny flash from Swope's camera would make the difference. However, he decided not to say so. Olson was beginning to stick his jaw out like the late General Patton. This was his moment of glory, why try to spoil it?

A man in olive drab, using approved jungle tactics, sneaked up to the car and tapped lightly three times at the heavy plate-glass window on the chief's side. Olson's driver, who so far hadn't said a word or even glanced back at Peter and Cronkite, touched a button that opened a little slide in the glass.

"Troops all deployed according to plan, Chief Olson. The captain says to tell you we're ready when you are."

"Good. Now where's the SWAT leader?"

As if on cue, another man stepped out from behind a tree. At least Peter assumed it was a man. Head, body, arms, legs, hands, and feet were covered in protective gear of various sorts. Peter saw Cronkite brighten, and began to feel a bit easier himself. If this was what they'd be dressed like up on the ridge, that walk to the ammo dump might be clumsy going but it could hardly be dangerous unless they happened to step on a land mine. Peter studied him, her, or it in growing fascination as he, she, or again it reported that the SWAT team was also in position and on the qui vive.

"Then let's move," said Olson grimly. "Thirty seconds to take cover, then we smoke 'em out."

"Can I take a picture now?" whispered Cronkite.

"No," barked Chief Olson. "Stay where you are and don't move a muscle."

He was listening for shots, Peter assumed. There were none to be heard. Some bluejays were making a fuss and Peter did think he heard a Blackburnian warbler, but that was all.

"Stubborn buggers," grunted Olson. "We'll show 'em. Gun 'er, Bert."

Peter stiffened, and not in fear. "This is what we've been waiting for, Swope! We're heading down the home stretch."

Cronkite flashed Peter a startled look but didn't try to say anything in reply. He wouldn't have been able to make himself heard. Chief Olson was proving to have a natural affinity with bullhorns.

"All right, you buggers, we've got you surrounded. Drop your weapons and come out with your hands up or you'll damn well wish you had."

The car was on the move. They were in full sight of Woeful Ridge now, heading straight up that natural escarpment Peter had noticed on his earlier visit. This car must have spiked tires, he thought, or else treads like an army tank. Swope was holding his camera up to the window, ready to start snapping at the crucial moment.

But there didn't seem to be any crucial moment. The SWAT team was crouching there, ready to charge, but had nothing to charge at. Not a survivalist was in sight.

"They're hiding, the crawling yellow-bellies," snarled Olson. He yelled into the mouthpiece, "Come out, you lily-livered cowards, before we blow you out."

They waited what seemed like an endless time, but nobody came.

"This is it, then! Ready, SWAT team? Go get 'em. Ready, National Guard? Fire one!"

Howling ferociously, the SWAT team went over the top. From all around Woeful Ridge, rifle shots resounded. Olson turned around, all agrin.

"Don't get your water hot, Professor. One means fire into the air."

"Thank you for telling me," Peter responded politely. "The—er—enemy don't seem very responsive, do they?"

"They'll respond, don't you worry. They damned well better."

Olson let forth another blast which Penrod Schofield would have recorded in a whole paragraph of dashes. That didn't work, either. After a while, the SWAT team started walking toward the car. Furious, Olson flung open the door and stuck his head out.

"What the hell's the matter with you stumblebums? What are you coming back here for?"

"We can't find anybody," whined the SWAT leader. "There's no sign of them anywhere."

"Are you crazy? Get me the National Guard captain."

"They can't find anybody, either. I already asked."

Olson swiveled around in his seat and glared at the two in the back. "Swope, are you sure we got the right place?"

"Of course I'm sure! How the heck many Woeful Ridges do you think there are around here? We didn't see any sign of anybody the first time, either, till that guy caught us in the ammo dump. Then all of a sudden there was a whole swarm of them tearing the staff car apart. I told you right at the beginning how it happened. They must have an underground hideout or something."

"Yeah, or something." Olson was sneering. "Come on then, you two. Lead me to this ammo dump, pronto."

"You mean just the way we are?" stammered Cronkite. "Without any riot gear or anything?"

"Without any riot gear or anything," mocked the police chief. "Okay, Munch, give this little boy here your riot gear. You'll have to button his buttons for him and tie his itsy-witsy shoelaces 'cause he ain't old enough to know how. Maybe you'd like to run home and get your teddy bear for company, Swope. Come on, you blubbering jellyfish, we haven't got all afternoon. I'm not scared, why the hell should you be? Let's get this farce over with."

"A splendid suggestion," said Peter. "I'll be happy to join you, Chief Olson, if your man there will kindly push whatever button opens this confounded door. Ah, thank you, sir. Coming, Swope?"

"Sure, Professor, if you are."

Spurning the riot gear that the SWAT man was playfully holding out to him, Cronkite sprang over the top of the ridge. "Let me know if I'm going too fast for you, Chief Olson."

"You go as fast as you've a mind to, sonny. I'll keep up, never you fear."

And, by George, he would, Peter thought. Those chunky

little bowlegs of Olson's could cover the ground at an amazing rate. This whole situation was pretty amazing. He ought to be scared stiff, he supposed.

"It's right through here. See, there's the cave opening."

Cronkite paused for just a moment. Olson moved up. "Scared, sonny? Let me go first."

"Wait a minute, Chief," said the leader of the SWAT team. "We'd better go first, with the riot gear and all."

He'd redonned the protective garments Cronkite had spurned. Without them, he'd have been an unimpressive character, Peter thought, the sort who might be found in any mob. With them on, he was formidable. Even his chief was willing to step aside.

"Okay, if you want," Olson conceded. "I guess that's what you're getting paid for. So what's the drill, Professor?"

"You'll find the cave appears to end very quickly in a blank wall. On the right-hand side of that wall, you'll see a darkish patch about chest high. Push on that patch, and the whole wall pivots."

"I'll be damned. Come on, men, let's move!"

Holding their shield in front of them, half a dozen SWAT men moved cautiously toward the cave. They were not challenged. Inch by inch, they made their way inside. Then they erupted like a swarm of angry hornets.

"This guy's nuttier than a fruitcake," yowled the leader. "There's nothing inside but a heap of fallen rock."

"Let me take a look," said Peter.

"Sure, look all you want. Take a few chunks home with you for souvenirs." The National Guard captain was looking bewildered.

Olson was furious, and showing it. "Swope, I'm going to get you for this."

"What are you jumping on Swope for?" Peter demanded. "It's perfectly obvious what's happened here. Those so-called survivalists got wind of your projected raid, evacuated their stores, and blew the place up. If you're going to get anybody, get a demolition expert out here to show you how it was done."

Olson explained in lurid physiological detail precisely what Peter Shandy could do with his demolition expert. "You're damn right it's obvious," he added when he'd blown off enough steam to be coherent. "This young punk friend of yours got the bright idea of faking a raid to get a big story for his lousy paper and take the heat off his brother. And he conned you into backing him up, Shandy, because you're a goddamn bleeding heart like all you college kooks. Maybe you can fool Shandy, Swope, but you're not fooling me one bit. I'm taking you in on a charge of obstructing justice and committing a fraud, and I'm arresting your brother Brinkley as soon as I get back to Lumpkinton."

Cronkite gritted his teeth. "On what charge, Chief Olson?"

"You know damned well what charge. On the charge of setting fire to the Lumpkin soap factory and killing Caspar Flum. Arson and manslaughter, that's what charge. I ought to go for first-degree murder, but seeing Brink's a local boy, I'll try to get him off easy. Not that he deserves any clemency, and neither do you. I've known for the past fifteen minutes that you lied to me. And you want to know how I knew? Look what my boys found over here!"

Shooing Swope and Shandy in front of him like a couple of errant turkeys, Olson herded them to the byway where they'd last seen Swope's 1974 Plymouth being pounded to pieces. "You told me last time you were here, your car was demolished by the survivalists, right?"

"I told you we'd seen it in the process of being demolished," Cronkite amended. "They'd ripped off the doors, they were smashing the windows with clubs, denting the top and fenders. The trunk was sprung and hanging open, and they had the hood up, ripping out the wires."

"Yeah, sure." Olson gave the young reporter a shove that sent him stumbling forward. "Go take a good, close look."

There sat a green 1974 Plymouth sedan, not in the best of shape but with its doors and windows intact, its body undented, its hood in place, and its trunk properly shut. The painted words BALACLAVA COUNTY FANE AND PENON were clearly visible on both doors and across the back.

"That's not my car!" Cronkite shouted. "It can't be."

"That so? You got the keys and registration on you, by any chance?"

"I certainly do. Check that car out for yourself."

"Damned right, I will." The chief took the keys Cronkite thrust at him and handed it over to the SWAT leader. "Here, Munch, like he says, check it out. Careful, there might be a few sticks of dynamite or something wired to the starter."

"Sure, Chief, or a couple of live alligators in the driver's seat."

In great spirits, the team bounced over to the car. Peter and Cronkite followed. By now, Peter was firmly convinced that the registration and serial numbers would be found correct, and they were. He knew the key would fit, and it did. When Cronkite still insisted this couldn't be the newspaper's staff car, Peter squeezed his arm.

"You'd better let the matter drop, Swope. It would appear that Chief Olson has an airtight case here."

"But can't you see?"

"Certainly I can see. Can't you see?"

Swope gaped at Peter in astonishment for a moment. Then, surprisingly, he grinned. "Yeah, I see. Sure I see! So now what do we do?"

"M'well, since Chief Olson was kind enough to offer us a lift on the way in, I believe I'll invite him to ride back to Balaclava Junction with me. You can follow in the—er—staff car, Swope."

"What the hell would I want to go with you for?" growled Olson.

Peter glanced around as if to make sure the SWAT personnel were out of earshot. "I thought that perhaps on the way you and I might have a little private chat about some of our mutual acquaintances."

"Such as who?"

"Such as Roland Childe and his four trolls, for starters. I gather you haven't yet seen today's newspaper."

TWENTY-ONE

"All I can say to you, Shandy, is this had better be good."

The mere fact that Olson was now sitting in the front seat of Peter Shandy's car was all the assurance Peter needed that it would be. What he said was, "Read it for yourself."

Peter passed over the *Fane and Pennon* he'd retrieved from the backseat. After one glance at the headlines, Olson gave a pretty good impression of having been struck with something other than a rubber bullet. He read the article through without making any comment, but his face was bright cerise by the time he got through.

"So? What's this, another of those journalistic fairytales? They haven't got any proof, have they?"

"Not unless you count the testimonies of two attempted murder victims and one eyewitness, plus the fact that the gang brought the stolen weather vanes on board with them when they came to hijack the boat. You may be interested to know that when they were being interrogated, they all put cyanide capsules in their mouths, except for Roland Childe. His turned out to be a lemon jellybean."

"Why, that—" Olson tripped over his tongue and had to start again. "That's a damned hard yarn to swallow, Shandy."

"You may wish to check it out with Ensign Blaise and the crew of the Coast Guard boat that picked them up. I have the boat's number written down somewhere. I'll give it to you when we get to Balaclava Junction. You could also talk with

Eustace Tilkey of Hocasquam, Maine, who owns the boat they hijacked and wrecked, and with those members of the gang who've turned state's witnesses. They all spat out their cyanide capsules, I should explain, and seemed quite relieved to do so. Peru and Argentina were doing most of the talking when I last saw them."

"Peru and Argentina? You trying to be funny or something?" Chief Olson was clearly not amused.

"Those are code names," Peter explained. "I find them as absurd as you do. Childe is Brazil, and the ringleader of the operation is known to us so far as Paraguay. He wasn't among those apprehended in Maine, but he'll be easy enough to nab."

"Oh yeah? You sound pretty damned sure of yourself, Shandy."

"With reason, Chief Olson. For one thing, we've obtained an excellent description of him from—er—a reliable source. He's said to be short, fat, bowlegged, and given to the wearing of ostentatious uniforms, among other things."

"What other things?"

"I couldn't begin to tell you at this point, but there's a fairly comprehensive dossier in the diary."

"Whose diary?" Olson was beginning to simmer.

"That of the woman who calls herself Elisa Alicia Quatrefages. She's Paraguay's—er—light of love."

Olson was now at full rolling boil. "Where's that diary?"

"Right now it's in my house at Balaclava Junction. My wife's in the midst of making a full written translation."

"The hell she is! I want that diary."

"I'm quite sure you can't have it," Peter demurred. "I'm not sure of the protocol, but I rather think it has to be sent back to the sheriff at Hocasquam, then go through the—er—proper official channels. My wife is going to give a copy of the transcription to District Attorney Wetzel. I don't suppose she'd be breaking too many laws if she slipped you a copy, also."

"Shandy, I've got a damned good notion to run you in. Who's seen that diary besides your wife?"

"Several people have seen the diary, myself included. So far, though, my wife is the only one who's been able to read it. Ms. Quatrefages wrote backwards in a mixture of French, Spanish, and a few other things. To complicate the matter further, she appears to be a poor linguist and a worse speller."

Olson made a menacing noise deep in his throat. "Does Swope know about this?"

"Oh yes. My wife told him when he came to the house to tell me about the upcoming raid. We discussed it further while we were riding out to Woeful Ridge together."

Olson thought that one over for a while. "Huh! I guess Swope figured he'd better have some poor sucker along for protection when the crap hit the fan. God, how I hate that young punk! He's going to need somebody a damn sight bigger than you when the D.A. hears about this little party he fixed up. Do you realize what it cost to bring the National Guard out like that? His lousy paper's going to get sued for every cent of the money, you can bet your boots on that."

Olson went on in much the same vein all the way to Balaclava Junction. Peter made no effort to answer back. The man was obviously in a state bordering on apoplexy. As far as Peter could see, Olson had every right to be. Peter was thinking seriously of indulging in a mild snit himself as soon as he got the chance. At least he didn't have to worry about picking up a speeding ticket on the way with one police chief in the car and another, God willing, at his house.

Yes, Fred Ottermole was there. As he turned up into the Crescent, Peter was immensely relieved to see Balaclava Junction's lone police car in front of his house. What with time's decay and its infinite variety of dents and bangs, the vehicle looked about the way the *Fane and Pennon*'s staff car had before that incredible metamorphosis. Incredible being definitely the operative word, Peter decided as Cronkite Swope pulled up in the Plymouth behind his and Fred's car.

Olson wasn't about to stand on ceremony. He leaped out of Peter's car before it was fairly stopped, charged up to the front door, and began pounding on it with both fists.

"Open up!"

To Peter's secret joy, Chief Ottermole had got the door open before Olson could balance himself. Fred held out a kindly arm.

"Oopsy-daisy, Wilbur. What you been drinkin'?"

"Don't get funny with me, Ottermole. Where's Mrs. Shandy?"

"Right there. Can't you see her?"

Helen was halfway down the stairs; she'd started as soon as she heard the commotion. "Are you all right, Chief Olson? That doorstep's rather tricky, I'm afraid. Peter and I have been meaning—"

Olson was in no mood for chitchat. "Where's that diary? I want it and I want it now. Come on, hand it over."

"It's up in the den," Helen told him. "But you can't—"

The hallway was tiny, the stairway going straight up from the doorway with only a few feet between, as is often the way in small old houses. Helen was still on the stairs since there was really nowhere else for her to stand. Olson brushed her aside so roughly that she missed her footing. Peter rushed to grab her. Ottermole grabbed Olson. The Lumpkinton chief struggled, but it was no contest. Ottermole was twice his size and twenty years younger.

"What's the big idea knocking a lady around in her own house?" yelled Fred. "Mrs. Shandy's charging you with assault and battery. Aren't you, Helen?"

"I certainly am, Fred, and thank you for reminding me. Peter dear, could you please help me to the sofa? That brute gave my ribs an awful whack, and I think I've sprained my knee. It hurts like the dickens. Honestly, Chief Olson, I must say you're setting a fine example to the youth of Balaclava County. Cronkite, I hope you got a photograph of him shoving me."

"I sure did, Mrs. Shandy!"

"Gimme that camera!" yelled Olson.

"What's the matter with that man?" Helen was using her most librarianly tone now. "Perhaps we should consider hitting him over the head with the fire shovel to quiet him down. It doesn't count as assault if the prisoner's resisting arrest, does it, Fred?"

"That's okay, Helen, I can manage him." Ottermole did something particularly nasty that caused Olson's knees to buckle. "Take that pair of handcuffs off my belt and hook 'em around his wrists, will you, Cronk? For Pete's sake, Wilbur, hold still and quit yellin'. You know the protocol, you've made enough collars yourself. Cripes, I should have brought a straitjacket. When you're finished with the handcuffs, Cronk, you'd better call up Budge Dorkin at the station and ask him to bring that other pair of handcuffs. I'm going to secure the bugger's feet. Wilbur, if you kick me in the shins once more, I'm going to snatch out your false teeth and bust 'em on the sidewalk. What's he all steamed up about, Professor?"

"He's afraid we'll read what Elisa Alicia Quatrefages has written about him in her diary."

"Him?" Despite the pain she was in, Helen began to laugh. "That's Paraguay? Well, they do say everybody looks good to somebody. How did you sniff him out, Peter?"

"I didn't have to. He blew his cover high, wide, and handsome out there on Woeful Ridge. I have to say I'd been wondering about Olson for some time, but I couldn't convince myself he had the brains or the energy to organize a large-scale criminal operation. Today's raid on Woeful Ridge convinced me he at least had the energy. He'd called out the National Guard, got hold of an armored car, even put together a SWAT team."

"How grandiose!"

"Oh, it was all that and then some. So now we know how Olson's mind works. He wasn't satisfied with hiring a few thugs to do his dirty work when he ran into an opportunity to pick up some easy money, such as looting and burning the Binks estate. He didn't even stop at corrupting half his own police force. He went ahead and set himself up a whole paramilitary operation. And you have to admit he made a damned good job of it, using that so-called survivalist colony as a cover."

"He certainly had the brains to pick the perfect aide-de-camp in Roland Childe," Helen agreed. "A psychopath with a cloak-and-dagger mentality was just the man Olson would have needed to organize his ammunition dump and run his drills and pull off his crimes according to plan."

"Yeah," said Ottermole. "Wilbur could manage the cover-ups easily enough, but he'd have had to keep his nose clean when it came to the rough stuff."

"And Elisa Alicia was too busy being his inspiration and his messenger and fencing his loot for him," Helen added. "I can see why an adventuress in search of adventure would have been attracted to a man like this. I suppose he's quite impressive, in his way, and he certainly fits her idea of the perfect male specimen. He's not quite swarthy enough and I don't suppose he's much good on horseback, but one can't have everything. Does she really call you Paraguay, Chief Olson?"

She probably did, for he started to bluster again. "I don't know what you're talking about. You're going to be damned sorry for this, all of you!"

"Oh, I hardly think so," said Peter. "I'd say we've got you pretty well dead to rights. Childe's going to fall apart, you know, if he hasn't already. Those mentally unstable types usually do, once they're made to face reality. So will the SWAT team, I expect. You made a serious mistake using the same chaps who'd been playing survivalists the day they roughed up Swope and me and wrecked the *Fane and Pennon* car. They won't stand up long to interrogation, I shouldn't think. By the way, Ottermole, who gets to grill them?"

"Beats me, Professor. Maybe the Lumpkinton Town Council will appoint an acting chief, if they can find anybody on the force who hasn't been one of the survivalist gang. District Attorney Wetzel must know what to do."

"Then we'll leave her to it, though I expect we ought to get on the phone and let her know there's some more to be done."

"I'll do that right now," said Cronkite Swope. "I guess I know pretty much what you're going to say next anyway, Professor."

"M'yes, I should think you might. Use the phone in the

kitchen, so you won't be drowned out if Olson decides to start bellowing again. As I was about to mention, Chief Olson, I found it a highly suspicious circumstance that the ammunition dump had been cleaned out and demolished. Since so much emphasis had been placed on keeping the raid a secret, this implied inside information, and nobody could have been farther inside than you. I shouldn't be surprised if the ammunition were found in the police station's basement, or under your guest room bed. You were probably hard put to find another hiding place in a hurry, and with your kind of moxie, you'd never have dreamed of getting caught."

Olson had turned to stone, which was perhaps the best thing he could have done in the circumstances and a great deal easier on his captors than his former frenetic behavior. Peter hurried to finish before the ex-mastermind started up again.

"Of course you had to move on Woeful Ridge after Swope had told his story to Attorney Wetzel. It was really brilliant of you to stage that three-ring circus and then expose the whole show as a hoax Swope was trying to pull in order to get his brother out of trouble. It was clever of you to frame Brinkley by planting the gun-powder on the cannon. Your only mistake was in trusting Elisa Alicia Quatrefages to do the artwork on that 1974 Plymouth you faked up to replace the one your playful cohorts had trashed. Not that Elisa Alicia didn't do her usual expert job, you understand, but as I remarked a while ago, she's a lousy speller. So are you, evidently, or you might have noticed in time that she'd left out one of the *n*'s in *Pennon*."

"Jeez!" said Ottermole. "Even my kids would know better than that."

"He's a liar," Olson wasn't quite out of steam yet. "It was always that way."

"Save your breath," said Peter. "I'm sure the *Fane and Pennon*'s files have enough photographs showing the original staff car to prove this one's a doctored-up fake. Very skillfully doctored up, I have to admit, which may open up a new field of interrogation concerning the correlation of

Lumpkinton's auto-theft rate with the scope of your—er—enterprise. I believe that's Budge Dorkin coming up the walk. Excuse me a moment."

It was, and Budge had the handcuffs with him. "Who's the pinchee, Fred? I mean, Chief."

"Him," said Ottermole.

"Chief Olson? Wow!" It took a lot to awe Budge Dorkin these days, but now he was definitely awed. "What's he done?"

"He's a master criminal."

"That old bucket of guts? You've got to be kidding."

"You must remember, Budge, that one person's bucket of guts may be somebody else's Errol Flynn," Helen said, though she didn't look any too convinced herself. "What happens now, Fred? Not that I'm trying to get rid of you, but we have out-of-town guests who'll be along in a while, and I do think Peter ought to get some rest between times."

"I dunno," Ottermole replied. "Hey, Cronk, you find out anything?"

Young Swope came in from the kitchen. "Yup, it's all set. Mrs. Wetzel says to park Chief Olson in the lockup and she'll be over with the warrant as soon as her cake comes out of the oven. I had to track her down at her house. It's her kid's birthday and she took the afternoon off to get ready for the party. She says she doesn't know how in heck she's going to get the cake frosted in time."

"Call her back and tell her to bring it here," said Helen. "Iduna's a whiz at birthday cakes. No, I'd better call her myself. I'm sure you'll want to take photographs of Chief Olson being lugged off to the lockup."

"When are Guthrie and Catriona coming back?" Peter asked her. "Have you heard anything from them?"

"Yes, they called from New Haven a little while ago. They had no trouble picking up Elisa Alicia. They just went down to the waterfront and there she was, sitting on a bollard, disguised as a jolly jack-tar from the *HMS Pinafore*, waiting for her ship to come in. They had a couple of Connecticut policemen with them so the arrest was no problem. Of course, it does mean the police from three states are now involved. She'll have to go through the usual channels, whatever they are, but I expect you'll be allowed to see her at the arraignment, Chief Olson. Now if you people will excuse me, I'll go make that phone call."

"I have a right to telephone my lawyer," Olson was shouting as they shoved him into the police car.

Fred Ottermole was yelling back that he could call from the station and to quit making a public spectacle of himself. Cronkite Swope was blissfully snapping photographs and making mental notes for the lead article he was going to write as soon as he got a chance to sit down. Budge Dorkin was trying to figure out how the gears on the fake *Fane and Pennon* staff car worked so that he could drive it down to the station. Mrs. Wetzel would be wanting to impound the car as evidence as soon as she and Helen had got the business of the birthday cake sorted out.

Peter decided he wasn't needed any longer and went back into the house. He collapsed into his armchair, stuck his feet up on a cricket, and shut his eyes. Helen came in from the kitchen, stood watching him for a moment, then began to tiptoe out of the room. But he stopped her.

"Whither, my love?"

"Hence, was my intention. I thought you'd gone to sleep."

"No, I was just cogitating. What do you suppose Olson was planning to do with all that money he's been piling up?"

"Flee to Paraguay with Elisa Alicia and raise hand-decorated police dogs, I should think. Or else set up a separate kingdom on Woeful Ridge and have himself crowned as emperor, which seems the likelier course. Could I interest you in a little tea?"

"You could interest me in a little wifely consolation."

"So I could, but not just now. Mrs. Wetzel will be along with that birthday cake. If she caught us in the act, she'd probably arrest me for tampering with the evidence."

"Tea, then," said Peter. "Did you think to get in touch with Iduna and let her know she's been volunteered?"

"Of course, darling. She's going to do a sunbonnet baby

with yellow ruffles and a bunch of daffodils. Mrs. Wetzel's daughter is eight years old, her name's Abigail, and she goes to day camp."

"Eight seems a trifle elderly for a sunbonnet baby these days, wouldn't you think?" Peter demurred. "Wouldn't Abigail prefer a rock star with a purple and orange punk hairdo?"

Helen shook her head. "Little girls are still little girls, no matter what anybody tries to make you believe. Abigail will adore the sunbonnet baby. If you don't intend to sleep, how'd you like to come out to the kitchen and help warm the teapot?"

TWENTY-TWO

Breakfast had been going on for quite a while. Catriona and Guthrie had remarked a few times that they ought to be getting back to Sasquamahoc, but nobody was taking them seriously, least of all themselves. Iduna had been over with a pan of hot cinnamon rolls and stopped long enough for a cup of coffee, but she'd had to leave because Daniel's plane was due in at noon and she didn't want to be late getting to the airport.

Fred Ottermole had dropped by to let them know former Chief Olson had been transferred to the county jail, the missing arsenal had turned up in the room over Olson's garage, and Mrs. Olson was being treated for nervous prostration and compound fracture of the self-esteem. He'd eaten a few of Iduna's rolls and drunk a large glass of orange juice because he felt the need of some extra vitamins, then charged off to bask some more in the glory of having bagged a genuine, grade-A master criminal.

The Shandys were more than content to let Fred do the basking. They'd been pestered with so many phone calls from interested neighbors that they'd been forced to turn off the sound so they couldn't hear the rings. The really important calls, such as the ones from Huntley Swope's wife and Cronkite's brother Brinkley, had come last night.

As for Cronkite himself, they hadn't seen him all morning. It was not until Guthrie had refused a fourth cup of coffee and told Catriona in a firmer tone than heretofore that they really must be going that the *Fane and Pennon*'s star reporter hurtled up the Crescent on his motorcycle and rushed into the house, too excited to stop and knock although Cronkite was a well-mannered young man as a rule. He was waving a long sheet of paper.

"Hey, Professor! Look what just came off the computer from Associated Press."

"Let's see it, Swope." Peter adjusted his glasses, read a few lines, and began to chuckle. "By George! Can you beat that?"

Helen gave him a poke in the ribs. "Peter, don't be infuriating. Tell us."

" 'Power Outage in California Cryonics Laboratory. Residents Thaw But Nobody Wakes Up'! The gist is that a small group of elderly people, including Balaclava County's only multimillionaire, one Jeremiah Binks, willingly participated in an experiment which involved their being deep-frozen by some—er—arcane technique. The idea was that they'd be defrosted at a future time when a method had been discovered to reverse the process of aging and they could be restored to eternal youth."

"What the hell for?" demanded Guthrie. "I can't imagine a more horrible fate than having to stay twenty-five years old forever. How did they get thawed?"

"It appears that the laboratory had been left unattended for several days, it being not unreasonably assumed that there wasn't much to hang around for. When somebody finally did drop in to check, it was discovered that a minor earthquake had caused a power outage. The participants had not only thawed but also—er—mildewed."

"My God! So now what?"

"There are several lawsuits pending against the laboratory, not to mention possible criminal charges. At the local level a special complication has arisen. The Binks property has been held in a trust pending the anticipated renascence of its owner. Now that it's obvious Mr. Binks isn't going to come back and collect, the scramble is on to find the sole heiress, a Miss Winifred Binks, who disappeared mysteriously a couple of years ago after having spent her last cent trying to claim possession of her grandfather's estate."

"Holy jumping catfish!" cried Catriona. "But what if this Binks woman never shows up?"

Peter smiled a sly and secret smile. "Oh, I think she'll probably come to the surface. How about a glass of orange juice for the vitamins, Swope?"

"That would be great," said Cronkite. "I just remembered I forgot to eat any breakfast this morning. You wouldn't happen to have a spare egg or two left, Mrs. Shandy?"

"Of course. No, Cat, sit still. I'll do it. Fried or scrambled, Cronkite?"

"Whichever's faster. We've got to get over to Woeful Ridge, Professor."

That broke up the party. While Cronkite was wolfing his belated breakfast, Catriona and Guthrie collected the few belongings they'd brought with them and made their farewells. They were practically out the door when Guthrie stopped short.

"Oh, I forgot to tell you folks. The New Haven police had the FBI do a fingerprint check on Elisa. It turns out she's actually Alice Lynch."

"Then Cat was right," said Helen smugly. "Miss or Mrs.?"

"Mrs. The Lynch who appears to be still her lawfully wedded husband or was when she married me, which is what counts, is doing twenty years at Dannemora for manslaughter and grand larceny. Elisa got off on a technicality but there was no doubt in anybody's mind that she'd been in it with Lynch all the way. So I'm still a bachelor and Elisa's facing a bigamy charge among other things. I guess I'd be pretty sore if I weren't so relieved. Well, now that you folks know the way to Sasquamahoc, you'll be coming again soon, I hope."

"You can count on it," Peter assured his old friend. "We'll all go whale watching together."

After a good deal more laughing and hugging, Guthrie and Catriona went off in another rented car.

"See," said Helen. "I told you all's well that ends well. Now, Cronkite, if you've quite finished eating, I do think you're right about getting on out to Woeful Ridge. Goodness knows what may be happening at the Binks estate once the news gets around, and that poor woman won't have a clue as to what it's all about."

"Do you want to come with us?" Peter asked.

"I'd love to, but I still have to finish typing that translation, then go over to the library and run off some copies. Mrs. Wetzel's planning to stop by in a while and pick hers up. I'll send another to the sheriff at Hocasquam by express mail, and save one for us just in case. I have no idea who's supposed to get the original diary, but no doubt somebody will tell me sooner or later. Go on, you two. Give my regards to the heiress."

"I'm sure glad it's good news we're delivering this time," Cronkite remarked as he and Peter started off in the Shandys' road-stained car.

"Let's hope Miss Binks also thinks it's good news." Peter grunted.

"What are you talking about, Professor? Ninety million bucks would be good news to anybody."

"We'll soon find out. She does appear to have worked out a pretty satisfactory way of life for herself, in which money doesn't figure at all."

"But don't you think the way she lives is sort of a waste?

I mean, a nice, bright woman like her down in that wood-chuck hole all by herself?"

"I may think so and you may think so, but what counts is what Miss Binks herself thinks. My only hope is that we can find her before the stampede begins. You did locate that bicycle cache easily enough, though, didn't you?"

"Well, I located it. I can't say the finding was easy, even though I did have the driveway and the cellar hole to orient myself by. Say, Professor, that hidden well we climbed out of wasn't far from where we got the bikes."

"M'yes, I've been thinking about that. The only problem with trying to get to Miss Binks's lair via the well is that what she called her drawbridge had to be lowered from the tunnel side. I suppose in a pinch we could simply drop into the water and swim across. It would only be a stroke or two."

Neither of them found the idea of being immersed in that black hole particularly attractive. They were almost relieved to find they'd have to find a different means of ingress. A couple of cars were already parked by the cellar hole and their drivers wandering around the area with cameras, wondering what to shoot. Peter raised his voice in loud complaint.

"No sense wasting our time here, there's nothing to see. Let's go over to Woeful Ridge and find out where they staged that big shootout yesterday. Quick, before those yahoos over there beat us to it."

That started a stampede, of course. Peter and Cronkite made a feint of going, too, then doubled back and slipped into the woods.

"Our best hope, I suppose, is to try to find those two big trees. She may be up in her aerie, where we found her the first time. If she isn't, we can leave a note."

"I've already got Mr. Swope's note," murmured a voice out of a bush. "Follow me, please."

TWENTY-THREE

They couldn't see so much as a flash of deerskin, but they could hear a slight rustling noise, so they followed that. It wasn't until they were well into the woods that Miss Binks showed herself, and then only to beckon them down one of her holes. She stopped up the opening with a neatly cut chunk of sod that had a small shadbush growing out of it and scuttled ahead of them along a tunnel that had to be traversed at a crouch.

Eventually, they found themselves back in the underground lair where they'd spent that memorable night. The banked fire wasn't casting enough of a glow for them to see by comfortably so Miss Binks uncovered the embers, added a fat pine knot or two, and set her teakettle across two flat rocks.

"Now, gentlemen, can I offer you a cup of sassafras tea, or are we in too much of a hurry to stay for the kettle to boil? There have been some exceedingly strange doings over at Woeful Ridge since our last meeting. But perhaps you know more about that than I do?"

"I expect we do," Peter replied. "No, there's no rush. Sassafras tea sounds most attractive."

While Miss Binks fussed around her midget kitchen, he and Cronkite gave her an account of what the disturbance had been all about. She expressed surprise and gratification.

"That is really excellent news, gentlemen. Now I shall feel

free to range over my domain without let or hindrance. Thank you so much for coming to tell me. Honey with your tea, Mr. Swope?"

"Uh, thanks, Miss Binks, but that's not what we came to tell you. I mean it was, but there's more. You'd better do it, Professor."

Peter cleared his throat. "It's about your grandfather, Miss Binks."

"My grandfather? You do surprise me. Don't tell me he's already been resurrected?"

"No. Er—quite the contrary. There's been a power outage at the cryonics laboratory. He and the other—er—occupants were accidentally defrosted and it—er—didn't work."

Miss Binks set down the teapot very, very carefully. "Are you absolutely certain of this?"

"Oh yes," said Cronkite. "I telephoned California to get the details as soon as the news came in over our AP line at the paper. Mr. Binks is pretty ripe and kind of squishy, and there's bright green fuzz an inch long growing all over him."

"I see." Miss Binks sat perfectly still for a moment, staring into the fire. "Poor, dear Grandfather! All his dreams of rejuvenation turning to bright green fuzz. This is a poignant moment for me, as I'm sure you must be aware."

"I'm afraid it may be more poignant than you realize, Miss Binks." Peter decided this was no time to beat around the bush. "The news item to which Swope refers also mentioned that the search is already on for the missing heiress who disappeared mysteriously after losing her court suit to gain custody of the old man's property. If you don't resurface right away, claimants are going to be crawling out of the bushes and you may have another nasty court fight on your hands."

"That is a point to consider, certainly. I have been so happy here. But as you say, if I don't claim my inheritance, someone else will. And that, I expect, would put an end to my being able to live here. Whoever got it would want to develop the land, no doubt."

"Very likely."

"Eviction by bulldozer. Not the sort of end I'd foreseen to

my peaceful sylvan existence. There is, as I recall, a great deal of money in the trust."

"Ninety million dollars was what it said in the news release," Cronkite amplified. "I don't know how much would be taken up in taxes."

"A good deal less than you'd have to pay if the money weren't in a trust," said Peter, "and if you hadn't been named as your grandfather's heiress. You're going to be an extremely rich woman, Miss Binks."

"There's irony for you." Miss Binks took a sip of her sassafras tea and gazed around her snug dwelling with sadness on her face. "I've been feeling myself an extremely rich woman out here already. I've owned nothing worth fretting about and lacked nothing that I've needed. Now I'm supposed to exchange this idyllic existence for infinitely more than I need and a great deal to worry about."

The thin shoulders inside the badly made deerskin tunic lifted in a shrug. "But what alternative is there? One must play the hand that's dealt one, as my Uncle Charles used to say. This philosophical attitude made him a sucker for card sharps, as you may imagine. Very well, if I must be rich, I suppose I must. The prospect does have its positive side, I must admit. What would you suggest, gentlemen? Shall I merely stroll out of the woods crying '*Ecce femina*,' or would a more businesslike approach be advisable?"

"What about the lawyer who acted for you in your lawsuit?" Peter ventured. "Did you two—er—part friends?"

"Oh yes. It wasn't Mr. Debenham's fault we couldn't crack the trust. He was perhaps overzealous on my behalf, allowing personal regard to sway his judgment as to the favorable outcome of the suit, but one can hardly fault a man for liking one. And I wasn't actually much worse off after we lost. He refused to take a fee and even offered to pay the court costs, poor man. Of course, I couldn't allow that, but now there's a chance at the big plum pudding, Mr. Debenham certainly deserves to have his slice. How shall I get to him? On my bicycle?"

"What I'd suggest, Miss Binks, is that you put on

your—er—shore-going clothes and let Swope and me drive you. We could stop at my house near the college long enough for you to do any—er—titivating you may feel inclined for. My wife will be delighted to make your acquaintance. You could then explain to the lawyer that you've been visiting friends who prefer not to be named because they don't want to be involved in the publicity which is bound to result from your—er—emergence. Unless you can think of something better."

"Anything but the truth, eh, Professor? I quite understand. I must be careful not to give any other possible claimant an opening for having me declared of unsound mind. Isn't that what you're thinking?"

"M'well, it's a point to consider."

"You are quite right. They'd have me in a padded cell quicker than a chipmunk can wink its eye. I shall say I've been staying at a small winterized camp in a secluded area where I was able to live very cheaply on what little money I had left from the sale of my aunt's effects. As to where it was, I shall refuse to tell on the grounds that I don't want my former neighbors to be pestered by ill-mannered curiosity seekers. That should suffice, wouldn't you think?"

"Heck yes," said Cronkite. "You don't have to mention that your neighbors are skunks and woodchucks."

"And a rather churlish Mr. Badger." Miss Binks did have a delightful smile. "You see, I don't want to lie any more than I absolutely have to. Once I've been put in possession of the funds, it won't matter a jot if the truth does come out. Anybody with ninety million dollars to disburse as she sees fit can be as eccentric as she chooses and nobody will dare raise an eyebrow."

Miss Binks poured them another round of sassafras tea. "So let's drink to the great god Mammon! Naturally I've entertained myself from time to time wondering how I should spend Grandfather's money if I ever got the chance."

"I don't suppose you'd care to give some thought to rebuilding the soap factory?" Cronkite suggested diffidently.

Miss Binks's smile became a chuckle. "I should be

delighted, and it's not going to cost me a cent. All I shall have to do is back Sam Snell into a corner and give him a sound tongue-lashing about performing his civic duty."

"Huh. You'll have to catch him first. Right now he's off someplace on his yacht, thinking it over."

"Is he, forsooth? Cheer up, Mr. Swope, he won't stay long. *Entre nous*, our valiant yachtsman gets seasick at the mere sight of a wave over three inches high. We have but to keep an eye on the weather reports and accost him as soon as he sets foot on shore. Once he finds out I've got my hands on Grandfather's money, he'll be groveling at my feet and licking my shoes. Which reminds me, I must buy some for the occasion. Trust me, Mr. Swope. Settling Sam Snell's hash will be a mere bagatelle. And, I may add, a labor of love."

"Miss Binks, you're fantastic!"

"So I've been told before, but never in that tone of voice. Thank you, Mr. Swope. Let's see, where were we? Oh yes, still stuck with all those superfluous millions of Grandfather's. You know this dustup with those absurdly named survivalists has set me thinking. What strikes one at the beginning, of course, is their total unconcern with survival— at least, with anybody else's survival. Grandfather was really concerned with survival, but his approach appears to have been ultimately as self-defeating as theirs. However, we must not therefrom infer that the basic concept of survivalism is wrong."

"One could hardly say so," Peter agreed, "since we've been working on survival ever since we struggled out of the primal ooze."

"Ah yes, 'when you were a tadpole and I was a fish in the Paleozoic slime.' Or is it 'time'? I shall have to refresh my memory for nonsense verse. For nonsense in general, I suppose, if I'm to resume my place in polite society. But anyway, what I'm getting at is that I've learned a great deal about survival during these past few years. I believe the best way to keep Grandfather's memory green—oh dear, that's an unfortunate turn of phrase, but no matter—would be, as I was about to say, for me to spend his money passing on to others what I now know about staying alive."

"That sounds like a great idea, Miss Binks," said Cronkite. "What will you do, give classes on how to make amaranth pancakes?"

"Classes would be part of the program, certainly, but we'd have to operate on a far wider scope for the plan to convey any meaningful benefit to the general public. It's not just a matter of showing people how to take a pointed stick and scratch the ground for edible roots, you know. There are too many of us, and not enough roots in the places where they're needed most. A holistic approach to survival these days is a far more complex business than it was in ages past. What with acid rain and neutron bombs and supply and demand and poisons in the groundwater, we've got ourselves into such a mess that we can't even count on having another age to fiddle around in. We've got to get it right this time."

Miss Binks laughed a little at her own intensity. "Well, gentlemen, I didn't mean to bore you with my trivial ponderings. My aim would be to deal with the simple facts, and to start where I find myself. We here in this country have picked our apples before we let them ripen, and we're suffering now from an economic bellyache. The ache's going to get a good deal worse before it gets better, in my personal opinion. In the meantime, bellies will still have to be filled and heads will need roofs over them, our climate being what it is. Food's to be had if you know what to look for, and shelter can be contrived in more ways than we generally think about. There's a lot to be said for a hole in the ground, you know. The big thing is to keep the earth closet far enough away from the water supply. And you see, I can explain all that."

"By George, so you can!" Peter was liking this. "None better. And how do you plan to do so?"

"First I plan to ask your advice on whether it would be possible to affiliate with Balaclava Agricultural College. This would add credence to my venture and provide me with access to a brain trust such as yourself and the distinguished

Professor Enderble, whose marvelous book, *How to Live with the Burrowing Mammals*, has been such a source of inspiration and enlightenment that I've actually worn the covers off."

"John will be delighted," Peter assured her, "and I'm sure President Svenson will be glad to discuss whatever thoughts you may have on the subject. I'll arrange a meeting as soon as he gets back from Sweden, if you like."

"Excellent. I shall have a more concrete proposal ready by then—and, I hope, cash in hand to get started with. My proposal will be essentially to turn Grandfather's land into an annex of the college, reserving a small plot on which I'll build a modest house for myself to live in. On the site of the original house, I'll erect whatever buildings are needed for carrying on the various activities we decide to pursue. One of these will be a television station devoted entirely to educational programs connected with survivalist themes."

"A television station?"

"Oh yes, that's the only way, don't you think? It's all very well to read in a manual of edible plants that in order to avoid being poisoned, one must gather the edible shoots of pokeweed before they're more than six inches tall, but when the plants are that small, how can the reader be sure they're really pokeweed? On the other hand, suppose you take a person out into a field and show him or, needless to say, her. 'See, this is a young pokeweed. It's small enough to pick safely. That one over there is too big, forget it. And this plant isn't a pokeweed at all, it's monkshood and it can kill you, so leave it alone.' Then the person will know precisely which is which, and that's the sort of thing one can do best on the grand scale through the medium of television. Furthermore, one could follow up with a demonstration of what to do with the pokeweed once it's picked. Pokeweed salad, for instance, or simmered pokeweed shoots with day-lily-pollen biscuits and wild elderberry jelly."

"And you could show somebody getting sick from picking the monkshood instead of the pokeweed and having to eat day lilies or something for an antidote." Cronkite was getting into the spirit of the thing.

"It would take a good deal more than day lilies to cure you of monkshood poisoning, young man! Our whole thrust will be to teach people to pick the right stuff in the first place. Anyway, gentlemen, the ramifications are endless, but that gives you a small idea of what I want to do. Henceforth I shall devote my abilities, such as they are, to making sure that Grandfather will not have defrosted in vain."

"Bravo, Miss Binks!" said Peter. "We're with you all the way."

"Then perhaps you can start by persuading Professor Enderble to speak a few words on behalf of the local fauna at the funeral service? Oh dear, I do hope Grandfather's not too soggy to cremate. It would cost a fortune to have his body shipped back from the West Coast in its present condition. But then, I do have a fortune to spend, don't I? I shall have to give careful thought to the funeral. One hates to be vulgarly ostentatious, but a multimillionaire mustn't be chintzy. Dear me, I find myself quite looking forward to affluence. Frailty, thy name is Binks. By the way, Professor Shandy, what happened to the soap-works weather vane?"

"My wife got it back."

"Oh, jolly good show! Now we can always go and see which way the wind is blowing. An excellent thing for us survivalists to be aware of, shouldn't you think? Let's see, we have to collect the ninety million dollars, arrange to bury Grandfather, browbeat Sam Snell into rebuilding the soap factory, and do our bit for the pokeweed. Well, that should do for a start. We'll tackle the big jobs later. Now, gentlemen, give me five minutes to titivate, and we'll be off."

MORE MYSTERIOUS PLEASURES

HAROLD ADAMS
The Carl Wilcox mystery series

MURDER	#501	$3.95
PAINT THE TOWN RED	#601	$3.95
THE MISSING MOON	#602	$3.95
THE NAKED LIAR	#420	$3.95
THE FOURTH WIDOW	#502	$3.50
THE BARBED WIRE NOOSE	#603	$3.95
THE MAN WHO MET THE TRAIN	#801	$3.95

TED ALLBEURY

THE SEEDS OF TREASON	#604	$3.95
THE JUDAS FACTOR	#802	$4.50
THE STALKING ANGEL	#803	$3.95

ERIC AMBLER

HERE LIES: AN AUTOBIOGRAPHY	#701	$8.95

ROBERT BARNARD

A TALENT TO DECEIVE: AN APPRECIATION OF AGATHA CHRISTIE	#702	$8.95

EARL DERR BIGGERS
The Charlie Chan mystery series

THE HOUSE WITHOUT A KEY	#421	$3.95
THE CHINESE PARROT	#503	$3.95
BEHIND THAT CURTAIN	#504	$3.95
THE BLACK CAMEL	#505	$3.95
CHARLIE CHAN CARRIES ON	#506	$3.95
KEEPER OF THE KEYS	#605	$3.95

JAMES M. CAIN

THE ENCHANTED ISLE	#415	$3.95
CLOUD NINE	#507	$3.95

ROBERT CAMPBELL
IN LA-LA LAND WE TRUST   #508 $3.95

RAYMOND CHANDLER
RAYMOND CHANDLER'S UNKNOWN THRILLER:
   THE SCREENPLAY OF "PLAYBACK"   #703 $9.95

GEORGE C. CHESBRO
The Veil Kendry suspense series
VEIL   #509 $3,95
JUNGLE OF STEEL AND STONE   #606 $3.95

EDWARD CLINE
FIRST PRIZE   #804 $4.95

K.C. CONSTANTINE
The Mario Balzic mystery series
JOEY'S CASE   #805 $4.50

MATTHEW HEALD COOPER
DOG EATS DOG   #607 $4.95

CARROLL JOHN DALY
THE ADVENTURES OF SATAN HALL   #704 $8.95
THE ADVENTURES OF RACE WILLIAMS   #723 $9.95

NORBERT DAVIS
THE ADVENTURES OF MAX LATIN   #705 $8.95

MARK DAWIDZIAK
THE COLUMBO PHILE: A CASEBOOK   #726 $14.95

WILLIAM L. DeANDREA
The Cronus espionage series
SNARK   #510 $3.95
AZRAEL   #608 $4.50
The Matt Cobb mystery series
KILLED IN THE ACT   #511 $3.50
KILLED WITH A PASSION   #512 $3.50
KILLED ON THE ICE   #513 $3.50
KILLED IN PARADISE   #806 $3.95

LEN DEIGHTON
ONLY WHEN I LAUGH   #609 $4.95

AARON ELKINS
The Professor Gideon Oliver mystery series
OLD BONES   #610 $3.95

DOUG HORNIG
WATERMAN #616 $3.95
The Loren Swift mystery series
THE DARK SIDE #519 $3.95
DEEP DIVE #810 $4.50

JANE HORNING
THE MYSTERY LOVERS' BOOK
  OF QUOTATIONS #709 $12.95

PETER ISRAEL
The Charles Camelot mystery series
I'LL CRY WHEN I KILL YOU #811 $3.95

P.D. JAMES/T.A. CRITCHLEY
THE MAUL AND THE PEAR TREE #520 $3.95

STUART M. KAMINSKY
The Toby Peters mystery series
HE DONE HER WRONG #105 $3.95
HIGH MIDNIGHT #106 $3.95
NEVER CROSS A VAMPIRE #107 $3.95
BULLET FOR A STAR #308 $3.95
THE FALA FACTOR #309 $3.95

JOSEPH KOENIG
FLOATER #521 $3.50

ELMORE LEONARD
THE HUNTED #401 $3.95
MR. MAJESTYK #402 $3.95
THE BIG BOUNCE #403 $3.95

ELSA LEWIN
I, ANNA #522 $3.50

PETER LOVESEY
ROUGH CIDER #617 $3.95
BUTCHERS AND OTHER STORIES OF CRIME #710 $9.95
BERTIE AND THE TINMAN #812 $3.95

JOHN LUTZ
SHADOWTOWN #813 $3.95

ARTHUR LYONS
SATAN WANTS YOU: THE CULT OF
  DEVIL WORSHIP #814 $4.50
The Jacob Asch mystery series
FAST FADE #618 $3.95

ED McBAIN
ANOTHER PART OF THE CITY   #524 $3.95
McBAIN'S LADIES: THE WOMEN OF
   THE 87TH PRECINCT   #815 $4.95
The Matthew Hope mystery series
SNOW WHITE AND ROSE RED   #414 $3.95
CINDERELLA   #525 $3.95
PUSS IN BOOTS   #629 $3.95
THE HOUSE THAT JACK BUILT   #816 $3.95

VINCENT McCONNOR
LIMBO   #630 $3.95

GREGORY MCDONALD, ED.
LAST LAUGHS: THE 1986 MYSTERY
   WRITERS OF AMERICA ANTHOLOGY   #711 $8.95

JAMES McLURE
IMAGO   #817 $4.50

CHARLOTTE MacLEOD
The Professor Peter Shandy mystery series
THE CORPSE IN OOZAK'S POND   #627 $3.95
The Sarah Kelling mystery series
THE RECYCLED CITIZEN   #818 $3.95
THE SILVER GHOST   #819 $4.50

WILLIAM MARSHALL
The Yellowthread Street mystery series
YELLOWTHREAD STREET   #619 $3.50
THE HATCHET MAN   #620 $3.50
GELIGNITE   #621 $3.50
THIN AIR   #622 $3.95
THE FAR AWAY MAN   #623 $3.50
ROADSHOW   #624 $3.95
HEAD FIRST   #625 $3.50
FROGMOUTH   #626 $3.50
WAR MACHINE   #820 $3.95
OUT OF NOWHERE   #821 $3.95

THOMAS MAXWELL
KISS ME ONCE   #523 $4.95
THE SABERDENE VARIATIONS   #628 $4.95
KISS ME TWICE   #822 $4.95

RIC MEYERS
MURDER ON THE AIR: TELEVISION'S GREAT
   MYSTERY SERIES   #725 $12.95

MARCIA MULLER
The Sharon McCone mystery series
EYE OF THE STORM   #823 $3.95

FREDERICK NEBEL
THE ADVENTURES OF CARDIGAN   #712 $9.95

WILLIAM F. NOLAN
THE BLACK MASK BOYS: MASTERS IN
   THE HARD-BOILED SCHOOL
   OF DETECTIVE FICTION   #713 $8.95

PETER O'DONNELL
The Modesty Blaise suspense series
DEAD MAN'S HANDLE   #526 $3.95

SUSAN OLEKSIW
A READER'S GUIDE TO THE CLASSIC
   BRITISH MYSTERY   #728 $19.95

ELIZABETH PETERS
The Amelia Peabody mystery series
CROCODILE ON THE SANDBANK   #209 $3.95
THE CURSE OF THE PHARAOHS   #210 $3.95
The Jacqueline Kirby mystery series
THE SEVENTH SINNER   #411 $3.95
THE MURDERS OF RICHARD III   #412 $3.95

ELLIS PETERS
The Brother Cadfael mystery series
THE HERMIT OF EYTON FOREST   #824 $3.95
THE CONFESSION OF BROTHER HALUIN   #808 $3.95

ANTHONY PRICE
The Doctor David Audley espionage series
THE LABYRINTH MAKERS   #404 $3.95
THE ALAMUT AMBUSH   #405 $3.95
COLONEL BUTLER'S WOLF   #527 $3.95
OCTOBER MEN   #529 $3.95
OTHER PATHS TO GLORY   #530 $3.95
OUR MAN IN CAMELOT   #631 $3.95
WAR GAME   #632 $3.95
THE '44 VINTAGE   #633 $3.95
TOMORROW'S GHOST   #634 $3.95
SOLDIER NO MORE   #825 $4.95
THE OLD *VENGEFUL*   #826 $4.95
GUNNER KELLY   #827 $4.95
SION CROSSING   #406 $3.95
HERE BE MONSTERS   #528 $3.95
FOR THE GOOD OF THE STATE   #635 $3.95
A NEW KIND OF WAR   #828 $4.95